Alpha Boys

An Erotic Anthology

Edited By

Mickey Erlach

Herndon, VA

Published in the United States by STARbooks Press, PO Box
711612, Herndon, VA 20171. Printed in the United States

Many thanks to graphic artist John Nail for the cover design.
Mr. Nail may be reached at: tojonail@bellsouth.net

Herndon, VA

Published in the United States by STARbooks Press, PO Box 711612, Herndon, VA 20171. Printed in the United States

Many thanks to graphic artist John Nail for the cover design. Mr. Nail may be reached at: tojonail@bellsouth.net

Herndon, VA

Titles Edited by Mickey Erlach for STARbooks Press

Contents

ALPHA WOLF
By Logan Zachary

Logan Zachary (LoganZachary2002@yahoo.com) lives in Minneapolis. His new book, *Calendar Boys*, is now available, and his stories can be found in several anthologies.

Christian Thomas never ran faster in his life. Faster than in the Friday night football game, faster than the championship game, faster than the time his car rolled down the hill and almost into the lake.

This time, he was running for his life. The wolf growled and snapped at his legs as he raced through the woods. He leapt over a log, but slipped on the wet moss. He landed hard on his chest, and it knocked the wind out of him. He rolled over and came face to face with the wolf's snarling mouth, lips curled back to expose sharp, yellow teeth.

Its foul, hot, fetid breath filled his nostrils. It crouched low, its muscles tense and ready to attack.

Christian raised his arm as it pounced. White pain flooded his body, hot blood sprayed his face, and a violent tug pulled him across the ground.

A gun shot rang out, and the pain was gone. Christian fell flat on his face. A cold wave washed over his body. Had he been shot? Was he dying? He blinked as he tried to get his ears to hear. The sharp echo of the bullet still rang in his head. In the distance, he heard a whimper and the rustling of the dry leaves as the four legs clawed to escape …

And then, nothing.

# # # # #

1

Coach Ramsey stood over the hospital bed. "I spoke to your parents, and I promised them I'd watch over you until they arrive." His brown eyes scanned his student's body lying in the bed.

Christian squinted from the neon lights in the room. An I.V. bag with a clear fluid hung on a pole next to the bed. The tube entered his hairy arm while his other arm was wrapped in gauze. The hospital gown wasn't tied at his neck, and his hairy, muscular chest peeked out of the opening. "Thanks."

"When did they say you could go?" Coach stepped closer to the bed.

"The nurse said as soon as my ride came." Christian swung one hairy leg out of bed. His head swam as he tried to prevent himself from passing out again. His hospital gown fell forward, exposing his whole chest. His hair thickened and darkened the lower it went down his torso.

Coach's eyes darted to his lap. Christian's junk was covered, but a huge bump was easily seen beneath the sheet and gown. "I brought you sweats. The nurse asked me to bring them. They're mine, but I know they'll fit." He offered him the paper bag he carried.

Christian took it just as a nurse walked in. "Is he your ride?"

Both men nodded.

"Let me get that I.V. out of your arm, and then I'll get your papers ready." She walked around the bed and clamped off the tube. With quick fingers, she unscrewed the plastic connector, pealed down the paper tape, and pulled the port out of his arm. She applied a bandage over the spot and threw the plastic port away. "Will you be signing him out?" she asked.

"Yeah," Coach said, as he shifted on his legs.

She nodded and left the room.

Christian opened the bag and pulled out the grey sweats. He pulled his gown off and unfolded the sweatshirt.

Coach caught a glimpse of his thick pubic bush as Christian pulled the shirt over his head, his long, lithe muscles rippled under his tan, hairy body. Each muscle finely defined as he moved. A stirring occurred in his jeans. He needed to adjust himself, but couldn't.

Christian pulled his other leg out from under the sheet and sat on the edge of the bed. His head swam as he struggled to stay conscious.

Coach moved over to the bed and stabilized him. "Are you okay?"

"Just a little dizzy, can you spot me?" Christian picked up the sweatpants and started to put them on.

Coach took them from him, knelt down, and helped start them over his big feet. His hands glided up his hairy legs as he brought the waistband to his knees.

The men's hands touched as they met there. Hot and hairy, a spark arced between them. Coach looked into Christian's eyes and saw the hazel pupils shrank to a pin point and then dilated to as big as it could swell. A golden glow flashed inside his iris as an electric charge seemed to form over their bodies.

Christian stood on unsteady legs; his cock was semi-erect and sprang up. He pulled the sweats up as fast as he could, but he felt Coach's burning gaze on his arousal. He inhaled and smelled the masculine excitement of Coach. He smelled the sweat, his musky balls, day worn briefs...

The nurse returned, and Christian sat down hard. "Here are your clothes, tennis shoes, and the papers you need. Make sure you follow up with your doctor next week, and don't hesitate to call us if you have any concerns over the next few days." She handed the clipboard to Coach. "Sign this, and you can go."

He signed the form and handed it back as an orderly brought a wheelchair to the door. He took the dirty tennis shoes and slipped them on Christian's bare feet. "I'll bring the car around and meet you at the front door."

Christian grabbed his hand as he was about to leave and squeezed. "Thanks."

# # # # #

"This extra room has clean sheets and towels if you want to shower before bed. I can stand by if your legs are still a little unsteady."

Christian felt a stirring in his sweats. Going commando allowed everything to swing freely, and a raging hard-on would easily tent the fabric. He tried to push his cock to the side, willing it to lay flat against his body. "I could use a hot shower …" he began.

Coach opened the bathroom door and flipped on the light. He strolled over to the shower and started the water. "It takes a bit to warm up," he said as he pulled the curtain closed.

Christian had kicked off his dirty shoes at the door and walked barefoot into the room.

"I can get a plastic bag to put over your arm." Coach took off.

Christian made his way slowly to the shower. He pulled the sweatshirt over his head.

Coach returned with a plastic bag and tape. He quickly covered the wrapped forearm and waited.

Christian turned his back and pushed down his sweats. His amazing ass, firm, smooth, tight and white, pushed out at Coach as he bent over to step out of them. His cheeks spread just a little to reveal a thin line of hair and a perfect pink pucker.

Coach held his breath.

Christian pulled the curtain back and stepped into the shower.

"Did you need me to hang on to you?" Coach rolled up his sleeve as he moved to the foot of the tub. He slipped it into the stall, feeling the moist heat and over spray. His hand brushed against Christian's back. Instantly, his hand opened and caressed the wet flesh.

Christian turned and grabbed into his arm, enjoying the security of his strength. "Thanks."

Coach moved a little and pulled the curtain back more, so he would be able to see where his wounded charge was. His dick swelled, and he adjusted it with his free hand.

Christian stepped to the back of the tub to get the shampoo bottle, his hairy chest brushed Coach's hand.

Coach's fingers closed like a suction cup to his body, refusing to let him fall. As Christian moved, his grasp shifted and ran over one of his pecs and cupped a nipple.

Christian held still as his nipple slipped between two of his fingers. He felt them scissor together and pinch the sensitive nub. He closed his eyes, savoring the sensation. He held the shampoo bottle, but wasn't able to open it with a bag on his hand. "I need help with the shampoo bottle."

Coach reluctantly let go and grabbed the bottle. He flipped the lid and tipped it over. Through the curtain opening, he saw Christian's hand, and he squeezed the bottle.

Christian soaped his hair and worked up a lather. Foam flowed over his head and down his back. As he completed his head, he worked over his furry chest and lower torso. He felt the heat and the shampoo work its healing magic. His arousal stood straight out in front of him. He scrubbed his low hanging balls and washed along his thick shaft.

Coach's hand held firmly against his shoulder blade. He moved his hand lower as Christian turned to rinse his chest and soap up his ass.

Christian's hand slipped between his cheeks and cleaned his crease and washed his hole. He spun in the spray and rinsed all the soap and foam down the drain.

Coach's hand twisted around his body. His fingers combed through the water soaked mat on his body. His finger tip trailed over his six-pack and dipped into his belly button.

Christian stepped forward to rinse deeper into his crack, as his body moved, Coach's hand slipped lower, through his pubes and rested on top of his shaft.

The water rinsed and revived him, the heat warmed him to the bone, and his energy returned.

He turned the water off and pulled the shower curtain back half way. "Do you have a towel?"

Coach pulled a thick bath sheet off a shelf and handed it to him.

Christian let the curtain fall back into place as he dried himself. The soft towel rubbed circulation back across his body as he wrapped around his narrow waist. As he stepped out of the tub, his plastic bag leaked.

"You got water on your bandage," Coach untaped the bag and pulled it off; the gauze on Christian's arm dripped. "We need to change that."

Christian sat on the stool. One of his hairy, muscular legs came out of the slit in the towel. He tucked the edge around his balls.

Coach carefully removed the wet bandage. Dried blood had soaked through wrap, layer after layer. More and more blood appeared on the dressings the closer it got to the wound. "Does it hurt?"

Christian paused for a moment. It didn't hurt. It didn't hurt at all. No pain. He flexed his arm muscles and tensed, but no red, ripping, burning pain shot through his arm. Nothing.

The last layer of gauze peeled off. Only two pink lines crossed his forearm. No open, gaping, bleeding injury was found. The wound was closed and almost healed. He turned his arm over and inspected the underside, same thing. A pink line ran over his arm, but its zigzagged appearance looked two months healed. The ring of a large mouth and the points of their teeth were visible in the bite mark, but the skin was intact and healed.

Coach threw the dripping bag and wet gauze into the garbage. He took Christian's warm arm in his hand and felt the warmth of his skin as he rubbed across the hairy forearm. He shook his head and said, "I guess you don't need that anymore." He looked at his watch, his raging hard-on throbbing in his jeans. He inhaled Christian's clean scent and almost licked his lips.

Christian looked at his arm and slowly shook his head. The men walked into the bedroom.

Coach pulled back the sheets. "Did you need anything else before you head to bed?"

Christian walked to the bed and sat down, his towel opened up wide.

"I'll bring you a glass of water; you can set it by the bed." Coach left before he could say anything else.

A few minutes later, Christian was under the covers, his discarded towel on the floor. Coach set the glass of water down by the bed and picked up the towel. After returning from the bathroom and turning off the light, he asked, "Did you want me to leave a light on?"

He snuggled deeper into the bed. "I'll be fine. Thanks for everything."

Coach's mind flashed on the naked body in between the sheets, how he longed to slip in between them and join him. "Do you want me to stay until you fall asleep?"

Christian smiled as he rubbed his chest with his hands. "I'll be fine."

"Call if you need anything, I'll be down the hall in the next room."

"Good night."

"Night." Coach left the door open slightly and headed to his room.

Coach stripped and slipped into bed with only his boxers on. His hard-on oozed and ached from how long he had been aroused. He reached under the sheets and rubbed his sensitive flesh. His fingers curled around his shaft and pulled slowly up and down. He felt the pre-cum flow out of his cock as he stroked.

Images of Christian's naked body, soapy foam flowing over his muscles, his beautiful ass, his huge, thick dick flooded his mind. He listened hard but heard nothing from the other room. He pushed the front of his boxers down below his low hanging balls. He jerked fast and furiously, enjoying the rising climax in his cock. His thrust his hips into his fist as he jacked. It didn't take long with such a powerfully sensuous vision of manhood in his mind.

The explosion started deep in his balls and pulled them up alongside his shaft, the white hot flow of lava sprayed across his body as wave after wave of pleasure poured out of him. He continued to stroke, milking out every drop from his balls. He bucked his hips and rubbed until he couldn't take the stimulation any more. He gasped and lay spent under his sheets.

He pulled his boxers up, cover his wet load, absorbing the majority into the cotton. A few minutes later, the joy faded, and he was asleep.

# # # # #

Coach felt the presence even before he opened his eyes. He felt a heavy weight at the foot of his bed. Slowly, he opened his eyes and saw a hulking figure crouched on his bed. The figure was back lit, but he knew Christian's body.

Christian's nude body.

Coach lay perfectly still; he watched and waited.

Christian inhaled deeply and twisted his neck in strange contortions.

Coach realized that his bed partner was naked and aroused. He had seen him play football for the university. His hulking form scared many men on the field, but his demeanor was always polite and kind. He listened to all that Coach ordered, following each and every command, but Coach sensed something different about him, something primal, something wild and powerful.

The sheet and the blanket were ripped off, and Coach's body lay exposed on the bed.

Christian had moved so fast, he was back in the same position as if he hadn't moved. The scent of man sweat and semen hung in the air. He inhaled deeply and emitted a low growl from deep in his throat.

Coach tensed, and the aroma of fear arose from his damp body. His boxers stuck to his skin and pulled on him as he moved.

Christian pounced and the boxers were removed in one fluid motion. The cotton was discarded to the floor as the athletic body crawled over him.

His erection met the huge one above him. His body was pinned down, more so by fear than any power or show of strength, so far. Every strand of hair stood out on his body and bristled against the fur above him. His pulse throbbed in his temples, and his tender neck felt too exposed, too vulnerable. He prayed he hadn't been noticed, but he knew better.

Christian dipped his head and licked down the side of Coach's face. Sweat, fear, and man played across his taste buds: exploding salt, sour, and sweet. He continued down his cheek, along his neck, over his collarbone and lower. His lips found the sharp point and suckled. His teeth bit on the nub and rolled it.

Coach lay as still as he could, allowing Christian to do what he desired. Fear held him in check, but the sensory overload made every nerve scream for more.

Christian crossed over to his other nipple and teased it before working lower. He found dried, salty-sweet spots across his hairy body. He licked off the blobs and traced his tongue along the midline of his trunk to the belly button, which was still moist and gooey. He lapped at the contents, cleaning out every last drop.

His bristly chin brushed the oozing tip of Coach's cock as it bobbed up and down.

Christian ran the stubble along the shaft and nuzzled his balls. He inhaled deeply and licked with a broad, flat tongue. He sucked one low hairy ball into his mouth and tried to swallow it whole. His nose poked his cock. Slowly, he released the fleshy orb and sought out the other one. He gobbled it in with a twist of his head; drool flowed over his pelvis, running down between his cheeks.

Coach let his head fall back as his pelvis rose and pressed into Christian's hungry mouth.

Christian spread his legs wide with his hands and reached beneath him to pull his ass up and off the bed. He sniffed the ripe hole that rose to him, meeting him in a new way. All of his senses read new and exciting colors and flavors.

Coach felt awkward with his ass open, but as Christian rose and swallowed his cock whole, he thought he'd shoot another load deep down his throat.

Another powerful growl resonated through Christian and into Coach. His hard-on almost shrank from the fear, but seemed to swell even bigger with the pleasure. "Ahhhh," escaped from him.

As his inch by inch exited Christian's mouth, he asked, "Do you like that?"

Coach couldn't emit a sound. He nodded frantically.

"You haven't seen anything yet." Christian dove down to his hole and twisted his tongue inside.

Pre-cum flowed down Coach's shaft as his balls rolled between Christian's fingers.

Christian twisted the hairy sac and controlled all of Coach's pelvis' movement. He was now in complete control. He felt Coach give himself over to him and instantly took over.

A condom and bottle of lube were on the nightstand as if the someone expected this to happen, and then they were used. Coach's ass was greased and ready as Christian sheathed his cock. He stroked its length a few times to lube it and traced Coach's crack to his waiting hole.

With one jump, Christian was on top of and inside him. His hips glided like a sleek animal as the two men became one. His thick cock filled Coach.

Coach didn't know what hit him. He was pinned and then filled. Before his body could feel the pain, a warm feeling took over his ass. The warmth grew to heat and then to pleasure deep inside.

Christian's hand let go of his hips and reached between his legs. He found Coach's fleshy hard-on, as he ran his hand to the tip, more pre-cum flowed over his fingers. He squeezed as he stroked and felt Coach's body go wild under his touch. He plunged into him as he pulled on his penis.

Coach moaned and thrust his hips to match Christian's. So many times he'd seen this young man's body in the locker room and shower. How many times he wished to just touch? Taste? Anything? And today, tonight, he had it all, by his parent's request.

Christian pounced harder. He had more strength, more energy surging through his body. He didn't feel that same, but so much better, more alive, more aware. His senses were keener, and he savored each thrust as if it were his first. His hands burned from Coach's body heat, and he wanted more, more, more.

Coach reached up and combed his fingers through the hair on Christian's body. It seemed thicker and longer than it did in the shower. He found his nipples and pinched them. He rolled them as hard as he could. It seemed to encourage his capturer, doubling his pace, his force, his strength.

Coach couldn't last any longer, he felt his prostate gland slammed one more time by Christian's cock, and his balls pulled up and expelled their contents. Thick cream shot out of his dick and poured between Christian's fingers.

Christian knew what the hot explosion was. He threw his head back and howled, long and loud, letting all of his sexual energy out and all of the pleasure, too. He filled Coach's ass, pumping into him again and again, until they collapsed on the floor.

Both men lay in a heap, panting. Sweat and semen ran over their hot bodies, mixing and dripping.

Coach finally moved and asked, "What was that?"

Christian just smiled a toothy grin.

"I don't understand. Where does this leave us?"

"As I see it, you can control me on the football field, but I'll control you in the bed." Christian grabbed his balls and twisted.

"Deal, but I have one question to ask."

"What?"

"What bit you?"

"Don't you mean who?"

The doorbell rang before Coach could ask any more. He rose and wrapped a towel around his waist and went to the front door in the living room. He looked out the peek hole and saw Dante, Ethan, and Lucky from his team.

Christian's naked body spooned Coach from behind. Christian licked his ear and whispered inside, "Open the door and let the rest of the pack come in … and play."

Coach didn't need to be asked twice.

THE BIG BAD WOOF!
By R. W. Clinger

R. W. Clinger has a bear at home, who goes, "Woof!" He can be reached by e-mail at <u>kenitorico@verizon.net</u>.

1. THIS LITTLE PIGGY

So maybe I am a little piggy. What's the big fucking deal? I like to sleep around and can't get enough fag-sex. Dicks are my life. Some guys are just like me. No, let me correct this, a lot of queer guys are like me in this fucked up city. We like firm pecs, long dicks, and man-asses a little too much. Line these jocks, mechanics, Marines, daddies, bears, accountants, and cowboys up … and I will fuck every one of them, any way they want me to, until they drop with satisfaction. Of course, I will take them on like a train, if I must. I'm a little piggy, and damn it, I have a reputation to uphold.

You're wondering my name, aren't you? Zander Gunn. I'm German with blond hair, blue eyes, and I sing like an *American Idol* winner. I'm five-ten, weigh approximately 175 pounds, have a muscular build, a dimple in the middle of my chin that collects jacked ooze when guys come on my face, and I have a dick the size of the Empire State Building. You want me? Of course you do. Every guy does. This is nothing new for me. I have this power over men and boys that I seem to have no control over. Something I like to call Alpha Boy Syndrome or Piggy Power. One look at me and … you'll drop to your knees, open your mouth, and beg me to slide my ten-inch shaft down the back of your throat, feeding little fucking peacock you my meat — exactly how you desire it.

I have an attitude, if you haven't guessed. To survive in New York City, you have to. If you don't, you're destined to be fucked over. No one is going to sing the blues for you, man. No one is going to save your ass when you're in deep shit. And no one, I mean no one, is going to open their heart up to you, unless you pay them with cash, your ass, or the stiff and juicy cock between your legs. I might only be twenty years old, but I'm a pretty damn smart twenty years old, if you know what I mean.

People in this neighborhood (The Bronx) say I'm a motherfucker. You want to know me, but you shouldn't know me. I'm the guy who will steal your car, money, and your boyfriend. I'm the guy you call a friend, but I'm not friendly at all. I call everyone a motherfucker, but what it boils down to is simple: I'm the biggest motherfucker out there. Your mother warned you about men like me. Stay away from them. Stay away from me. If I can find a way of breaking you ... I will. I've warned you once. It's all up to you now, of course. Don't be a dumbass and fall for me, or my game of life.

What I do? I'm a professional dealer. Not with drugs. Not with the races. Not with the lottery. Not with a list of ladies or gents I sell my body to make the green. I deal with art. Big time art. Nice art. Expensive art. Watercolors. Frescoes. Oils. Pencil drawings. Collages. Renaissance. Cubism. Pop Art. Whatever fucking art I can get my hands on. I sell it down at my father's gallery, The Gunn House. Fuck you if you don't think I can wear a monkey suit to work in. I rather look dick-stroking hot in a pressed shirt, silk tie, and an expensive pair of shoes and slacks. Brooks Brothers all the way. H&M all the way. Gucci all the way. A dapper, young man who looks like model material. Magazine-perfect. Edible and handsome and robust. It's only after work hours when I turn into an asshole. I'm like two people: art dealer during the day and a smug, bitch-boy at night. Get this straight. Learn it.

So Dad is pretty rich, but he doesn't give me a dime. He makes me work for it. Every penny. Every nickel. Every quarter. Mom doesn't even save my ass when it needs to be. My family has a strong work ethic. We get what we work for. No handouts.

No pity parties. No checks written out for hardship. You earn it, and it's yours. When you share it with others, it better be a fucking tax write-off. It's a hard pill to swallow, but you can get used to it after growing up with the concept. Count on it. I'm living proof.

Here's the deal: I work my ass off, and Dad pays me what he pays the average Joe. He says when I obtain an art degree from a city college, he'll pay me more. In the meantime, I'm fucked. Honestly, I haven't made this move in my life as of yet. College is not my thing. I'm a little too rough for it. A little too stubborn. A little too obnoxious. And a little too shitty for the stuff. I'm not ready for it, and know this. When I'm ready, I'll be the first in line to sign up. Until then, fuck off.

Here's the problem: I'm in debt. I owe over ten thousand dollars on my Visa, have numerous debts to friends, and can't manage my money worth a shit. I'm behind on my rent a total of three months. My apartment's cupboards have no food in them, and Dad isn't about to give me a raise anytime soon. I'm a stuck pig. One that squeals at the top of its chinny-chin-chin voice — this is me!

This brings me right back to being a little piggy. Listen. Pay attention. This is where the real and unbelievable Zander Gunn makes an appearance. This is where you're going to drop whatever you're doing and say, "Holy fuck!" to yourself with complete astonishment. Right here and right now is where you're going to admit to yourself: He's not lying. It's all true. He is an asshole. He is the biggest motherfucker. And he is a little piggy. I want him. All of him.

So listen.

Pay attention.

I'm not going to tell you twice.

2. HUFF AND PUFF

It's sometime in June, twilight with a purple-azure hue on the horizon, just before the vampires in the city decide to come out and play. I'm watching a naughty XXX Hot House DVD of men in the shower, soaping each other down in white, soapy suds. Beefy guys with giant nipples, long shafts, and beautiful faces. I'm relaxing after a day at Dad's gallery and hustling the paintings. The only goal I have in mind is to get my rocks off. Blow a load. Churn out some cream on my ab-lined torso, and call it a good time. Who needs friends and a fag bar, right?

Just when a boner rises in my briefs, and I begin to get all hot and bothered, there's a knock on my apartment door, which I ignore; I just want to be left alone for the evening with my ten-inch spike and its pent load. No bothers. No worries. Just me. The knocking on the apartment door ensues, though, which really starts to throw me into a pissy spin. I really don't want to be bothered. I try to ignore it for as long as possible, flick the naughty DVD off, press my boner away, and end up at the door in nothing more than my cotton underwear.

On my travels to the door, I yell, "Coming!" but not in a good way. "Jesus, Mary, and JoJo, hold your fucking dick on, man!" I finally get to the door, twist the three Yale locks counter-clockwise, pull the door open, and ...

Here he is, a teddy bear with the biggest prick on the planet. Mr. Stanley James Wolfe: six-three frame, 220 pounds, rich brown eyes, cocoa-colored military buzz cut, gold hoops in his earlobes, beautiful complexion at the age of forty-four, big hands, bigger feet, and a mound of cock under his Levi's denim that has professional porn star all over it. Wolfe is handsome in a dirty way. Think blue collar type with a hairy chest, uncut shaft, and muscles out the wazoo. Think Titanmen material. Think XXX Colt star. A working man all the way. The superintendent of the building. The fucker who collects rent payments.

Both of us know why he's here. The guy wants his dough from me, my back rent and this month's rent, which he is not too pleased about going out of his way to collect. The look on his adorable and rugged face says that he's going to kick the shit out me: strained eyes, tight cords along his neck, pursed lips. Immediately, he rattles off, "What do I want from you?"

I'm a smartass by nature, grab my balls with my right palm, give them a tender squeeze, and reply, "You came by to suck my dick, asshole."

"Besides that," Wolfe admits.

So the bulky guy surprises me, blowing me away by his confession. I'm taken aback and have to let it sink in for a few seconds that he finds me attractive. I have to allow this tidbit of information to roll between my temples and sit there in a ball for the next few seconds. Now, I decide to turn around, jiggle my rear, and reply, "You came to lick my ass-crack, didn't you?"

"We can do that later, Van. Right now I need money from you. This is why I'm here."

I quickly spin around, face him, and get an idea from his honest, yet mysterious comments, realizing in full that he likes my skin and pretty boy looks. What if I trade my chest, dick, and ass for a month's rent? Can I use him this way? Will my Alpha Boy qualities assist me in gaining what I want? Can I be a little piggy and let him fuck the rent out of me? I think about this for a few seconds in his presence, wink at him, smile, and demand, "Why don't you come in here, Wolfe. We have shit to talk about."

He's apprehensive at first, which I expect. Now, he inquires, "What kind of shit?"

"Money, and a hot little ass like mine to fuck. What do you think?"

A grin spreads across the man's butch face. His rich brown eyes light up with interest, which proves I have him right where I want his horny mind frame.

Wolfe decides to strut inside my apartment, showing off his masculinity. I tell him to have a seat on my yard sale sofa, but he chooses to stand. Now, I face him with the apartment door closed, pull down my briefs, show him a speedy glimpse of my deflated cock, and say to him, "This is the shit I can give you for the rent that is currently due. What do you say?"

He is in lust for my abs, pecs, firm nipples, the narrow treasure trail beneath my puckered navel, and the semi-exposure of my cock. He licks his lips, continues to smile, and admits, "I want more."

I push my ruby red briefs down to my ankles, kick them off, bend over like a gymnast, pick them up and off the floor, and present them to the man in front of me. I hold out the briefs for him, and say, "Smell these, faggot. Get a good whiff of them and bring them back when you want to fuck my tight ass for this month's rent. Do we have a deal?"

Wolfe takes in the limp cock between my legs: veined and uncut with a mushroom-shaped head, five inches soft, half the size it becomes when its fully charged and excited in the company of a sexy man such as the super.

He takes the cotton-blend fabric and rubs it against his nose, mouth, and a cheek. He huffs and puffs with excitement and inhales my underwear's aroma, which consists of sweat, dried semen, and piss residue. Wolfe pulls the underwear away from his face, shakes his head, and asks, "What about the other three months you owe?"

My reply is direct and to the point, "I'm sure we can make some kind of arrangement together regarding all of the money I owe you."

Again, he licks his lips, takes another deep inhalation of my briefs, nods his head, and agrees. "Yeah, maybe we can work something out."

3. LET ME IN, LITTLE PIG

Just when I think our arrangement is agreed upon, and he is going to leave, exiting my apartment with my cotton-blend underwear in tow, he admits to me, "I think it's only fair to try out the goods before I truly commit myself to this deal."

"A test-run?" I question, rub my chin, having no inclination that this would arise between us but know exactly how to work with it.

Wolfe nods his head. "Yes. A test-run ... or whatever you want to call it."

He thinks he has me by the balls, but doesn't. Remember, I'm the fucker of fuckers. I'm in control here. I'm the naked one with all the power. The Alpha Boy kicks in and I prattle, "Wolfe, how do you intend to carry out a test-run on me?"

"That's up to you," he says, beaming with an ear-to-ear grin that tells me he wants to get his rocks off.

What better time is there to rip off his clothes, drop them to the floor, and tell him to sit down on my sofa? Here it is: the perfect specimen of man for my needs, right before my eyes with his hairy brown chest exposed, nipples the size of quarters, six-three frame of all muscle, and a cock that's seven inches limp between his furry thighs. Hungry for his offered meal, I move up to him, drop to my knees in front of the sofa, peer up the slope of his rugged and nicely developed torso, and suggest, "Let me make it rock-hard for you, pal."

"Don't hold back, Van," he woofs, since I already have the tip of his hose between my lips, hardening the device for my selfish and piggy use.

Honestly, I'm quite surprised that his eleven inches of flag slides down the back of my throat and blocks off my lungs with such ease. I can't believe I don't pass out from losing oxygen because he's this long and wide in the prick department. Both of us learn quite quickly though, that he's not a challenge for me, just a toy for my Alpha Boy needs/game/gig. I take all of his girth and length into my mouthy hole, drive my nose in the brown and curly thatch of his V-shaped pubic hair region, and eventually pull off, obtaining air for just a few seconds.

Of course, I blow him with expertise. My lips, tongue, and throat all work together in synchronized motion. Pandemonium begins between us as my head shifts up and down between his thighs. I don't gag, choke, or lose consciousness. In fact, the complete opposite occurs: I have full control over the situation that links our flesh together in this wicked passion between a young and old man.

Wolfe huffs and puffs under my care. His hips rise into my face, fall away, and rise again, which transpires for the next few minutes. Sweat builds on his hairy torso. His nipples drip with perspiration, which falls to his gym-crafted abs. The man heaves for air beneath my oral piggish pleasure and …

Before he claims he's going to come, before he accidentally pops a load off into my mouth, before he coats my throat and insides with his white cream, gunning to have his orgasm, I pull off and away from him, stand, and utter in full charge, "Done, asshole. I want to ride you now."

He gives his rock a good yank and says, "Hop on, pal … Don't be shy."

Of course, I'm not going to be shy. Why should I be? The man is my sexual target, a meat-marionette on my sofa, someone I want to give instructions to, slap around, and have power over, just so I can get my rent paid, in full. Not just a month. No fucking way. The entire amount.

"Condom," he says. "I don't fuck around without using protection."

"Of course," I reply, and fetch one from my jeans on the floor.

"Roll it over my shaft," he says.

"Fuck you," I say to him. "Do it yourself." I toss the plastic in his direction, gaining control over him yet again.

Wolfe tears the condom wrapper open with teeth, rolls it down over his massive, tank-sized cock, and says, "It's all ready for you, man."

Game on. I turn around and face my Sony. I grab the lube that just happens to be there and grease up my hole. Now, the animal has a view of my broad shoulders, suntanned back, and tight, greased up ass. I cock one foot on the edge of the sofa, lift my weight, cock the other foot up on the edge of the sofa, and lower my weight onto his inflated and upright tool, ready to provide him with the ride of his life. Once I have half of his lumber inside my asshole, I lean back, find the rear of the sofa with my gripping palms, and hang on for dear life.

The connection we share is not about sex, lust, or attraction between two males. Instead, it's about rent money due and how I'm paying for it. His eleven inches of fun inside my core is nothing more than a joyride for free rent; a bill that needs to be paid; a fun-filled adventure for my bottom to make sure I have a place to live; a sex-romp and sport of seduction, so I don't get booted out of my likable apartment. This is life. This is the Alpha Boy in full action. This is my ulterior motive at its finest process. This is manipulation to the fullest potential. Fuck you if you think badly of me. Fuck you if you don't agree with this designed bond between a super and his tenant. And fuck you if you think I give a shit about you, or Wolfe. This is my gig. I call the shots. Let the tirade continue ...

4. BLOW YOUR HOUSE DOWN

I'm not afraid to be me. The rough boy. An Alpha Boy who likes to tell people what to do and demand certain things from my friends. I'm not afraid of a man's smile, laugh, intelligence, or cock. I'm not afraid to sleep around and devour as many cocks as I can up my piggy ass or convince older guys that they need to be fucked by my ten-inch prick. I'm Vander Gunn and damn proud of it. Someone who is always in control. Committed to no one but myself.

I have Wolfe exactly where I want him, underneath my weight, inside my rear, practically immobile, and obviously enjoying his time spent with me. I don't doubt that after I get him off, physically convincing him to shoot his load, I won't owe him a cent. I'll be in the clear. My payment slate with be clean, and I will have a zero balance regarding the money owed to him. In the meantime, though, I have work to accomplish; a deed that needs fulfilled; ass-action for my debt.

Overtop Wolfe, I ride his tool with authority and a limitless hunger. My bottom builds up suction on his club that is unbreakable. I bob up and down in a feisty and nonstop manner, waving above him. A north and south ride continues on his eleven inches of firm stick, which pulverizes my bottom with skill, need, and unending motion. Here, I rise and fall, doing all of the work for both of us, controlling my super's orgasm. And here, atop him, jostling up and down with tumultuous speed, he begins to howl beneath me. One fall on his cock turns into a few dozen falls, again and again, pleasuring the man to his fullest desire, so very willing to pay off my bill.

Beneath me on my dilapidated sofa, Wolfe bonds his palms with my hips and blasts inside my core. He huffs and puffs like the wolf he is, and calls me, "Pig," while fucking me. An animalistic howl of sorts escapes his mouth again, filling the apartment. His lips meet my spine, and he gnaws at my back with short but abrupt bites. His meaty piston drives into my rear, partially falls out, and drives inside yet another time. This act between us transpires for the next few minutes, sending us into united bliss.

In front of him, having my balls and cock bounce up and down because of our commotion, keeping my rump-bopping consistent on his flesh-post, I become somewhat out of breath, and challenge, "Is this a good test-run for you, man?"

He grunts his answer behind me, "I haven't made up my mind yet. Keep it up."

To my utter surprise, as I lift my weight off his post and drop it back onto his rammer, enjoying my ride and how his tool bangs my internal organs, he reaches around me with his right hand and discovers the ten inches of tool between my legs. His fingers and palm circle my shaft and take a ride of their own as I hump him.

The simplistic language of lust between two males continues here, of course: swift movement with our bodies; my arching back; grunts and growls within the apartment; an unending and driven spirit that flows sporadically throughout our bodies; the likeness of sex compounded together by two men; an up and down sport of necessary bliss; wolfish howls; piggy snorts; humping his dry and wrinkled fist, selfish for my own orgasm; sweat mixing on the sofa, sealing our naked bodies together; the pain that cradles my rear by his consistent hammering; north and south euphoria — this is what transpires; this is the scene we carry out as temporary partners, performing our deal; this is how we bring our man-play to its final act.

When do I explode? Twenty minutes into our gig? Twenty-three minutes into our gig? Twenty-nine minutes into our gig? Time becomes superfluous in my fucked up mind. A wave of hyper emotion that is steamy-hot circulates throughout my middle. My breathing intensifies as I continue to rock up and down on the man's stem. A sexual tempest occurs between my legs as my balls flap up and down by our concurrent and intensified motion. Flesh and muscle feel as if it burns off my bones. A relentless moan escapes my clenched teeth, and my chest begins to shake. Pleasure is discovered with such ease, and creamy-white man-spray flies out of my hose, arcing to the floor where it lands in puddles.

Here, atop him, feeling abrupt elation, coming in a state of pure bliss, I continue to ride his tool until the super/animal/werewolf is ready to fire out his own churn. Here, I fake a second orgasm, continuing to moan, still having control over my meat-puppet, and prompting the man beneath me to shoot his load. Here, I stray from my city boy life and fill the role of a little piggy, bucking up and down on his stiff stallion, sending him into a cataclysmic action from which he will never return.

"Blowing!" Wolfe exclaims beneath me as I yank my bottom free from his post. Having my ass positioned just a few inches above his staff, he removes the condom from his solid piece of wood. The plastic is tossed to the floor, landing in one of my cum-puddles. Beneath me, the man jacks his pole with three quick tugs, murmurs my name in utter satisfaction, and a white stream of his wolf-fluid zooms out of his prick's tip and mixes with my own on the floor. White puddles grow larger on the commercial-grade carpet, pooling between the sofa and the Sony television where I sexually devour my XXX movies by Falcon, Hot House, Colt, and Titanmen.

# # # # #

Following our stupendous mind- and cock-blowing performance, we do not kiss. Instead, I jump off the sofa, dash to the bathroom for towels, and return to Wolfe's side. Within seconds, I pass him the cotton and confess, "How much rent money does that take care of in your opinion?"

Silence. Stillness. Something. Is the asshole actually calculating an algebraic formula between his fucking temples?

Are numbers and equations skiing from one side of his brain to the other, forming an answer to my question?

"Wolfe?" I question him, perhaps pulling the man out of his mental math. "Answer my fucking question."

He smiles at me: greedily, hungrily, without any emotional attachment to me whatsoever; exactly how I want this situation and his lack of feeling to seem. The smile is seared on his face, and he finally replies, "A quarter of the amount you owe me."

"You get three more fucks then, right?" Again, I control the man, unwilling to perform more than my suggested three times, booting him from my fucked up life until I need to pay my rent again in August … September … October … or close to the holidays.

The man nods his head, cleaning off his cock with the cotton towel I have so courteously provided for him.

What comes over me next is nothing sinister. In truth, my behavior is rather spontaneous, and proves that I will not let the hulking and sexy man fuck with me. I walk up to him, swing my right arm in his direction with a swift motion, open its palm, and nail a smack to his right cheek.

Wolfe's head flies to the right, just as I intend. He gives me a look that questions: What the fuck was that about? But, he seems to like the hit at the same time, greedy for a few slaps.

My response is curt, rather alluring, and strong-willed, "I just want you to know who makes the rules in this apartment."

The man rubs his cheek, shares a confused look with me, and says, "Whatever, pal."

Our meeting ends abruptly, I realize. He dresses, takes a piss in my bathroom, tells me that he'll be back sometime soon for his second rent payment, and leaves my apartment with my briefs in a pocket of his jeans. Over his right shoulder, on his way out, he adds, "Fucking hottest ass I've ever bashed, Van. I can't wait until next time to do you all over again."

I ignore the fucker's comment, slam the door behind him, lock the locks, and decide to have a beer, celebrating my Alpha Boy tendencies, and how I plan on continuing to pay for my rent for the next year — or however long I decide to cradle Wolfe's steeping dick inside my tight man-trap.

DOUBLE-CROSSED
By Mark Apoapsis

Mark Apoapsis doesn't currently have a website but may be reached at mapoapsis@excite.com.

Jerry had not given me his telephone number, let alone the address of his lodgings — his pad, I supposed they called it these days — but that didn't stop me from finding him. It never does. So here I was, a week after we'd met in one of those bars that had become increasingly easy to find in San Francisco in recent years, standing on his balcony, peering through the perfectly formed panes of glass in the sliding door to catch a glimpse of his perfectly formed body in the darkness of his bedroom.

He lived close to one of the many college campuses that had sprung up around the Bay Area over the last five or ten decades, and I wondered if he was a student. With so many people continuing their education past high school these days, I find that half of the men in the age range I usually go after are still in school. Although in this case, it could be argued that Jerry had been the one who'd gone after me. He'd ignored several very attractive young men who'd seemed close to his own age, and had come up to talk to me instead. He probably figured me for twice his age, assuming his eyes could make out the gray threading through my black hair in the dim light of the bar. He seemed to be one of those fellows who are attracted to distinguished-looking older men. On the other hand, he'd also ignored a number of men who looked older than I, easily old enough to be his father, and after talking to him for a few minutes, it was clear to me that he wasn't one of those young guys who have a daddy fetish and are hoping to be spanked. Not that I haven't played along with that in my time, to get what

I really wanted. But not Jerry. No, he couldn't wait to get me into a shadowy corner the back room and down on my knees, where he wanted me to suck him off. Which, technically, is just what I had done. It was refreshing. I like it when I find someone as self-assured and aggressive as he was. It's so much more satisfying to take a strong-willed man like that and reduce him to my submissive plaything.

My eyes having long since adapted to darkness, I could see everything in his room, down to the details on the poster with a photograph of that new foursome from Liverpool. I could see Jerry himself lying in bed on his back, smooth face completely unguarded in sleep, covers drawn up to almost cover his bare shoulders. Finally some instinct told him he was being watched, and he woke up, looked around, and seemed startled to see the silhouette of a man lurking at his window. He sat up in bed, rubbing his eyes, his long hair almost brushing his shoulders. Long hair was finally back in style for young men, after a post-war period when whole generations had affected the current military-regulation hair styles. Personally, I associated long hair with freedom, as he no doubt did; a shorn man was a humiliated, submissive man. Maybe I would make him cut it.

He swung his bare legs out of bed. He was clad only in boxer shorts. There was something to be said for modern fashions of sleepwear, which left almost his entire body exposed for my inspection. For too long men had worn pajamas, long johns, or nightshirts. He was slim in the way that only those well under thirty ever seem to be. His nearly hairless chest was nicely muscled, his arms sinuous. I'm something of a connoisseur of men's muscles, and seeing him without his clothes for the first time, I could tell at a glance that he'd acquired these by a systematic program of lifting weights, not by working on a farm or carrying a heavy shield. I've stripped enough farmhands and soldiers to know the difference.

He padded up to the sliding glass door and unlocked it, as they always do. He slid it open, shivering a little as the cool air hit his bare chest.

"Hey, man," I greeted him, trying my best to sound like I was from his generation. "Remember me? Last week, at the …"

"I remember. What the fuck are you doing on my balcony, man? How the hell did you even get up here?"

"I couldn't stop thinking about you," I said, which was not entirely a lie.

"Well, get in here so I can close the door. I'm freezing."

That was all I needed to hear. I stepped across the metal tracks the door slid along and effortlessly slid the door shut behind me without turning away from my intent examination of Jerry.

"Look, man," he said, "it's not that I didn't enjoy what you did in the bar. That was an intense scene. It sure wasn't an ordinary blow job. But you have to admit it's a little weird for you to come to my apartment in the middle of the night looking for seconds. If you'd called, then maybe …"

"I'm calling now. Oh." I glanced at the telephone on his nightstand, its base, receiver, and long coiled cord all a matching shade of yellow that would have seemed garish a few years before but was probably the most muted shade in Jerry's whole room. "You never gave me your telephone number."

"I guess that's true. How did you find me?" He moved toward the wall switch that I knew from experience would turn on an electric light, but I quickly stepped in his way.

"Um," he said, "just let me put some clothes on, and we'll talk."

"No," I said. "I won't let you put some clothes on."

He looked astonished at my boldness. Then he grinned and said, "OK, cool, what the heck. I'm cool with that; I'm awake now and horny anyway. Let's get you out of your clothes." He reached for the top button of my shirt.

"No," I said again, grabbing his wrists. He tried to break away. He was strong, but not strong enough.

"Whoa!" he said, grinning. "You're even strong than you look. I'd love to see what you've got under all those layers of clothing. We did it in such a hurry last time; I didn't even make you take off your shirt. It'll be nice to take our time."

"We do have all night," I agreed, "and I intend to take my time." I let go of his wrists and lifted him by his armpits, pinning him against the wall with his bare feet dangling about the carpet.

"Whoa!" he exclaimed again. And then he could only make soft involuntary sounds of pleasure as I explored every exposed part of his body with my lips, tongue, and finally teeth.

It was less than two hours before dawn by the time I left him, quivering naked on his bed. His boxers were gone; I'd eventually ripped them off with my teeth. I was still fully clothed. "You're mine now," I whispered to my semiconscious young conquest, running my fingertip one last time from his throat down to his navel. "I'll be back in a week or two." I paused to lick a few stray drops of precious fluid that had run down into the hollow formed by his rising and falling belly. "You'll have recovered by then."

# # # # #

I continued visiting a few hours after sunset, every week or so. Whether in resignation or because the sun was setting earlier, he began waiting up for me and stopped locking the door to his balcony. Probably resignation, since he never knew which nights I would come; I liked to keep the timing unpredictable, and didn't bother keeping track of days of the week now anyway, since I was no longer working. On the one hand, finding him awake meant I no longer had the pleasure of watching him reluctantly approach the door in his boxer shorts, but on the other hand, I had the even better pleasure of slowly stripping off his clothes with my own hands. The look on his face as he let me peel off his tie-dyed T-shirt and unzip his ripped jeans was always priceless. I could tell he was used to being the one who decided when his clothes came off, if they ever did, and how long he'd leave the other fellow's clothes on. Sometimes, depending on my whims and degree of self control, I would leave him merely shirtless and drained; other times I would leave him utterly naked and smeared with his own delicious juices.

# # # # #

Despite having been reduced to my plaything — or more likely because of it, to compensate for being another man's plaything — he maintained an active sex life. So in hindsight, it was just a matter of time, as winter deepened, before I interrupted something.

I heard two men's voices in the living room as soon as I entered. Voices, and the not-unfamiliar sound of leather slapping against meaty bare flesh. I couldn't make out the words, but I recognized the taunting voice as Jerry's. The other voice, the one with the pleading tone, punctuated by involuntary grunts and whimpers, was a stranger's. I knew that in this day and age, any torture going on in the next room would be playful and consensual. The days were long gone when Jerry could have bought a real sex slave on the open market, or even the black market. The two had probably even prearranged a code word that would end the torture, leaving the submissive one free to beg as much as he wanted to without being taken seriously. That custom went back even to my time; when I was a young man wrestling with my friends for dominance, the universal code word indicating submission was the word for "father's brother." Unless Jerry's sex partner spoke their agreed-upon code word, they could both pretend Jerry could do whatever he pleased, and he was utterly at his mercy. I would enjoy changing the rules of their little game by asserting my ownership of young Jerry right in front of the man he was dominating.

I rounded the corner — and recoiled in horror. There was a time when I would have turned and fled the building, but by now I was mature enough to summon up enough self control to stand my ground. It wasn't that Jerry was busy whipping a prisoner, or that the prisoner had been stripped completely naked and was tied up and helpless. I'd expected something like that. It was the way he'd been tied up. I wouldn't have blinked if the prisoner, a brawny, hairy man who looked at least ten year's Jerry's senior, had been spread-eagle on the floor or strung up by the wrists. But he'd been secured to an upright wooden frame that held his arms and legs spread out — a *crux decussata*, in the shape of the numeral "ten." I shuddered. Intellectually, I knew it was all in play, but any kind of torture device made of two wooden crossbeams fills me with visceral revulsion — really freaks me out, as they say nowadays. Back in my day, they used to be a standard way to execute common criminals and captured enemies, and the sight of one always brings back memories that still haunt me after all these years, of watching six comrades slowly dying on those things over a period of days. While I, as naked and helpless as they were, was doing the same thing. They'd used a different style on us, the kind with a vertical stake and a horizontal crossbeam, but I'd seen men die equally painfully on both styles. I had spent my last days watching men I loved and had fought alongside being slowly torn apart under their own weight. My last days, but as it turned out, not my last nights. I woke up later at the bottom of a pile of the cooling bodies of my friends, and had to claw my way out. So after watching my buddies die in literally excruciating pain on one of those infernal devices, excuse me if I still suffer from a touch of post-traumatic stress to this day when I see anything resembling that shape.

Summoning up the hard-earned self control I'd learned over the centuries, I recovered quickly by focusing on the obvious realities of the here-and-now. The toes of the naked man before me were curled in the plush modern carpet, his weight supported by his feet, and only straps secured his strong arms and legs. He wasn't hurting, only helpless, and he obviously liked it that way; he was fully erect. He'd heard my gasp and was now glaring at me, looking slightly embarrassed and greatly annoyed at the interruption — not desperately hopeful, as I knew any real prisoner would have looked when there was any unexpected interruption. Jerry suddenly noticed that he no longer had his captive's attention and also turned around to face me. He, too, looked annoyed, even angry, but it was a helpless sort of rage.

"How convenient," I said, hiding my discomfit and taking a brave step toward the crux. "You've arranged a captive audience for what I'm going to do to you."

Jerry was holding a leather belt. He'd been flogging his captive with what was probably the fellow's own belt, since he himself was still wearing one. I took the belt from his unresisting hand. Then I took away the one he was wearing. He was fully clothed in a leather jacket over a black T-shirt, both of which I also took away from him. Facing growing red, he glanced back at the man who was watching us helplessly.

By the time I'd finished having my way with him, Jerry was naked, trembling, and drained. Then I made him kneel in front of his prisoner. With one hand I coaxed the older man's flaccid penis back to the state it had been when I'd walked in, and with the other I guided Jerry's head close to it. Few things are more humiliating than a master forced to pleasure his slave. I kept his hair wound around my fist until he'd brought the bound and naked man to climax, then made him swallow. Finally, I let him slide to the ground, released the prisoner, and wrestled the burly man onto the ground on top of Jerry to do some more sucking of my own.

As always, I left them weak but alive. Not only did this self control allow me to keep coming back for more, it was actually the safer strategy these days. Society had changed in my lifetime; people now took unexplained dead bodies a lot more seriously, and wild stories of monsters a lot less seriously, than anyone had even as recently as a century ago. So now I usually played with my food, and always stopped when I was no longer hungry, not when I was satiated.

# # # # #

When I next returned, about a week after humiliating him by making him pleasure his own "slave," Jerry was once again alone and all the lights were off, just the way I liked it. He was awake and still dressed, in jeans and a white T-shirt streaked with bright purple and yellow dyes. As soon as he saw me, he jumped up and walked quickly to a switch on the wall. A light bulb lit up, in the instant way those electric light bulbs do, but instead of the usual yellowish white light, the room was bathed in a dim purple light, dimmer than a full moon, although certain of the posters on the wall began glowing colorfully from within, as though they too had hidden lights embedded. Despite the apparent dimness of the light, it felt like the sun had just risen. The strength began seeping out of me.

Not for the first time, I regretted conforming to current fashions. Back when I was a soldier, I'd worn a red cape, and for a long time after that I'd been in the habit of wearing various styles of capes. Say what you will about them being cumbersome and extraneous, I could have used one right about now to shield my face and other exposed skin from that mysterious purple light. Instead, I was wearing a button-down shirt with nothing underneath, and I'd left the top couple of buttons deliberately unfastened so that my chest hair curled over it, something I'd recently found to be helpful in attracting men when I went to the right sort of bars. It left my throat completely exposed to the enervating light and even let a little light hit my chest. I hastily tried to button it up, turning my back on the light, which I could still feel seeping in through the back of my thin shirt.

Jerry, the white parts of his T-shirt glowing with an unnaturally blue glow, brighter even than the parts dyed in neon colors, somehow brighter than the very light that illuminated it, lunged at me and ripped my shirt open. I was slow to react, and he spun me around so that my bare chest was bathed in dim purple light. I tried desperately to draw my shirt shut, but he pinned my weakening arms behind my back, and my shirt fell completely open, exposing my entire chest and flanks to the strange light. My knees grew weak, and I sagged in his arms. After a few moments, he let me sink to me knees and roughly stripped the shirt off my back entirely.

He walked around to face me, careful not to cast his shadow across me, as I knelt there at his feet, bare to the waist. "I've been wanting to get your shirt off since I met you. Wow, you really are built. I'm a little surprised, now that I know what you really are."

"I used to be a warrior," I said.

"Yeah, well, now you're a vanquished warrior. How does it feel to be the one at another man's mercy?"

"Familiar," I said miserably.

"What? No way!"

"Back in my day, we didn't have the Geneva Convention, or the British Articles of War, or any of those modern reforms. Prisoners of war could expect to be stripped, flogged, tortured, humiliated, enslaved, even used as sexual playthings by their captors. Everyone did it back then. I did some of that myself, more times than I can remember. And once in a while I was on the losing end of it."

"It sounds almost you like it. I think that's your scene."

"Not at all. Does a boxer like being beaten senseless in front of an audience? What I liked was winning, but I knew I always risked being taken prisoner if I wasn't killed in battle. I just never expected it to happen again, now that that life is over."

"Well, it's happening." He knelt behind me and put his arms around me under my armpits, with his fingers interlocked against my chest, and began laboriously dragging me backwards.

"Where are you taking me?"

"Where do you think?" he grunted, pausing to rest.

I realized he was dragging me directly toward the *crux decussata*. "No! No, please! Anything but that! I'll be your slave for the rest of your life! Anything! Just don't put me on that thing! Do whatever else you want. Tie me to the bed, string me up by the wrists, just not ... not ..."

"Hey, man, chill out, it's okay," he said, suddenly gentle. "Is that really the only thing that freaks you out about being my prisoner? Hey, are you crying?" He was kneeling at my side with his arm around my bare shoulders.

"Please, I'm begging you," I sobbed. "I know I'm in your power, and I can't stop you from doing anything you want to me. Please just promise me you'll never put me on one of those, and I'll do anything you want."

"OK, I promise. Just as well. This is killing my back, just dragging you over to it. I'm used to more cooperative prisoners, to tell the truth. Let's get you onto the bed."

Between us, we managed to get me over to the bed and roll me onto it, where I lay on my back, exhausted, as he bound my wrists over my head, removed my shoes and socks, and lashed my ankles together. He needn't have bothered; my bare chest was still bathed in the strange purple light, and I was getting weaker by the moment. Also, I'd given my word to be his slave for the rest of his life. A bit rash; that could be fifty years, even eighty, which was a long time even for me. With luck, he'd tire of me within a decade. At his age, even the four years he was spending in college must seem like a significant time.

He left the room and came back a few minutes later with a sharp knife. I whimpered, thinking he was preparing to torture me for hours in ways that would quickly kill an ordinary man. But he only made one shallow cut across my upper chest that barely stung. "Is it true what the stories say?" he asked me, as I felt a wet trickle slowly running toward the center of my upper chest to pool between my pectoral muscles, matting down my chest hair.

"Some of them," I said weakly. "Which stories?"

"I guess I'll find out. I've got to try this just once." He bent over me and began licking my chest as I squirmed helplessly.

# # # # #

"Man, you're the perfect pet for a college student, aren't you?" Jerry said teasingly as he dragged me out of the walk-in closet where I'd spent the last several hours, or was it days, draped uncomfortably over a wooden footlocker, bound and gagged and still bare-chested, with my head wedged between a water pipe I'd once found him using to smoke marijuana and a pile of winter coats that he must have brought with him from a colder part of the country. The journey from the East Coast was trivial these days. It had taken me eight months, on a wagon train that lost an unusually high number of young men to coyote attacks, but it had been worth the trip. Most of the '49ers never struck it rich, but for me, as for Levi Strauss and Wells Fargo, the men themselves proved to be a gold mine.

Jerry removed the gag, asking teasingly, "Are you sure I don't need to put you on a leash and take you for a walk?"

I blinked against the late afternoon light that stole in around the edges of the carefully drawn curtains. "I don't need to relieve myself, if that's what you mean. Ever. But I do need to be fed a few times a week. Please."

"A few times a week? You're better than a goldfish." He pulled off his tie-dyed T-shirt and knelt down beside me, pulling me close until I could feel the warmth of his chest against my own, and his musky young scent against my nose, irresistible as always. The difference was that this time he was in control, and I knew I would never again get as much of him as I wanted.

# # # # #

Over the next few days, or months, he emptied out the clutter until there was room for a wooden chair. He kept me tied to it, still shirtless and barefoot, and replaced the bare electric light bulb in the ceiling with one of the dim purple bulbs he'd ensnared me with. The light was brighter than a full moon inside, but most of it came not from the purple bulb itself but from the blue glow it magically drew from every T-shirt hanging behind me, every threadbare patch of blue jeans, even from ordinarily invisible specks of lint on the floor. Spilling down my bare chest, it also magically drew every ounce of strength out of me.

Periodically Jerry would come and gloat over me and sometimes make a fresh cut across my chest and followed the trickle down my sternum to my belly with his tongue. The cuts always healed within minutes, as all my wounds do. The captors who had crucified my comrades and me had whipped our backs and buttocks to shreds with straps embedded with sharp rocks, but I had woken up to find my skin smooth and whole again, and even the holes clear through my wrists had already started to scab over and heal without a scar within a night or two — although it seemed like I spent weeks picking splinters out of my back. In the centuries since then, I've recovered from even worse wounds.

I couldn't tell whether Jerry's visits were hourly or weekly. I had no outside light to judge by, was perpetually groggy in the strange purplish-blue half-light, and the only bodily function I had to give me clues to mark the time was thirst, which he slaked by allowing me small sips of water and, all too rarely, even smaller sips of something much tastier and stronger — himself.

Over a dozen times before I stopped counting, I heard male voices and laughter, muffled by the closed door, often followed by moans and pleadings further muffled by gags of their own, punctuated by the light slap of leather against exposed backs and buttocks. In between men, he used his belt on me, too. The pain was nothing; he was holding back, and even if he'd really laid into me, it was only leather. But the humiliation was like nothing I'd experienced in a long time — longer than he'd been alive.

One day he wanted to show me a new toy he'd acquired. He untied my ankles from the chair legs. My wrists had also been bound together as always, twisted behind the back of the chair, and he released the rope that tethered them to the chair but left them bound. He hoisted me to my feet — he was stronger than I'd realized — and helped me stagger across the room. I saw one of the purple light bulbs on in the bedroom, in addition to the ordinary bright yellowish lights. It hardly mattered; my muscles were twisted in knots, and in any case, I was sworn to him for life even if I did get a chance to escape.

There was no sign of the *crux decussata*. He'd installed a horizontal metal bar across a doorway, probably designed more for chin-ups than the types of exercises he apparently used it for. He raised my arms over my head as I leaned against him weakly, and tied my wrists to it. I wasn't technically strung up, since the bar was not all that high; my bare feet were still firmly planted on the carpet.

The new toy turned out to be a wooden paddle with three uppercase Greek letters carved into it. They didn't seem to spell any word I knew. Admittedly my Greek was a little rusty, and that language was probably changing as fast as English was.

"I made the guy I had over last night leave this with me," Jerry said. "He probably wasn't supposed to even bring it with him. But his fraternity probably isn't supposed to have those traffic signs decorating their walls, either. He also wasn't supposed to let someone other than the pledge master and other frat brothers use it on him. He told me they don't pull his pants down when they do it. What's the fun in that, I say?"

He undid the button fastening my pants and began toying with the zipper. I moaned, already anticipating the smack of solid wood against my naked buttocks.

# # # # #

He never did give me my pants back after that, although just before taking me down he pulled my boxer shorts back up — not before a long and possessive inspection of my genitals. At least my sore butt wasn't in direct contact with the hard wooden chair, although the thin layer of cotton didn't offer much padding.

It was days before the physical ache faded. At least, I judged it was days, because I heard the usual muffled male conversation and laughter and other sounds twice in that time. It would take much longer for the humiliating memory to fade. The only consolation was that there had been no one there to witness how completely in Jerry's power I was when he had strung me up and pulled my remaining clothing down to my ankles and spanked me until I had begged him for mercy.

Then one day, I heard one of the muffled conversations approaching my makeshift cell, until I could make out words.

"It's true," I heard Jerry say through the door. "That's what the black light's for. I'll prove it. I've got him right here."

He opened the door. His guest was a man even younger than he, with long hair held back by a headband. The stranger wore nothing above his waist but an open denim vest and a string of beads — love beads, I believe they were called. He had a lean, tanned chest that I longed to sink my teeth into.

"No way!" the stranger said in delight. "But how do I know he's not some regular guy?

"I'll show you." Jerry turned to me. "You've been looking pale lately. If I untie you and let you have a snack from Gilbert here, will you promise not to finish him off? And do exactly as I say?"

"I promise, *dominus*," I said with unfeigned meekness. It had been a long time since I'd called any man that; it meant something along the lines of "master" or "possessor" or "dominator." It certainly fit our current relationship.

He picked up my chair, with me in it, and backed slowly out of the closet. Then he untied me. "Kneel at Gilbert's feet and do it like you did to me the first night we met."

The young man, Gilbert, pulled his pants down, but left his underwear on. I nuzzled the bottom of his red briefs, savoring the scent of his smegma even through the cotton, and then closed my mouth on his lean upper thigh. He gasped.

I was even thirstier than I'd realized. Gilbert gripped my bare shoulders tightly, supporting himself as his knees began to buckle, but seemed unwilling to pull away.

"Enough!" Jerry said firmly, stepping in and dragging me away. "Gotta leave some fight in him, or he won't be any fun at all." His young friend staggered, and Jerry caught him and easily lifted him in his arms and carried him to his bed. I didn't see what they did after that, since Jerry came back and retied me to the chair and moved it back into the closet, closing the door.

# # # # #

"Now that I'm in a real house, you'll have your own room," Jerry said as he helped me out of the crate in which I'd been transported, bound and gagged with my nearly naked body packed in sawdust, by two professional movers whose strong virile bodies I could almost smell right through the sawdust, tantalizingly out of reach.

My new room, which had no windows, was of course equipped with several of those dim purple lights that kept me weak and helpless even at night, as well as ordinary lights. It was empty that day, but in the end he didn't give it over to me entirely as my prison; he installed exercise equipment that he used himself, shirtless and just out of reach, as I watched, my mouth watering. I never knew when he would offer me a drink. He also filled it with various bondage devices, which he used both on me and on about one out of three of his guests; the others he played with in some other room I never saw. Some exercise devices served double duty.

When he brought a man into my room, I waited to see whether he'd just brought him in to admire his prisoner or whether he would strap him down and play with him in front of me. If he did so, I could usually count on being offered at least one drink.

My boxer shorts were long gone by now. They'd gotten ragged, and finally the last tatters had been ripped away by one of the men Jerry allowed to torment and pleasure me. It had been one of the younger ones, even younger than he. Some years must have passed because Jerry's face and body had gotten slightly thicker. Not as many as it felt like, because his hair, which he'd eventually cut much shorter and then repeatedly gotten trimmed, showed no signs of graying or thinning. Surely he'd get tired of me in a few more years, or failing that, as he entered middle age. Clothing styles had changed several times; bushy mustaches had gone in and out fashion, and there was a brief period I rather missed now, where men wore their shirts unbuttoned halfway, apparently right out on the public street, judging from their tan pattern.

I told myself I'd get my freedom back sooner or later, when Jerry's life, or at least his youthful vigor, inevitably ebbed away. How much longer? How long had it been? He hadn't aged much so far. I had no idea how long electric light bulbs lasted, but certainly he'd replaced each of the bulbs in my room countless times. The newest ones were not bulb-shaped at all, but were swirled like soft ice cream, and the "vanilla" ones were bluish while, not yellowish like the old bulbs.

The latest guest was even older than Jerry's usual taste, his hair mostly gray and receding, and he was plumper than Jerry usually liked them. "Dude, I don't believe you've kept him all this time!" the older man said. "And he looks exactly the same, even more so than ... Whoa, this is so awesome!"

I'd heard other guests use that last word once or twice recently and was beginning to realize it had a new watered-down sense. I gathered that "dude" could now mean any man; it used to reliably lead me to lean, muscled surfers, and then for awhile it referred to disappointingly scrawny, socially inept men. It was harder than ever to keep up with all the language changes now that I was in captivity, to the point where I sometimes couldn't follow at all. Like now.

"You remember Gilbert? We wreak 'n' neck did on line." The syllables sounded like English, but I had no idea what Jerry was saying. And I certainly didn't recall the names of the endless parade of men he'd subjected to me or subjected me to.

"You go first, Jerry," Gilbert said. With a bittersweet smile, he watched the younger man take off his shirt. Then suddenly he said, "Wait a second. Let me get my phone." That made no sense unless the word was no longer short for "telephone": we were in Jerry's house, not his, and instead of leaving the room he began fishing around in his pocket. He added incomprehensibly, "This is totally going on you, too, brighter way."

45

CLIMBING THE MAST
By HL Champa

HL Champa is an extensively published writer of erotic fiction. Find out more at http://heidichampa.blogspot.com.

The three worst words that can ever be uttered in the work place had just been spoken in my office; again. Team building exercise. We all tried to stifle our sighs and groans, but it didn't work. Each one of us was leaning out of our cubicles, staring at our boss, who was holding a stack of brochures for our next forced adventure. I closed my eyes and pinched the bridge of my nose between my thumb and finger. As the boss droned on and on about how highly regarded this place was and how exciting it was going to be for the rest of us, I cast my mind back to our last team building exercise. And, the one before that.

Morale had never been high at our office, but lately, things had dipped to an all-time low. Two more tortured souls had just quit, leaving the rest of us even more overworked and still chronically underpaid. The first attempt to bring us all together Kumbaya style, was an obstacle course almost a year ago. That day ended in tears for some and mud stained clothes for all. Then, three months later, there was the trust seminar, the mandatory softball league and finally, a few months back, the empathy training. None of them had succeeded in doing anything but wasting our time and putting us even further behind schedule on our work. I was officially too old for this shit.

This time, we would be sailing aboard a replica tall ship that was moored in a nearby harbor. According to the brochure that the boss had dropped into my lap, we were going to learn the basics of sailing and be charged with getting the ship from point A to point B without sinking or running aground. I only hoped that the boat company had good insurance. *The Southern Star* claimed to be able to bring any group of people together in pursuit of a common goal, all while having fun and learning. They promised a lot. Clearly, this boat had never seen an office environment like Murphy and Paula Designs. In our little group, *The Southern Star* may have just met its match. The only reason we all agreed to do it was the promise of the open bar and buffet after we completed our mandatory sailing instruction. We all begrudging signed on; knowing that a few hours of bullshit would be worth eating our weight in free shrimp.

We arrived at the dock around noon one Tuesday, none of us in any way prepared for what was about to occur. Most of my co-workers had downed a few drinks at our pre-sail lunch, to help calm their nerves. Some of them were starting to regret their choice of beverage, thinking about the effects those glasses of wine and beer would have on their stomachs once we got moving. If there was a less sea-worthy group of people on earth, I'd like to meet them.

We were welcomed aboard the beautiful boat, which appeared in every way the real deal I'd only ever seen in movies and history books. Except for the engine and the bathrooms located below deck. There had to be some concessions to the modern world when dealing with tourists and reluctant team builders like us. We stood on the deck in a semicircle, while the crew, all dressed as if it were still 1850, appeared before us. They were all in knickers that fell to just below their knees, flowing white shirts and blue kerchiefs, tied loosely around their necks. None of them had shoes on.

As we met our "captain" for the day and were given preliminary instructions, I found myself distracted by a young, handsome member of the crew that seemed just as disinterested as the rest of us. He shifted restlessly from side to side, his bare feet sliding a bit on the teakwood deck. His muscular calves were bare, protruding from his short pants, covered in a smattering of dark hair. As my eyes moved up, I took in his solid frame, before settling my gaze on his face. He was looking at the captain as I studied his dark features, the slope of his nose and the deep brown of his eyes. There was a bandana tied around his dark hair, only a few stray curls managing to escape out the back. It showed off his thick neck and part of a tattoo that started somewhere below the line of his shirt.

Suddenly the boat lurched, the wake of another boat making ours move before we were ready. I was so busy staring at the cute deck hand, I reacted too late and found myself down on my knees in a heap. My co-workers didn't even bothering to help me up. So much for the team. The rest of the group followed the captain as he began to explain the finer points of hoisting a sail. Luckily for me, my new favorite sailor turned out to be my knight in shining armor as well. He extended his hand, which I took without thought and stood up, hoping I wasn't blushing too much after my embarrassing fall. He gave my hand a squeeze and despite my return to my feet, he didn't let go of my hand. I could hear the captain, regaling everyone with tales of the sea, but I stayed right where I was, right in front of my very own sexy sailor. I wanted to say something to redeem myself, to make myself sound smoother than I obviously was, but no words would come out. He saved me yet again by speaking first.

"Looks like someone doesn't have their sea legs yet. It's going to be a long day for you."

His voice was deeper and raspier than I thought it would be for someone who looked to be only about twenty-one or twenty-two. It also contained the hint of a New Jersey accent, which was the last thing I expected to hear on a replica tall ship. He didn't speak in a fake British accent like the captain, and there was no attempt to keep up with traditional language or diction. I was glad he wasn't playing along. In that moment, it was nice to be talking to a real person and not some guy who took his job way too seriously.

"I don't think I'll ever have them. We haven't even left the dock yet. I'm in trouble. And, there's no chance of getting help from my colleagues. They'd sooner drown than help me out. We aren't exactly a close knit group."

"Don't worry. We'll do our best to look after you if no one else will. And, if you fall overboard, we have ways of getting you out of the water. No worries. I'm an expert at mouth to mouth."

His devious smile made the heat return to my face. Two of his bottom teeth were crooked, but it only gave him more charm.

"How come you don't have to stay in character like the captain does?"

"I'm supposed to, but I'm not really very good at pretending to be from the past. They hired me for my sailing skills, not my acting. Plus, I get college credit for it. I leave the real acting stuff to the drama kids they have on board. Don't worry. You'll get all the old time flare you can handle. I'm Lou, by the way."

"Travis."

Our hands were still locked together, so there was no need for a traditional handshake. He finally let me go, much to my disappointment. We joined the rest of the group, just in time to be divided into our two teams. Neither of them appealed to me, but I still took it personally when I was picked second to last. There was no way I was a worse sailor than some of my colleagues, but my profound indifference might have been my undoing. Once we were divided, each team was assigned members of the crew that would oversee our voyage and show us the ropes, so to speak. My luck continued, as my young friend, Lou, was in charge of my team.

The boat finally left the safety of the dock, and we set out into the more open water. The lunchtime drinks had another effect on some of my brethren. A few of the ladies started madly flirting with the member of the sailing team that happened to be standing closest to them. *The Southern Star* crew must have gotten this kind of thing all the time as they all seemed to take it in stride, but I was still embarrassed to be a part of such a display. As much as I wanted to fawn all over the handsome deckhand now showing me how to hoist a sail, it seemed out of the question in a work environment. Decorum didn't stop Lou from winking at me, however, causing me to lose concentration at a critical moment and nearly costing my team valuable points. For the first time all day, I had galvanized my co-workers, giving them a common enemy to work against. The intensity soon dissipated, however, when one member of the other team had to be excused to throw up overboard.

I tried to follow Lou's instructions and be a productive member of my team, but that wasn't easy with him distracting me. With his every move, he seemed to touch me in some way or brush up against me. During our turn at the helm, Lou was behind me the whole time, at one point his whole body pressed against me while we worked on the rigging. His innocent contact turned out to be fine until his hand grazed over my ass while no one was looking, right before our team took a break. When I turned to look at him, his expression was one of desire, all air of professionalism gone from his adorable face. His lustful gaze dropped to my lips, just for a few seconds before coming back to my eyes. The rest of my group was in their own world, trying to stay out of the other team's way. Lou and I stood next to each other, both of us pretending to be interested in the proceedings. To the outside world, it looked innocent enough, but when the words came out of his mouth, they were anything but. He spoke softly, so only I could hear him, leaning just a bit closer as he did.

"Later, once the party starts, I'm going to fuck you, Travis."

I looked at him, unable to respond at first.

"Unless you're not interested, Travis. But, something tells me that you are."

My voice came back to me just in time. I knew I shouldn't say it, but I just had to.

"I'm very interested, Lou."

His eyes dropped to my crotch, the evidence of my interest plain to see. He leaned just a bit closer, until his voice was directly in my ear. His tongue flicked across my earlobe before he breathed his last words.

"Good. Glad to hear it, Travis. I'll find you later."

He shot another wink at me before walking away; I couldn't stop my dick from stirring in my business casual khaki pants. I quickly found a place to sit, so I could conceal the evidence of my arousal. As our teams took turns navigating specific paths across the calm water, my thoughts were less focused on the task at hand and more focused on what would happen with Lou below deck at some point in the evening.

Both of our groups managed to sail better than anyone expected. There was only one near miss with a buoy, and the screaming and finger pointing was kept to a minimum as we formed tenuous bonds of teamwork. Sadly, my team didn't win and therefore didn't get the nifty certificates that my boss had printed out, but we held our heads high in moral victory, as none of us had gotten sick. When we finished up, Lou put a hand on my shoulder and smiled at me before disappearing, just as the food and drink started to flow for our reward party.

I grabbed another drink from the free bar and downed it quicker than I should have. My co-workers and boss were knee deep in the canapés and shrimp, just as I expected. My eyes kept darting around the boat, in search of Lou, who seemed to have completely vanished. No small trick considering we were still in the middle of the water. The cheesy music the boat company had chosen to accompany our party made it hard to hear, which was a blessing when colleague after colleague sat down next to me and blathered on about how much fun they were having.

Just as the next wave of food made it to the buffet tables, I saw Lou appear, just over my bosses shoulder. When he smiled and crooked his finger, beckoning me to him, I could barely breathe. Using my unsuspecting fellow passengers as decoys, I made my way through the group, undetected by my boss, who still hadn't cornered me for our one-on-one chat yet. The last thing on Earth I wanted was to waste precious time listening to him drone on about togetherness when Lou was looking at me with those sexy eyes.

I had just slipped through the last of the crowd and into the quiet hall below deck that led to the front of the boat when I heard his voice. My heart jumped when I heard him, my cock stirring back to life.

"I was beginning to think you'd had a better offer, Travis. I don't like to be kept waiting."

Lou was standing in a doorway marked for employees of *The Southern Star*. Before I could respond, he grabbed the front of my polo shirt and pulled me into the small, dimly lit room. I found myself pressed against the thin wooden door, Lou's pelvis pressed firmly against mine. He turned the lock, the click loud enough to be heard over the terrible music.

"Sorry, Lou. I just had to avoid my boss, so I took the scenic route."

"Very smart. Wouldn't want you to get in trouble, now would we? Trust me, now that the prime rib is out there, no one will miss you. At least for a little while. You're all mine. Finally."

"You made it difficult for me to concentrate on sailing today, Lou."

"Well, I do what I can. You seem very good at following all my directions, though. I like that. Let's see if you can keep it up. Show me that cock, Travis. I've been wanting to see it all day."

Lou left his hand on my shoulder while I reached down and undid my belt with quick efficiency. My pants dropped to the floor, and I slid my boxers down after them. Lou lowered his eyes and licked his lips.

"Very good, Travis. Now make yourself hard for me. Jerk that cock."

When my hand touched my rapidly stiffening cock, I groaned, moving my fist up and down. My eyes stayed on Lou, his gaze moving over me slowly. There was a couch opposite the door. It sat right underneath a porthole that led out to the main deck and took up every inch of space along the wall. Lou sat down on it, still watching my every move.

"Take off the rest of your clothes, Travis. I want you naked."

I hesitated, my eyes going to the window above his head. The sound of Lou pounding his fist against the arm of the couch brought me back.

"I said now, Travis."

I pulled my polo shirt over my head, stepping out of the pants pooled at my feet. I tossed my shoes onto the pile and stood up. Lou slouched down, beckoning me with a crooked finger. I took one step toward him, but he stopped me with another gruff request.

"On your knees, Travis. Crawl to me."

His voice kicked me right in the guts and made another rush of blood flow to my cock. Despite my desire, I didn't know how to respond.

"What?"

"Did I stutter? I said, crawl over here, so you can suck my cock."

I stood stock still until the scowl on Lou's face compelled me to move. I dropped to my knees before I could think another thought, closing the small distance between us in an instant. As I knelt naked between his thighs, I felt a rush of heat all through my body. Lou ran a hand over my hair and smirked, tightening his fingers like a vice. The tug hurt, and I cried out at the pain.

"When I talk, I expect you to listen, Travis. Just like you did earlier today. Get it?

I nodded, as much as he would allow me to with my head pulled back. He let go of my hair, but his touch didn't leave me.

"Good. Now, take out my cock and suck me."

This time, I didn't miss a beat, and I undid his knickers as quickly as I could. His hand on the back of my neck left me no choice but to take him into my mouth, letting my tongue slid all the way down his shaft as I went.

"That's it. Take me deep, Travis. I want to hear you choke on my cock."

Lou had both hands on the back of my neck, forcing his dick all the way to the back of my throat. I took him; let him fuck my mouth however he wanted. I felt the saliva drip from the corners of my mouth, tears streaming down my cheeks at the force of his thrusts. My cock ached, and I moved to touch it, but Lou stopped me.

"I didn't say you could touch your cock, Travis. In fact, put your hands behind your back."

I clasped my fingers behind my back, doing exactly what Lou told me to do. Just like I had all day. His fingers twined again in my hair and gave a tug as his cock slid in and out of my mouth at a slow, steady rhythm. I moaned around him, which elicited a chuckle from Lou.

"Yeah, you like that, don't you Travis? I knew you would."

He yanked me back, leaving me gasping for air.

"Get up, Travis."

I scrambled to my feet, only to have Lou grab me by the wrist and shove me over the arm of the couch, my ass high in the air. He grabbed my arms, forcing them back to their previous position behind my back. My face rested against the cushion of the couch, and there was nothing I could do. I was completely at his mercy. And, I loved it.

His hands smoothed over my cheeks, my cock bobbing free, waiting for attention. I winced at the thick press of his fingers on my skin, the rough way he pulled my cheeks apart. I never felt more exposed, more at the mercy of someone else's whims. I waited for Lou to do something. Long seconds stretched out, the only sound in the room was our breathing and the muffled din from the party going on around us.

Finally, I felt a finger drag over my puckered hole, a quick tease, over as soon as it started. His finger returned; this time moistened with saliva. He circled my opening before pressing the tip gently inside me, his other hand closing around my cock. His fist moved up and down on my stiff dick, my moans escaping my throat for the first time.

"You want me to lick that sweet, little asshole, Travis?"

I desperately wanted to answer him, but my voice was not working. I heard Lou laughing behind me. His finger stopped moving, his hand disappearing from my cock. I whimpered in distress, but that only got another laugh.

"Come on, Travis. I need to hear it. You know you want it. Just tell me. I wanna hear the words come out of that mouth of yours."

"Lou, please. I can't."

"Sure you can. Tell me, or I'll walk out of this room right now. I'm sure I can find someone else to keep me company tonight."

I sighed, my body screaming out in protest, unable to bear anymore. I pushed my ass back toward Lou, my desiccated mouth forming the words my head was already shouting.

"Lick my asshole, Lou. Please, I want to feel your tongue on me."

"There was that so hard, Travis?"

I didn't have to wait long for Lou to oblige me. His tongue dove right in, nothing teasing or gentle about it. The tip went right for my center, pushing my asshole open little by little. His fist returned to my cock, which was aching to be touched. I couldn't stop myself from rocking back into him, trying to get more of his fat tongue in me. But, he stayed firmly in control, his tongue easing away, going back to feather-light licks around my rim. His hand stroked my cock at an erratic pace, keeping me guessing and frustrated. I groaned at the torture, but I loved every second of it. Lou was groaning, too, pushing his tongue back into my ass, wiggling and squirming his way deeper inside me. I was so close to coming, my whole body beginning to shake with strain. Lou replaced his tongue with his finger, his thick digit slipping inside to the knuckle without much effort.

"You wanna get fucked, don't you Travis? You wanna come with my big cock in your tight ass?"

"God, yes, Lou. I want you to fuck me. Please, fuck my ass."

"Wow, didn't have any trouble that time, did you, Travis?"

I heard the pop of the lube top open, and soon the warm press of his tongue was traded for the cool slide of his lubed fingers. Just as I got used to his intrusion, he was gone.

I heard the familiar crinkle of the foil condom wrapper, and I held my breath waiting for him to roll it on. The unyielding press of his cock against my asshole forced me to breathe again. Lou gasped right along with me when I felt my sphincter give way and let him in fully. The fingers that had been digging bruises into my hips released, the pain only making my cock swell more in my stroking hand. I knew I wouldn't last long and when he started moving inside my ass in deep, measured strokes, I cried out louder than I intended to, hoping no one outside the portal heard me. I squeezed my eyes shut, perspiration flushing my face and back as I took him. Lou threw gasoline on my fire with more dirty words.

"Jerk that fucking cock, Travis. I want you to come and squeeze that ass around my dick. Come hard for me."

My hips moved mindlessly back toward him, and my dick twitched in my hand, come spurting hot and sticky from the tip. Without conscious thought, my ass contracted around Lou's cock, just like he wanted. My head flew back, and I bit my lip to keep myself quiet. Lou was pounding me with more fury and force than I'd ever experienced before. I felt his sweat dripping onto my back, and as I milked the last drops from my dick, Lou drove into me to the hilt, his chest collapsing onto my back as he came violently behind me. His teeth sank into my shoulder as the last quakes rumbled through him, his panting breath hot on my already soaked skin.

I could barely move as Lou moved away from me. I finally managed to pull the rest of my body onto the couch, every muscle tired and sore. My eyes felt too heavy to open, my whole body sated and loose. Lou dressed quickly before tossing me my clothes, his voice jolting me back to life.

"Don't fall asleep on me, Travis. You'd never be able to explain that to your boss. Or mine, for that matter."

Reluctantly, I stood up and put my clothes back on. I checked myself in the small mirror on the wall before reaching for the door handle. Lou stopped me with a kiss, pressing a business card into my hand.

"Call me, Travis. I'd like to see you again. Maybe I can teach you how to sail for real."

"Only if you bring the costume, Lou."

"Deal."

I returned to the party while Lou went toward the front of the boat. Just as I slipped back into the throng, I heard my boss's voice and felt his hand on my shoulder.

"Well, Travis. What did you think of today? Should we do this again?"

"Absolutely, Sir. It was a hell of a ride."

HIGHWAY ROBBERY
By Landon Dixon

Dixon's writing credits include the several magazines and anthologies and two short story collections of his own.

I shoved the empty plate back, popped another notch on my belt. "My compliments to the chef — as always," I said, grinning and waving at the dark, pretty face smiling back at me from the food slot in the wall.

Lionel cooked a hell of a steak and had a hell of a beefsteak hung between his legs. He gestured at me with his greasy spatula, licking his plush lips with a neon-pink tongue. But I didn't have time for dessert, not this time. I was already behind schedule.

So I spilled some money out on the counter and swung around in my stool and ambled for the door of the truck stop. I'd have to find another way to work off that meal, maybe further down the road.

Out in the parking lot, I checked the padlocks and seal on the rear doors of the trailer. Everything was just as tight as Lionel's ass. I was hauling a load of furs, so I wanted to be sure.

I climbed into the cab of the tractor and keyed the engine to roaring life. I shifted into gear and rumbled out of the parking lot, onto the highway. Traffic was light, this stretch of rural road through the prairies not very heavily travelled. Just the swaying stalks of corn and sunflowers on either side of the asphalt ribbon to keep me company, as I punched the pedal and gave her gas, shifted up to hauling ass speed.

You get tired on the road, bored, especially after a heavy meal and a put-off cock-stop with one of your route regulars. So

I popped the tab on an energy drink and guzzled, punched up some porn on my dashboard-mounted computer.

It broke every rule in the book, as I broke out my hard-on to keep stroking time to the two guys fucking on-screen. But a man on the road sometimes has to live by his own rules, to avoid that white line fever running him right off the track.

It was my favorite scene download — a young blond guy getting "seduced" by a handsome, smooth-talking, silver-haired jackal. The blond beauty had just taken a dip in the old man's pool, and now he was toweling his buff, bronze body off. As the silver fox suddenly slid the guy's Speedos down from behind.

The kid looked around, his big brown eyes gone wide, plush red lips parting in a gasp of protest to reveal succulent pink tongue. The sugar daddy comfortingly wrapped his arms around the blond from behind, grasping smooth, humped pec and chocolate-dark nipple with one hand, smooth, outstretched, tan cock with the other.

The older man was naked, as well, his body lean and tanned and shaved smooth, remarkably wrinkle-free, his huge hard-on pressing in between the younger man's petulant butt cheeks, pumping. The blond moaned now, tilting his head back on daddy's shoulder, surrendering to his sensuous gay nature, to the other man's beating need that would not be denied.

I just knew the kid was going to get his ass blasted by that fox.

But then my dick froze in my hand, as I shot a quick glance up onto the open road. There was a man standing on the yellow gravel edge of the highway, about a hundred feet ahead and closing fast. An erection was sticking out of the front of his jeans. I just about jackknifed the big rig.

I'd thought I'd seen it all, after twenty years of towing freight on the highways and byways. But this was a new one — a hitchhiker eschewing his thumb for his dick. He had me sold.

I tucked my cock back into my pants and pumped the air brakes. I slewed all eighteen wheels over to the shoulder of the road, eyes glued to that beckoning hard-on. I came to humping stop about ten feet in front of the man and his roadside attraction. He grinned and waved. His cock bobbed delightfully in the baking sun, as he bounded over to the tractor and climbed up into the cab.

"Hi, I'm Adam! Thanks for stopping!"

He was blond and brown, no more than twenty. His wide, blue eyes twinkled in his boyishly handsome face, his smooth, bronzed arms flowing like sweet caramel out of the shirt sleeves of his tight white T-shirt. His faded, blue jeans were tight, too, spray-painted onto his shapely long legs and mounded butt. His cock beamed up at me from between his legs, hard and happy as mine was throbbing away in my pants.

"That's ... quite an unusual way you have of flagging folks down," I commented, throat cracking dry with the young hung so close and confined in my cab. His cock stretched up more than eight inches, slick-shafted and curve-headed, cut and clean just the way I like them.

"Yeah, well, desperate times call for desperate measures," he responded with a laugh. "No one was stopping for me. So I had to find some other way to attract attention, other than my thumb." He looked down at the huge hump bulging the crotch of my workpants. "Guess I got your attention?"

I nodded, swallowed. "Travelin' light but packin' heavy, huh?" He didn't have a bag or a backpack, just the beef.

"Best way to ride, I find." He reached over and ran my straining zipper down over my hard-on, pulled the pulsating appendage right out into the stuffy air with his hot clutching hand.

"Yeah!" I grunted, reveling in the soft heated swirl of his palm on my prick. I shifted into gear, muscled the rig back onto the road, miles to go and schedules to keep, Adam stroking my dong to ensure I didn't sleep.

"God, you're huge!" he kindly marveled, tugging me out to my full seven pressure-inflated inches with his pulling hand.

I grinned, gripping the wheel, watching, feeling him stroke. I was old enough to be the boy's dad, but I was still a sucker for compliments. He moved closer, giving me some wrist action with his right hand now, torquing my shaft, twirling his long slender fingers over my hood. Then he proved he was a sucker, too, by dipping his sunny blond head down and pouring his pouty red lips over my cap.

"Fuck!" I growled, bucking up into the boy's baby-wet mouth.

He rolled his sky-blue eyes up at me, batted his long lashes, lips sealing tight round my knob. Then he sunk his head lower, slowly, his mouth widening and lips stretching, consuming my granite-hard prong.

I jerked the drifting rig back onto the road, caught a honk and an obscene hand gesture from a vanload of nuns heading the other way. But God herself couldn't stop or slow me down now, or that gorgeous blond inhaling my pipe.

Adam didn't brake until his lips kissed my pants. His cheeks and throat bulged with dong, face stuffed. Then he grinned, so help me, winked, slithered out his tongue and wormed wetly at my balls.

I smacked the air horn with applause. He pulled up, slowly as he'd poured down, inches of gleaming, straining hard shaft oozing out from between his tight-sucking lips. He stopped the dizzying ascent at my cap, biting into the meaty knob, pumping hot humid air out of his nostrils and gazing at me.

My legs quivered, foot jumping on the gas, rig along with it, face bleeding sweat and blazing lust. As Adam dropped back down, pulled back up, sensually sucking on my prick. It was all I could do to keep one eye on the road and two on the cocksucker.

Fortunately, that stretch of highway was as flat and straight as most of the farmers who plowed either side. Unfortunately, I'd been highballin' a long time between spitstops, had plenty of pent-up gas in the tanks. Adam's soulful deep-throating was making my wheels wobble, my paint peel off.

He sensed it and sucked harder, faster. His head flew up and down in my lap, blond hair a blur. My groin was bathed in blistering, ball-rupturing heat, my cock a molten steel rod blown out of all proportion by the kid's velvety mouth and tongue and lips.

"Droppin' a load!" I bellowed, shaking, breaking.

My foot trod flat on the gas pedal, the rig shooting forward. As my spit-drizzled balls exploded, mouth-embedded cock blowing wild. I bucked up and down on the smooth stretch of highway, spraying the back of Adam's throat, spouting jet after jet into his mouth.

He didn't stop sucking, started swallowing. He bobbed his head up and down as before, in rhythm to his Adam's apple now, vaccing the hot, salty jizz right out of my hose. I shook, rattled, and rolled, spurting joy-juice, the kid draining my system dry.

Twenty miles further down the highway, he said, "Hey, let's stop for that guy. Two's good company, but three's a threesome." Who was I to argue with him? He'd proved his roadworthiness.

The new guy was just as young as Adam, built along the same sleek, streamlined lines. His name was Brian. He had short, silky black hair and light brown eyes, a handsome, suntanned face with a cleft chin ornament. He was wearing tight blue jeans and white T-shirt, carrying a gym bag in his right hand. He'd had his thumb out, not his dick; but that soon changed.

"Hop in!" I called across Adam, after he'd popped the door open.

But the blond had a better idea. "Why don't we all go in the back, where there's more room — to get better acquainted?" He gestured with his head at the company trailer hooked up to my tractor.

I was suddenly wary. "Well, uh, I've got a schedule to keep and ..."

"I'm game, if you guys are," Brian piped up, clinging to the door and the side of the cab, smiling warm and inviting at Adam and me.

Hell, there have to be more benefits to pushing a rig than on-time delivery.

I sprung the locks open on the trailer doors, the seal, invited the boys to step into my backroom. And there was room, in between the crates of furs, an aisle that I quickly carpeted with some extra rubber pads lying around. Then, as Brian and Adam started stripping off their clothes, I took a last look out the rear doors, at the deserted stretch of flat-top. Then I sealed things up nice and tight again, with me and the nice and tight boys inside.

I lit a lantern, hung it from an overhead hook. The warm, yellow glow made everything nice and cozy, provided ample illumination for the spectacular strip and sex show the two young men treated me to. I just stood there rubbing my re-aroused hard-on in my pants, watching Adam and Brian peel off their tees, kick off their shoes and pull off their jeans.

The boys hadn't packed underwear. Their cocks stood out high and hard from their shaven loins. It was enough to make a middle-aged man's mouth water and slit drip, which it did. I squeezed my dong affectionately, taking in every lean-muscled, sun-kissed lithe inch of the men's gleaming brown torsos and arms and legs, every bloated millimeter of their cocks.

They embraced, kissed, their soft, wet lips pressing passionately together, arms clasping nude bodies close, dicks sliding up tight. I unbuckled, unbuttoned and unzipped, drew out my measure of a man and stroked slow and sure, staring at the steamy sex scene — two young studs getting it on nude and lewd. This was exactly the kind of wildlife I loved up in my grille.

Their glistening pink tongues swirled together, entwined, hands clutching bunched shoulder muscles, clenching taut butt cheeks, erections undulating against each other. It was too good just to watch; I joined in. Sex ain't a spectator sport unless you're all by your lonesome, in my logbook.

The boys stripped me clean. Then treated their elder to the erotic. Brian gripped my balls and sucked on my right nipple. Adam grasped my cock and sucked on my left nipple. I hummed like a set of tires on a straightaway, motor racing.

Adam grabbed onto the back of my head and mashed his mouth against mine, flowered his tongue in between my trembling lips. As Brian dropped to his knees on the padding, in possession of both my cock and balls. He squeezed my sack, sucked on my dick.

The raven-haired guy's mouth was just as accommodating and sexually unforgiving as the blond's, his throat just as supple and skilled. He bobbed back and forth, blowing me wet and hot and tight, juggling my nuts like I juggled the cheat sheets.

Heat suffused my quivering body in waves, rising up from my sucked-upon cock and shimmering all through me. I blew hot exhaust in Adam's mouth. He swallowed my groans of pleasure, sucking on my tongue like Brian on my prick.

We shifted gears. I went to the lube, greasing my already spit-slickened dong. Adam and Brian went to the pads, on all-fours, presenting their golden bottoms to me in the upraised and stick-it-in position. I smacked their smooth, rounded buns with my stick shift, watching the ripened young flesh ripple, listening to the guys gasp. Then I shot two fingers of both hands into their butt cleavages, scrubbed the silky stretches slippery with lube. They groaned when I pressed fingertips into manholes.

"Fuck us!" Adam pleaded, shuddering his bum at me.

I put the hammer down, pushing my gleaming cap in between Adam's cheeks and up against his pucker, squishing through, inside. I sunk shaft into the kid's superheated anus, spearing two fingers inside Brian's chute and plowing them deep. My balls kissed up to Adam's trembling buttocks, cock buried full-length and throbbing in his ass; my fingers disappeared up to the hand knuckles in Brian's tunnel, embedded in their entirety.

The guys desperately kissed, frantically flailed their tongues together. As I drilled into their asses, dong and digits. I pumped Adam's sucking chute with my cock, plunged Brian's gripping anus with my fingers, banging off both sets of gyrating cheeks. Then I switched positions, poling Brian's ass, probing Adam's.

I went back and forth, in and out, over and over. Sweat filmed my body and eyes, my blood boiling and body burning and cock singing. The smack of damp flesh against steaming flesh filled the overheated trailer. The two young men could take anything this old road dog could dish out, deep and passionately, dish it right back with the thrust of their golden buttocks, the clench of their ass muscles.

"Fuck! Jesus! I'm coming!" I hollered, pistoning Adam's butt with my cock, sawing Brian's butt with my fingers.

My body burst with pleasure and my brain exploded. I blasted searing ecstasy into Adam, yanked out and plugged into Brian, spouted more brutal joy. I poured out my scorching lust into both men's anuses, flooding them, filling them, overflowing with feeling.

Shortly afterward, Brian pulled a shotgun out of his gym bag and pointed it at me. "Hand over the keys, old man," he said.

I gaped, dick hanging deflated.

Adam explained, "I spotted you barreling down the road with my pocket binoculars, stuck my cock out to make you stop. We knew what you were hauling, knew your peccadillo for young men, planned it perfectly so that you picked up both of us without suspecting a thing." He grinned. "You didn't think you could ride for free, did you?"

They drove off with my truck and the valuable cargo attached. Not before I hit the tiny transponder on the key ring, however. The Feds had alerted me to the possibility of a hijack, equipped me, and now I alerted them. They'd know the rig was stolen, be able to track it, be waiting for the boys wherever they felt like stopping them and their short-lived reign of highway terror.

Maybe I should've been more careful with the load, saved everyone and the company some trouble. Then again, I'd help capture the highway robbers. And, more importantly, I wouldn't have been able to drop a couple of my own loads, if I hadn't stopped for a pair of unscheduled pick-ups.

A BACKHANDED KIND OF BUSINESS
By Landon Dixon

Six months in Hollywood, and my goose looked cooked. I'd sunk about as low as a man can go without strapping a mattress to his back. I was dressing up like a bunny, serving slop at a Long Beach drive-in as a car "hop." I had my suitcase packed, the bus schedule back to Kansas memorized.

But I still kept calling into Central Casting every day, hoping against hope for some "extra" work. And I kept getting the same response, "Nothing." I could've strangled that dame with my phone cord. But I would've been at the back of that line-up, too. The end of the war had flooded Tinseltown with hunky ex-GI's looking for the easy life depicted on film.

So, when my roommate told me about a file clerk job at Western Pictures, I jumped at it like it was a car horn, figuring this was my last chance.

"You'll be working for Mr. Mullen," the wooden-faced hag of an office manager, Mrs. Kleinsasser, told me.

I could've kissed the splinters out of the old bat's face.

Bryce Mullen was a tall, distinguished-looking gent of around fifty-five. He had a silver screen profile and brilliantine hair and cold, dark eyes, a slim, well-proportioned body that seldom stooped down to the level of his office staff. He was a big-shot producer at the low-budget studio.

I seldom saw the guy, except when he made his grand entrance to his office in the morning. And most of what I saw of the movie business was from sneaking around back lots and sound stages during my lunch breaks.

71

But what I saw flushed the last of my illusions down the drain. The sets were just as phony as the people, the people a mess of neuroses and egos and raging superiority/sycophant complexes. This was Hollywood behind the scenes, and it wasn't pretty — the plywood and paper mache was showing, and everybody in the business seemed just as fragile.

I was sitting in the studio cafeteria one day with one of the typewriter slaves, when Mrs. Kleinsasser suddenly cast an ugly shadow over our lunch. "Mr. Mullen wants to see you in his office — immediately, Mr. Logan." She arched an eyebrow that hadn't seen plucking since the Silent Era, cueing me to big trouble.

"You fancy yourself a screenwriter, Logan!?" Mr. Mullen bellowed as soon as I slunk through his door.

He was ensconced in an English leather chair behind a polo field-sized desk, holding a story scenario in his hand. I recognized it as *Midwest Meets East*, the screwball comedy I'd taken the initiative in appending a sheet of story suggestions to, facts about the people and places.

I stared down at the plush carpeting and mumbled, "I was just trying to be helpful."

He tossed his aristocratic head. "Mr. Logan, if I want your contribution on a project, I'll get one of my flunkies to ask for it. And you can be damn sure I won't ..."

Just then leading lady Iris LaRose and her personal director, Sy Freelinger, marched into the office with a list of demands regarding *Wide Open Skies*, an oater Miss LaRose was currently co-starring in; sparing my fate for ten minutes and stirring Mr. Mullen into more of a snitty rage. He paced back and forth behind his desk with theatrical precision after the pair had departed.

Then he remembered me and charged. "You're still here!? You're fired! Get out!" He spun around, giving me both cold shoulders.

I smacked his ass.

He jerked up against his desk. His head turned almost completely around to look back at me. "What do you ..."

"That's what my mother back on our Kansas farm used to do whenever one of us kids behaved like a spoiled brat." I was good and fed up with the whole rotten deal. "And you can stick that in your movie and film it!"

"I don't ever want to ..."

I smacked his tight little butt again, and he jumped again. "That goes double for me. I'm leaving this laughing academy. You people are screwier than a hardware store, just as dull underneath."

His face reddened, his buttocks loosening under the hand-woven material of his pants. "Do that again."

"I said ..."

"Don't say it again! Do it again!"

"With pleasure!" I swatted Bryce Mullen's impudent rear-end with my open palm a third time. His cheeks rippled.

"Again!"

I moved closer, getting wise. He was breathing like a steam engine, his slender body trembling. Vulnerable like that, with his mannerisms dropped and emotions showing, he wasn't such a bad guy, for a pervert. I whacked his ass, hardest of all this time.

He was jolted from the tips of his leather-tooled shoes to the top of his twenty-dollar haircut, and he gasped like a little girl.

I shook my blond curls, still angry, but now just a little turned on. Nothing surprised me in this place. I smacked Bryce's bum, shivering his posterior and attachments, making him sigh.

He gripped the edge of his desk and arched his back and pushed his butt out at me. "Punish me! Discipline me!" he hissed. "I need a strong hand."

What he needed was years of psychotherapy or two weeks in a flophouse to straighten out his twisted values. But all he had was me and my avenging hand, and his bum was neat and trim and rounded just right. I licked my lips and slammed his behind.

"Yes! That's it!" he rasped.

"Quiet!" I snapped back, my face gone as red as his, my body quivering the same.

I was in control now, and I didn't want any backtalk, just the dirty talk I was giving to his backside. I spanked his ass, rocking him, really flailing his cheeks to the point where they gyrated non-stop.

"Take down your pants!" I ordered.

He obeyed quick as a whip. The emperor had no clothes on his lower half. His smooth, double-humped bottom blushed crimson where I'd hit it. I touched the heated skin, and we both gasped.

Then I raised my hand to the rafters and whistled it down onto his bare bum. The crack of our flesh, the shriek of our voices, blasted the crackling air apart.

"Yes! Spank me!" Bryce cried, his voice flaring like his butt.

"Shut up!" I retaliated, really getting into my role, crashing my hand down across his pert, proud buttocks again and again.

The palm of my paddling hand flamed up to the inferno temperature of Bryce's cheeks, as I whaled his bottom, fanning the fire in both of us. I was consumed by something wild and weird and wonderful; maybe the feeling of power, after getting shoved around for so long; maybe something deeper and more depraved, after denying my basic instincts for so long.

Either way, Bryce Mullen, big-shot movie executive, was on the receiving end of my proletarian rage. And he reveled in it, roiled with it, getting the heavy hand he so richly deserved and needed. His bum burnt brick-red to my beating tempo, and he moaned and groaned like he was going to shoot the works. The selfish bastard!

"On the couch! Over my knees!" I yelled.

Like all Hollywood big-wigs, Bryce had a deep leather couch in his office, for casting purposes more than resting purposes. He and I tottered over to it. I unfastened my belt, pulled it out of the loops, let my pants drop down like Bryce's eyes following them. He stared at my hard-on. I was aroused out to full-length, pulsating with an excitement usually reserved for Errol Flynn opening nights.

I sat down on the edge of the sofa, beckoned at Bryce and the big, long cock jutting out from his loins. He instantly draped himself over my knees, sinking my bare bottom into the cool leather, his hot, hard prick into my soft thighs and hard cock.

I looked down at his beaten bum, enjoying the view, the feel of our dicks pressing together. Then I beat his ass some more, with the belt. I flailed the flushed, trembling cheeks with renewed strength and urgency and purpose. He whimpered, his body jumping with each stinging lash, his cock throbbing into my pulsing cock.

I shimmered with tingling heat, making me dizzy, making me deranged. The crack of my belt on Bryce's bare bottom sang out in the stifling office, the man's padded back-end getting ravaged with pleasure and pain. I felt the pleasure, as well, all through me, the only pain the cramping in my arm from cracking the whip so harshly.

Bryce's cheeks whitened with numbness under my blasting belt, the skin losing its elasticity, gaining ridges. I could hardly believe he could take it, but he kept moaning for more. Until he was just moaning, his body jerking with more than my blows.

He groaned low and long, and I felt his cock spasm against my cock, heated sperm spurt onto my quivering thighs. He wasn't going to get off that easy.

I bounced up onto my feet, bumping the shuddering man off my knees and onto his feet. His cock stopped shooting, just leaking some semen from the gaping slit on his swollen purple knob, his eyes leaking tears as he stared at me. I let him simmer down for a moment, then grinned, gripped his dick, basted my hand in some of the sperm that he'd spilled. Then my cock.

His eyes shone, glistening with heartfelt joy and anticipation. He knew what the third act was going to feature. But I was still directing things on my terms.

I pushed him up against his desk. He grasped the edge, stuck his bum out at me. I got in close behind, whacked my slickened dick against one of his wounded buttocks.

"Yes! Sweet Jesus, yes!" he cried, hamming it up to the hilt.

The ravaged skin on his butt cheeks was rippling with genuine emotion, however. As I slammed my log into one, the other. I patty-caked his ass with my cock.

Then I speared the slick stick in between Bryce's quivering legs, up in between his quivering cheeks, caressing his crack with my hood, basting it with some of his hot sauce at the same time. The man's bum cleavage was just as silkily smooth as the rest of him. He could be a real arrogant ass, all right, but he had the plush derriere to back it up. I shivered with my own raw emotions, gliding my cockhead up and down in his hot-velvet crack.

"Fuck me! Stick your cock in my ass and fuck me!"

His plea for anal fulfillment was registered three studios over. But I hadn't called for any dialogue.

So I took a step back and smacked his butt with a bladed hand. "I'm calling the shots now!" I reminded him. "This is a Logan production!" I ranted. The power had gone to my head, both of them; the hot blood pounding in the pair.

I took a step closer, gripped my gleaming cock again and pushed the swelled-up tip between Bryce's buttocks. I hit pucker, and we both groaned. I gritted my teeth and got a second grip on one of the guy's legs, pushed harder with my prick. My meaty hood mushroomed his starfish, sunk in.

He clamped down tight on my cap with his ring. I thrust hard, thrust deep; shot shaft into his anus, inch after bloated, beating inch, filling the man's rectum, sticking and stretching his chute. It was a scintillating collaboration worthy of an Academy Award.

My thighs kissed up against Bryce's backside, balls pressing tight, cock fully buried. I let him feel the depths of his, and my, depravity, rutting around in his anus. His passion pit of an ass squeezed me in fiery heat, blazing up from my cock and sweeping through the rest of my body. He shook out of control on the end of my prick, buttocks gyrating all on their own.

I smacked his right cheek, his left, pumping my hips, fucking his ass. It was almost as tough as walking and chewing gum at the same time, only far more pleasurable, and physical. I spanked Bryce's rump with both of my hands, stuffing his chute with my cock.

He arched his back, his manicured fingernails tearing splinters out of his mahogany desk. His seat cushions clasped my cock tightly, rippling wildly with the beat of my thighs and palms. Sweat prickled my brow and stung my eyes, as I upped the pounding tempo still more, whacking ass harder, fucking ass faster.

Bryce wrenched a hand out of the wood and grabbed onto his wood, fisted in rhythm to the torrid pace I was exacting on and in his bum. He twisted his head around and stared at me, imploring with his glazed eyes for me to pour on the pain, the punishment, the nut-busting, chute-reaming pressure. I gave him that much, dishing out even more of my frustration onto his butt cheeks, hammering my angry cock into his soft, greedy anus.

"We're reaching the climax of the story!" I rasped. "The climax!"

It wasn't the best line I'd ever ad-libbed, but it captured the moment perfectly.

Bryce loved it. His body jerked, repeatedly, jolted by full-blown, ass-busted orgasm. He didn't take his swimming eyes off of me, as he striped his blotter with jet after jet of hand-cranked jism, applauding my anal efforts.

My own balls boiled, my body temperature soaring to fever pitch. I crashed my hands into Bryce's buttocks, banging out a frenzied bongo beat, pile-driving cock into his chute. I could feel his spasms of utter, excruciating joy, his ass muscles squeezing my pistoning rod even harder.

There was one final act of humiliation, however, myself cast in the starring role yet again. I yanked my thundering cock out of Bryce's ass and yelled at the man to fall to his knees.

He dropped his still spurting dick and spun around and hit the carpet on his knees at my dong, right on cue. I opened my mouth, he opened his. I speared my cock into his gaping maw, going as deep into this end as I had at the other.

He grasped my hips and frantically bobbed his head back and forth, chewing up the scenery and my cock. He took me into his mouth and throat and back out again, lips sealed tight to shaft, facial cheeks billowing and bulging. The sucking pressure was enormous, the heat and damp exquisite. The man had obviously swallowed a lot in his days at the studio, my cock just the latest.

I blazed with passion, balls bubbling furiously, prick wet-vacced beyond the point of no return. Then I felt nothing, but total, triumphant bliss.

I ascended to the heavens on white puffy clouds, propelled up and away by burst after burst of liquid ecstasy. My mind detached from my burning body, blown sky-high. The stuff that wet dreams are made of.

Bryce gobbled up and gulped down everything I had to give him, and then some.

I was promoted from file clerk to Head Story Editor that same afternoon. A real Tinseltown success story — a star-struck Midwestern boy who struck out on his own, and then out at others, and got all he desired.

Bryce will sometimes butt in during one of my story conferences, but I just have to hold up my hand, and I get my way.

THE SECRET OF MY SUCCESS
By Landon Dixon

Cody heard the door swish open, the sharp click of heels on hard tiles. A man entering the washroom. He grinned and spread his legs wider apart, gripped his cock tighter.

The crisp footsteps stopped at the urinals. Then the heels pivoted, headed for the stalls, the steps softer, more tentative, less business-like.

Cody was sitting on the toilet in the middle stall, leaning back against the wall, his torn and faded jeans down around his ankles. One small hand clutched the enormous erection bulging his white cotton briefs, while the other hand cupped a firm pec through his white cotton T-shirt. "I'm in here," he said.

The footsteps stopped, the man directly outside the stall door, hesitating. A tall, distinguished-looking man dressed in a pinstriped black suit that molded close to his long, lean body thanks to expensive tailoring. A power suit that accentuated his swept-back, silver hair, the bronze tan on his fine-featured face. He wore a brilliant pink tie and white shirt to go along with the suit, and gleaming black leather shoes. He looked exactly like the successful businessman he was.

Now, he bit his plush lower lip, as he reached out a shaking hand and touched the green metal of the stall door, pushed it open.

"Hi, Jameson," Cody said. He shifted his hand slowly up and down the massive outline of cotton-wrapped cock. "I thought I'd run into you here — sooner or later."

The slender fingers of the young man's left hand found the hard, poking bud of his left nipple through the thin fabric of his T-shirt, pinched the rigid protuberance. He bit his lip, smiling at the staring man.

"I-I thought I told you not to come here," Jameson stammered. The older man's normally deep, authoritative voice cracked under the strain of watching the young man stroke his huge cock, roll his hard nipples.

"You told me. But I'm here anyway. So, what are you going to do about it?"

Jameson licked his lips, took a quick glance around the temporarily empty washroom. Then, still gazing at Cody's clasped and clothed erection, the twin indentations in the young man's T-shirt, he pushed the door all the way open, slipped inside the stall.

"I could have you thrown out, you know?" His clear, blue eyes that had coldly and calculatingly stared down so many men and women in tense negotiations, didn't blink, focused on Cody's pumping hand.

"You could," Cody conceded. "But you won't."

He pulled his hand off his cock and leaned forward, peeled his T-shirt up over his head. He shook out his shiny, black hair, tossing the T-shirt aside. His torso was smooth as alabaster, the same color, except for the rigid, jutting pink tips that crowned the small, twin swells of his pecs.

Cody leaned back against the wall and cupped his pecs, crawling his fingers up to his nipples and squeezing the rubbery buds bare. A shiver ran through his young, clean, unblemished body, his cock almost bursting its straining confines.

Jameson shut the stall door behind him. His right hand quivered violently as he pushed it through his thick shock of hair. "Someone might ..."

"Someone might," Cody jeered. "But I know what you're going to do, big man."

Jameson's Adam's apple bounced in his long, slender throat. "What?"

"You're going to take your cock out, big man. Show me just how happy you are that I stopped by." Cody squeezed his nipples between his fingers, hard, pulled on them. His body arched with pleasure, the swollen purple-pink cap of his cock popping right through the elasticized waistband of his bright white briefs.

The older man shot the bolt on the door. But Cody shook his head. Jameson unbolted the door, then fumbled the zipper on his suit pants down, scrambled his cock out of his silk shorts and out into the open.

"Just like I thought," Cody said. "You don't mind me being here at all. Do you, 'big man'!?"

Jameson's erection stuck out long and hard from the opening in his pants. His cock was slender and smooth and tan as the man himself, hood and shaft clean-cut. He gripped his organ at the base, the cap sniffing up into the air with excitement.

Cody looked at the handsome prick with contempt. "Now, get on your knees, on the floor, at a real man's cock."

As Jameson's legs collapsed and he buckled to the floor, Cody lifted his bum off the toilet seat and slid his briefs down. His monster erection sprang free, shooting up into the air.

Cody's cock stretched halfway up his stomach, shaft thick as a man's wrist, pink as a baby's mouth, hood mushroomed meaty at the top. The light blue veins on his ten-inch appendage pulsated with the beat of his and Jameson's hearts. His large balls were shaven bare, seized up tight between his legs.

Jameson glared at the young man's cock, his normally shrewd eyes gone glassy. His hand strangled his own prick. As he reached out with his other trembling hand for Cody's cock.

Cody slapped Jameson's hand away. "Lick my nuts, you dirty old man."

The bathroom door swished open and footsteps echoed loudly, men's voices.

But Jameson hardly heard them, or the hot hiss of piss hitting the white porcelain of the urinals. As he crawled forward on his scuffed knees and dipped his silver head down, stuck his thick, pink tongue out and licked the bottom of Cody's sack. The young man grimaced, but didn't give away anymore of the sexual impact of the older man's tongue on his sensitive scrotum.

The men outside moved over to the sinks, zipping and talking. Water sprayed into enamel bowls. Jameson's name was mentioned.

The man himself was down on his hands and knees, smearing his budded tongue all around and over Cody's sack. He felt the heavy balls roll under his sweeping tongue. He painted the tight, wrinkled flesh with his saliva, gazing up at the towering cock that jutted out above his head, that shadowed his upturned face. The beautiful, bountiful erection jerked with each swipe of Jameson's tongue on Cody's balls.

"Suck my nuts … Jameson!" Cody hissed.

The men's voices outside abruptly stopped.

Jameson closed his eyes and opened his mouth wider and surged his red lips over Cody's bulged sack, mouthing the young man's scrotum whole. Cody's cock twitched. A shining pearl of pre-cum bubbled up into the gaping slit, rolled down the throbbing shaft.

Jameson tugged on Cody's balls with his mouth, lips sealed tight.

"Now suck my cock, Jameson! You're a cocksucker — so do what you do best!"

Footsteps scuffled outside, the men hurriedly exiting the washroom.

Jameson disgorged Cody's sack in a wet, glistening mass and jerked his head up, planted his wet lips on Cody's hood, flowed them down, and down, and down. Cody bucked, the older man's hot, lush mouth consuming his cap and almost all of his shaft. Jameson's cheeks and throat bulged with cock, his eyes shining.

Cody grabbed onto Jameson's head, gripping the man's hair. Then he thrust his butt up, pumping his hips, driving his cock back and forth in Jameson's mouth and throat, fucking the man's face. "Jerk your cock, while I fuck your mouth, little man!"

Jameson's eyes watered, his nostrils flaring for air. He gagged, spit spilling out of the corners of his crammed mouth, his lips stretched obscenely wide. He eagerly pulled on his own cock, as Cody pistoned his elastic mouth and throat with meat.

"Uh, Mr. Jameson? Are you in here?"

"Eat my cock, Jameson! Eat it!" Cody cried. He thrust in a frenzy, bum bouncing off the toilet seat, holding onto Jameson's head and slamming his cock into the man's face.

Jameson shuddered, his fisted cock erupting, spraying ropes of hot semen against the toilet, onto the tile floor. Cody cried out, his dong exploding in Jameson's desperately sucking mouth. He blasted sizzling, salty sperm down Jameson's frantically gulping throat.

"They're, uh, waiting for you in the boardroom, Mr. Jameson," the confused, plaintive voice from outside spoke up again. "The board of directors ... sir ..."

Cody spasmed one final time, then let Jameson suck his gently spurting cock dry, both men wallowing in the rich, erotic fulfillment of total release.

# # # # #

The steel-grey Lexus swung off the highway and onto the side of the road. It swept powerfully up to the young man in blue jeans and white T-shirt standing on the shoulder. The passenger-side door popped open, the expensive car purring.

"I-I didn't know you wanted to come," Jameson said, watching Cody slide into the black leather bucket seat next to him.

"Sure you didn't," the young man retorted. "I'm coming, all right, Jameson. Inside of you, in front of everybody."

Cody insolently spread his legs wide, and the dome light of the car illuminated the huge bulge at his crotch that threatened to burst the stitching on his fly. He rested a warm palm on the throbbing monster.

Jameson's mouth opened like he wanted to say something, perhaps protest. But Cody cut him off by saying, "Drive on, Jameson. We have a party to attend with all your big shot friends."

They arrived at Jameson's spacious, cedar-log lake house in under an hour. His foot was heavy on the accelerator, his eyes sometimes on the road, mainly on the stroked hump in Cody's jeans.

The house was ablaze with lights on the inside and lanterns on the outside, alive with the talking and laughing and drinking of forty or so important colleagues, friends, and business contacts. Jameson greeted some of them inside the rustic, well-appointed living room of the house, the rest of them out on the broad, manicured lawn that swept down to the lake. As Cody walked up the stairs to the second floor, saying hello to no one.

He knew where the master bedroom was — at the end of the hall — and now he entered it, flicked on the lights. The large, semi-circular pane of glass in the far wall offered a spectacular view of the moon-dappled lake, the lantern-strung lawn and the people milling about below.

Cody strolled over to the window, casually stripped off his T-shirt and pulled off his jeans. He stood looking out over the crowd, stroking the mammoth erection that jutted out from his loins.

Jameson glanced up, ran into the house.

Cody cupped his balls and gave them a squeeze, swirling his hand slowly up and down his engorged shaft, over his mushroomed hood. A smirk twisted his pouty lips, as he heard the bedroom door snap open, swiftly close.

Jameson stared at the young man's twin, taut, mounded butt cheeks, the pair smooth and ripe and creamy-white as the rest of the boy, split deliciously down the middle by shadowed crack. "Cody, please! You can't ..."

"Yes, I can." Cody turned around, pointing his cock at the older man. "Take off your clothes, Jameson. I'm going to fuck you."

Jameson licked his lips, his chest heaving. He was wearing a dark-blue silk shirt and black slacks, dress shoes. His silver hair shone, not a hair out of place, his tanned features gleaming under the lights — the lights that brightly illuminated the bedroom to the two men inside, and the crowd of important people gathered outside.

Jameson's hands moved on their own volition, guided into wanton action by his staring eyes on Cody's huge, handsome cock, the warm tingling in his body from the wicked thought of where that massive erection was destined. He stepped, naked, over to Cody by the window.

The older man's lean body was deeply tanned all over, a stunning color contrast to Cody's ivory skin. Silver hair adorned Jameson's narrow chest, sprinkled his hanging balls. His cock rose up in the air like a snake to its master's tune, bobbing as he approached Cody.

The two men looked down at the people below. "Please, Cody!" Jameson futilely pleaded. "This is an important ..."

"I'm going to stick my cock up your ass, Jameson," Cody said, hefting his sledge. "All of it. Fuck your pampered ass with my cock. So get up against the glass, so you can put on a real show for your guests. Two men transacting business — dirty business."

Jameson hesitated only a second. Until Cody picked up a bottle of lube from an antique end table and misted his prong, rubbed the slippery substance into his gleaming meat. Then Jameson sprang forward, planted his hands on the windowpane, his feet on the carpet, pushing his ass back and up at Cody.

Cody slapped the man's trembling buttocks with his cock, making Jameson jump. Then he skimmed some of the lube off his dong and greased Jameson's asshole, sticking a pair of fingers in between the man's cheeks and scrubbing clenched pucker. Jameson groaned, his palms squeaking on the glass.

"Think you can take it, 'big man'!?" Cody gritted, raising his cock to Jameson's ass.

"Fuck me! Fuck my ass!" Jameson hissed.

Cody split the man's cheeks with his club head, hit pucker, pressed hard, pushed through, swelling ass ring with his hood. He relentlessly drove his dong forward, into Jameson's wildly quivering ass, shaft stretching gripping chute, sinking home, stuffing superheated anus to bursting with his manhood. He didn't stop until his balls and thighs touched up against Jameson's rippling buttocks, his cock buried full-length inside the man's rectum.

The pane of glass rattled with Jameson's body. Some guests glanced up. They could see the grimly grinning face and burning bare torso of their host; then the rhythmic motion of his body, the expression of sheer erotic delight that twisted his refined features. As Cody thrust his cock back and forth in Jameson's ass, rocking, fucking the man.

Cody gripped Jameson's shoulders, torquing up his stroke. He banged against Jameson's gyrating buttocks, shunting his cock in and out of Jameson's sucking ass, faster and faster. The heat was inferno, the tightness vise-like, the pressure immense, building and building to the bulldozing of Cody's cock in Jameson's chute.

The whole window shook with the older man's buffeted body, the reaming he was taking, Cody pile-driving into his ass. Everyone below was looking up and watching now, staring at the panting man in the window; the guests inside the house cocking their ears at the sound of the rhythmic thumping and rattling, the low, animal-like moaning coming from the second floor.

Jameson squeezed his eyes shut, his mouth hanging open, his jarred body ablaze with the stoking stroke of that huge cock churning his ass. His own forgotten hard-on jerked upwards, suddenly spouted semen, erupting with an orgasm that Jameson could barely feel above the glorious pounding of Cody's dong.

Cody dove his hands down off Jameson's shaking shoulders and around and onto the man's gasping chest. He gripped Jameson's hard, jutting nipples, pistoning chute with his cock, pummeling ass. Until he jerked, seized up, his hard-thrusting cock detonating inside Jameson. He blazed sperm against the man's bowels, again and again and again.

Cody rutted around inside the steaming mess of Jameson's blasted rectum afterwards, as the older man struggled to catch his breath. "They say you shouldn't think with your cock," Cody breathed into Jameson's ear. "But it's worked for me."

Jameson swallowed and nodded. Semen dripped down his trembling legs, Cody's cock gently plugging his scorched and spermed chute making him shimmer with glowing pleasure. "You'd-you'd make a good businessman, Cody."

"I *do* 'make' a good businessman." Cody thrust his dong balls-deep into Jameson's ass again, hard. "That's the secret of my success."

OCEANUS'S STARE
By Derrick Della Giorgia

Derrick Della Giorgia was born in Italy and currently lives between Manhattan and Rome. His work has been published in several anthologies and literary magazines. Visit him at www.derrickdellagiorgia.com.

When the door opened, Aurelio forgot the short sentence he'd been rehearsing up the stairs and stood silent, holding the bag of milky liquid in which the buffalo mozzarellas swam. The high frescoed ceilings made him feel even smaller and more disarmed than he used to, when in front of Giotto and Arthur. Without changing the awkward position of his body, he stepped forward and stared at the interminable private darkness that separated him from the open window that framed the Trevi fountain. He had grown up by that fountain, which the tourists assaulted twenty-four-seven all year around, meters away from his family's cheese store. Yet now he looked at it from above, without being submersed by its massive bluntness. Oceanus didn't look as powerful, and he was trapped in the stone, too limited by distance and orientation to scare away Aurelio's dirty thoughts about the daring tritons and their winged horses. He wouldn't mind, now, having the mighty Titan watch. Nor would the god's austere beard mute the turmoil of his groin. He would walk into the water — as in his recurrent dream — and lure his men La Dolce Vita style.

Lost in himself, Aurelio surrendered to the almost inaudible flowing of the water and — with the usual submissiveness — welcomed the erection the wet statues were causing between his thighs.

"Happy holidays." The Roman young man unconsciously recited, offering the just awakened Giotto, simultaneously the mozzarellas and his turgid white pants. The rich musician was the only son of the kind duke who helped Aurelio's family start their business, and Arthur his American artist boyfriend: both of them as discrete and gentle as charming and beautiful. "Happy Holidays." The sweet and mature voice of the two intellectuals sounded familiar and safe to Aurelio. His fantasies were not in trouble with them. They both could be his father, but he'd never seen them that way. The ping-pong of emotions among them too erotic to be defined by simple age.

Responding to the current of air just formed in the apartment, the bedroom golden curtains swelled up veiling the sculptures as Arthur joined the duo in the corridor and initiated a series of reactions that made that Christmas Eve memorable. Giotto pushed Rome out of the scene behind the tall XIX century door, Arthur knelt and latched his still bedroom-warm hands on Aurelio's hips pulling the white erection closer to his senses. In the distance, the fountain was freed again, and Aurelio couldn't miss the correspondence: he was the sturdy standing Oceanus and Giotto and Arthur the two trustworthy tritons. In a moment of enlightenment, he brought the mozzarellas to his face and cooled down the heat spreading on his blushed skin. He knew Arthur's fingers weren't going to stop. He was waiting and willing to let them unbutton his pants and dig into them. His dick would have been presented in the frescoed room, his balls awakened from the caress of his groin. He felt the work outfit become looser around his waist and Giotto's breath exploring his loins. Winning his terror of Oceanus's stare, the shop boy refused to move and proudly stiffened his body, hoping the couple would make his solitary bedroom dreams come true right there. Lastly, he closed his eyes and inhaled as much air as he could, anticipating the lack of oxygen the future orgasm would provoke.

Aurelio was different. He had never been attracted to the procession of perfect young tourists who visited Mozzarella Trevi daily. Tank tops, muscles, long stares, blunt offers, insistent proposals didn't affect him. He wasn't able to explain why, nor had he ever tried or needed to, but his heart would only follow a certain kind of music. As with Oceanus, the sturdy men who knew about life were the ones with which he wanted to succumb. Stable, incorruptible hands like Giotto's, the touch he longed for. Imperative, eccentric orders, the commands he would obey. "Stay still, turn your head, think of something sad ..." An infinite list of moments he had shared with Arthur. Brush in one hand, the other almost pulling his greying short hair in despair and inspiration, the painter loved Aurelio's naked body. Milky boy's thighs and knees —as the couple referred to him — was in seven of the twenty-three paintings of the American artist's last exhibition. Being naked with them wasn't new. It was the ardent desire of sleeping with them that Aurelio hadn't been able to utter or satisfy yet.

To complete the magic, the notes of a trumpet climbed the walls of the third floor apartment and wound up to Aurelio's feet, where the cheese stained pants delicately rested as four lips sealed each second of the scene above his trembling knees. A glance, a smile, a long kiss between the two extravagant customers, and the mozzarella boy's briefs were forced down, too, releasing a pungent image in the discolored mirror on the side wall. In the front, Aurelio's black wool sweater crowned the white worker legs, brushing the dark pubic hair and the perfect cock pointing skywards; in the back, it teased the gluttonous melon size ass. Fulfilling his most secret erotic fantasies, Aurelio had become the purest object of the art of loving, *ars amandi*; the fire that was before burning the skin below his eyes descended now into his chest, dripped around his nipples and circled his navel, finally exploding into his fervent balls. For an instant, he was tempted to free his hands and grind Arthur's head into his groin, screw Giotto's mouth deep into his hole. But he was scared his dream would pulverize, and once again, he let the milky water bring relief to his skin, all over his neck.

Like the pupil who doesn't stare at his teacher for too long as a form of respect, Aurelio avoided looking down in the presence of the two men who were teaching him how to be happy. He challenged Oceanus's stare instead, for the first time with some arrogance. The arrogance of a young man who has been given the power to unveil life's secrets. The way he was being touched and handled was the right way. He knew he wasn't capable of doing the same with his own hands on his own body. He knew he couldn't obtain that pleasure, unless guided. The timing of Giotto and Arthur was not coincidence but fruit of knowledge and study.

In his ears, the fountain water kept flowing incessantly in a crescendo of intensity, inundating the oriental carpet he was standing on, the antique furniture and Arthur's Rome art books scattered on the floor. Aurelio was inside Arthur's mouth. Diving into his smooth flesh and pumping his head a little further with every thrust until his balls were pushed against the artist's skin. Immediately, the tingling invaded his limbs and mined his balance, giving the inexperienced lover the idea to take advantage of Giotto's laborious lips. He sat on the aristocrat's face and suddenly recognized the tip of his tongue. Intermittent unripe waves of pleasure scoured the seas of his insides and announced "the liquid," as Aurelio had baptized his juice in the warm silence of his room.

"Stand still." The painter ordered, this time not to finish up the canvas. Arthur wasn't trying to capture an expression or the contraction of a muscle. His only concern was milky boy's orgasm. No rush in his action, no selfishness. But Aurelio's knees trembled, uncontrollably. His tendons were weak and Giotto's creative hands blocked them. The pianist was more gentle. He emanated a kind of elegance that only accompanies classical music. It was with him, next to the black and white keys of the immense monster in the living room that Aurelio had decided what to do with his life. It was thanks to Giotto that Aurelio's father had understood the importance of studying and his son's inclinations. It was Giotto's naked chest that Aurelio had dreamed of through his initial masturbation acts. All that was poured into what was happening now.

The complex movement the three created concentrated between Arthur and Giotto's mouths, like the streams of passion running through the creases of Oceanus's loincloth. In his brain, Aurelio rediscovered a series of images he'd been treasuring through his years with the couple. Passionate kisses by the burning eggs, interrupted laughs under the shower, the distant moaning of the locked bedroom. Beyond age and status, Aurelio had always felt part of their carnality and their embrace. That was his last thought when taken away by the expanding of his senses, he dropped the mozzarellas that dilated on the floor in a white disaster. The tritons blew their shell-shaped horn to tame the storm and with the same vehemence Aurelio's member, to the zenith of a painful hardness, ejected short rivers of dense milk on his mentors' joyful smiles.

"Happy holidays to you, too, Aurelio!" Giotto and Arthur exclaimed at unison. "Aurelio? What's wrong?" They continued, turning their heads toward the window behind them to see what Aurelio was looking at in a state of trance. The Trevi fountain was so close that it looked as if it was in the apartment.

DADDY BEAR AND PUNK
By Donald Webb

Donald Webb has had short stories published in numerous gay magazines and anthologies. He lives with his life-long partner in Victoria, BC. Contact him at andon402@shaw.ca.

It being Saturday night, Cameron decided to drop into Colby's, a downtown gay bar. It was going on ten, and the bar was jumping when he entered the door. A number of men were on the dance floor under the glare of glittering strobe lights. Some had their Tees tucked into the backs of their jeans, exposing their naked upper bodies, but most were still fully dressed. Cameron's eardrums vibrated from the pulsing beat originating from two huge speakers. After pushing his way through the throng of hot bodies to the bar, he purchased a Bud, leaned against the counter, and looked around. Two hunks sat at a table for four, the other two chairs were vacant. He moved closer.

The elder of the two was sprawled in his chair, his butt at the edge, with his long legs stretched out beside the small table. A packed basket jutted out from his tight faded blue jeans. Muscular arms, exiting from the ragged edges of his sleeveless T-shirt, were raised above his shoulders, with hands clasped behind his head. Tufts of hair sprouted in his armpits and above the neckline of his shirt. His closely-cropped salt-and-pepper hair put him in his fifties.

The punk seated beside him sent testosterone pulsing through Cameron's blood vessels. With his brunette hair gelled into stiff spikes, dark eyeliner highlighting his smoky gray eyes, black leather motorcycle jacket, black Tee, tight black jeans — tucked into mid-calf black biker boots, and a wide black leather belt cinched around his narrow waist, he was a wet dream come true.

The young punk is probably in his mid twenties, Cameron was thinking, but in his current outfit, he doesn't look old enough to be in the bar. Cameron made eye contact with the older guy, but the guy quickly looked away. Cameron looked at the punk who was staring back at him. They locked eyes for a few moments and then the punk winked. Cameron returned the wink. The punk nodded toward the empty chair beside him.

Cameron walked over and said, "Anyone sitting here?"

The older guy averted his eyes. The punk shook his head.

"Mind if I sit?" Cameron said.

The punk smiled. Dimples appeared in his smooth cheeks. Pouty red lips — that looked as if they'd had a few collagen injections, parted, showing a perfect set of teeth. "Nope, go for it," he said.

"Busy place tonight," Cameron said.

"Sure is," the punk said, then after a beat, "I'm Jude, and my Daddy's name is Trey."

"I'm Cameron."

They shook hands and guzzled their beers. Jude rose and moved onto the dance floor. With eyes closed, and arms out wide, he moved sinuously to the music. When the tune changed, he approached the table, lifted his beer bottle, and gulped down the beer. He placed the empty bottle on the table and then resumed his bump and grind on the dance floor.

Trey rubbed his crotch. "That boy drives me crazy, can't get enough of him."

"I can see why," Cameron said. "I don't even know him, and he's driving me crazy." Cameron finished his beer. "Can I get you guys another?"

"Sure," Trey said.

When Cameron returned to the table with the three beers, Jude was still on the dance floor, and Trey's eyes were fixed on him. Jude ambled back to the table, saluted Cameron with his beer, took a big swig, and then headed for the restroom. Heads turned to watch his ass churning as he crossed the floor.

"Don't mind me saying," Cameron said, "but he's got a fabulous butt."

"You should see it naked," Trey said.

"He like to get fucked?" Cameron asked.

"Never has been. Still a virgin. He likes to get rimmed though. One of these days, I'll get in."

Cameron couldn't believe what he was hearing. It didn't sound right.

They watched the dancers. None came close to the pure sexuality that exuded from Jude when he was on the floor. The jingling of the chains and keys adorning Jude's outfit announced his return from the restroom.

"Busy in there?" Trey asked.

Jude nodded. "Packed. Someone wanted to blow me. Had to pry his lips off my dick. Told him I was saving it for my Daddy."

Jude leaned over, gave Trey a long kiss, dropped into his chair, and threw a leg over Trey's beefy thigh. Trey rested a hand on Jude's thigh, did a quick look around the room, and then gave Jude's dick a quick squeeze. "You're hard," he said.

"You'd be, too, if you'd just been through what I've been through."

"Can I check the restroom out?" Trey asked.

"As long as that's all you do."

Cameron and Jude watched Trey wend his way toward the restroom.

"He's got a nice muscular butt," Cameron said.

"You should see it when he's naked and lying on his stomach," Jude said.

"That I'd like to see."

"That can be arranged."

"Does he let you fuck him?" Cameron asked.

"You kidding? He's always begging for my big dick."

"You got a big one?" Cameron asked.

Jude placed two hands on the thick tube visible through his tight jeans and gave it a squeeze. "That's ten inches of Grade A meat, I'll have you know."

Cameron's dick stiffened at the thought of Trey getting fucked by his punk boy. After what seemed like a long time for a piss, Trey returned to the table. His fat dickhead, covered by a wet spot the size of a quarter, was clearly visible through the taut faded denim.

"You were right," he said. "It was a struggle to get out of there."

Trey's faced blushed when Jude said, "You were gone too long. I was getting ready to come drag you out of there."

Cameron's cell phone chimed. He opened it and read the text from a friend. "If you're free, come on over ... we're having a party."

"Your lover?" Jude asked when Cameron closed the phone and returned it to his pocket.

"No such luck. I'll be going home to an empty house tonight."

"You don't have a boy at home?" Jude asked.

Cameron shook his head.

"You poor baby. How come a hunk like you doesn't have someone?" Jude said.

"Unlucky in love ... I guess."

"Nother beer, guys?" Trey asked.

Jude and Cameron nodded.

After Trey returned to the table with the beers, Cameron decided it was time to empty his bladder. "Right back, guys," he said as he rose from his chair.

"Enjoy yourself," Jude said.

"Just goin' for a piss," Cameron said.

"We believe you, dude, but if you're not back in five, I'll send in a search party," Trey said.

The restroom, as advertised, was packed. Cameron squeezed between two guys at the trough, unzipped, and let fly. The guys standing beside him were hard. When Cameron's bladder was drained, he placed his hands on his hips to drip dry. The guy on his left immediately grabbed Cameron's dick and milked out the last drops of piss. Cameron's dick reached for the mirrored wall.

"Nice dick, bud," the guy said. "It'd be tough to swallow, but I'd like to try."

"Not tonight," Cameron said. "I've other plans for that baby."

With difficulty, Cameron stuffed his cock into his jeans, zipped up, and returned to the table.

"You're just under the deadline," Trey said. "But by the looks of it, you had the same problem we did."

"Sure did," Cameron said giving his woody a squeeze.

Jude smiled. "We've had enough for the night. Daddy has to work in the morning, and I have to get my beauty sleep. You wanna come home with us?"

Try and stop me, Cameron was thinking. "Sounds like a plan," he said.

They drained their beers and headed for the parking lot.

"You have wheels?" Jude asked Cameron.

"Yeah, I'll follow you."

# # # # #

"You wanna beer?" Trey asked when they were in the couples' apartment.

"Nah, I'll give it a pass," Cameron said.

"Me, too," Jude said.

Jude started a CD and then, in the middle of the room, he began the same sexy moves he'd displayed at the bar, only this time he did a slow strip. Cameron and Trey sat on the sofa watching the performance. Jude's jacket slowly slipped from his shoulders, exposing his muscular biceps and intricate colored tats on both upper arms, and then he pulled his Tee off and threw it at Cameron. Cameron held the Tee to his nose. It was slightly damp and gave off a leathery male aroma. He kept breathing in the heady scent, watching Jude watching him.

Trey laughed. "He's one sexy fucker, ain't he?"

"Sure is," Cameron said.

Jude lay on his back and lifted his boot clad feet, placing one foot on Cameron's knee, and the other on Trey's knee. Cameron following Trey's lead, removed Jude's boot and sock, then when Trey leaned over and licked the sole of Jude's foot. Cameron followed suit. After they'd feasted on Jude's toes, Jude jumped up and resumed his dance routine. After a few minutes, he dropped his pants and stepped out of them. Now naked, except for white bikini briefs that barely contained his muscular butt; he continued entertaining Cameron and Trey.

He turned his back on the two guys and, inch by inch, peeled his briefs down his legs, gradually revealing his gorgeous butt. Cameron let out a sigh when Jude bent over, removed his briefs and threw them at him. He held the briefs to his nose and once again breathed in the heady aroma. Except for the hair in his pits, a small pubic patch, and a thin line between his ass cheeks, Jude's body was completely hairless. His cock, free of the confining briefs, hardened up. He's right, Cameron thought, it is a good ten inches. It was uncut and curved up to Jude's abdomen and looked humongous on his small frame.

"Take your clothes off," Jude said to Trey and Cameron.

Once they were stripped, Cameron was once again struck by the difference in the two men. Trey's beefy chest and legs, and the huge stiff appendage sprouting from his body, somehow made Jude appear like an innocent young boy whom the older man could bend to his will. But that didn't seem to be the case. Jude seemed to be in control.

Cameron pushed Jude onto the sofa, lifted Jude's legs, and dived nose first into the damp spot between his cheeks. All night he'd wanted to rim Jude, and now he was finally doing it.

Jude let out a long groan. "Oh yeah, eat my ass, dude," he said pulling his thighs up to his chest.

Cameron gently nibbled on the exposed pucker, and then sent his tongue deep into the dilated chute. When he'd had his fill of ass, he licked Jude's perineum, and then deep throated his smooth dick.

Jude swiveled around on the sofa and hung his head over the edge. "Gimme that big dick," he said opening his mouth wide.

Cameron pushed his dick into Jude's mouth and watched Jude's pouty lips slide down his shaft. In that position, he had a clear passage straight down Jude's throat. He was picking up speed when Trey climbed onto the sofa. Trey planted a foot on either side of Jude's body, sat on the back of the sofa, and shook his dick at Cameron. Cameron leant forward and swallowed his dick. It was long and thick, but he had no trouble taking it all the way down his throat.

"Fuck, dude," Trey said. "You're just as good as Jude."

Jude and Cameron sucked dick for a few minutes, and then Jude extricated himself and said, "It's time for Daddy to get fucked."

Trey left the room for a few moments, returning with a fist full of safes and a container of lube. Cameron sat back on his haunches and let Trey roll a safe down his dick. He squirted some lube onto Cameron's dick, ran his hand up and down the shaft, then lay on his back on the sofa and lifted his legs. "Go for it," he said. "Gimme that big dick."

Cameron placed the head of his dick at Trey's open hole, and then with one push, he was balls deep in the hot cavity. As he deep poled Trey, he could feel his dickhead bumping into Trey's prostate.

"Ah, ah, ah," Trey cried each time Cameron hit bottom.

"That's what Daddy needed," Jude said. "Fuck him hard."

Cameron was building up speed, when Jude moved behind him, spread his butt mounds, and licked his hairy perineum. Cameron stopped moving and lay on Trey when Jude's tongue lapped at his hole. Cameron had been rimmed many times, but he'd never had it so good. "Fuck, boy," he said. "That feels good."

"He rimming you?" Trey asked.

"Oh yeah, he sure is."

When Jude's lubed finger slipped into Cameron's chute, Cameron jumped, knowing where this was heading. He'd been fucked a few times, and he'd enjoyed it, but he preferred to be on top. Jude kept poking away until he had two fingers worming their way up Cameron's tight chute. Cameron was feeling ambivalent. He'd wanted to fuck Jude, but it seemed Jude wanted to fuck him. Thoughts flashed through his mind. Should I let him? He's much bigger than I've ever had before. Will it hurt?

When the head of Jude's dick pushed at Cameron's tight muscle ring he thought, what the hell, and let it in. It was kind of exciting having the tables turned and being dominated by a punk boy.

"Oh fuck," Cameron said when Jude was fully embedded. "I didn't think I'd be able to take it."

Jude withdrew a little and then pulled Cameron back against his pelvis. Cameron — a quick study, got the message. He resumed fucking Trey, moving back and forth on the huge rod up his tight ass. The punk's hot gasping breath sent tingles down Cameron's spine.

It didn't take long for all of them to climax. Trey was the first. He spewed cum all over his chest and neck, and then Jude cried out, "I'm coming, dude. Shooting up your ass." Cameron picked up speed when he felt Jude's big knob vibrating in his chute. Within seconds, he was emptying his balls in the punk's Daddy.

Sometime later, when Cameron was dressed and ready to leave, he said, "Good fuck guys. Hope I run into you again."

It was going on 1:00 am when Cameron finally climbed into bed. Sometimes, he wished he had a steady. Someone he could cuddle every night, but then again, he thought, I'd have missed meeting Daddy Bear and Punk.

FUCKING LINK
MASTERSON
By Armand

Armand has published in more than a dozen anthologies. One day, he
hopes to develop a superpower that allows him to turn any man gay.

Link Masterson — yes, that was his on-air name — was a
cocky, randy braggart who supposedly fucked anything on two
legs. That is, if it had a vagina. I had only worked at the station
for two days when I saw his magnetism at work. One of the
interns from the local college, a cute sorority girl named Buffy,
couldn't stop rubbing her tits against him every time she asked
him an inane question or she brought him a cup of coffee. She
was a like a sluttier, less stylish version of Kim Kardashian.

I had just gotten my assignment — filming a promo for a
hair show that was going to be judged by the station's anchors
— when I caught Link wink at Buffy. Yes, he's a winker. After
she walked away, he caught me eyeing him and sauntered over.

"She's something else, isn't she?" he asked like we were best
bros.

"Uh, I guess." His expression was comical. He couldn't
understand why I hadn't replied, "I'd like to bang her in every
position in the *Kama Sutra*."

"Don't think we've met. I'm Link Masterson." He sounded
like that announcer who narrates every movie trailer.

I took his hand and shook it firmly. "I'm Alex Ryan, the new
camera guy."

"Ahh. Welcome aboard." He flashed a cheesy smile. "So
what do you think of Buffy?"

From what I could surmise in my short time, he was a total tool, but the women adored him, and I could see why. His dark brown hair was graying at the temples but was still thick with a perfect wave, and he filled out his turtlenecks and suits like an ex-football player. "She's not really what I'm into," I finally responded — an oblique way to say I don't like snatch.

Link was incredulous. He furrowed his brow and looked as if he was about to interrogate or berate me. Suddenly, his epiphany dawned. "Oh." Then he did something bizarre. He visibly puffed out his chest as if he was posing for a superhero poster. Damn this guy wanted everyone's attention. He swatted my arm and said, "Be seeing you around, Ryan."

I didn't give a shit if he was calling me by my last name or couldn't remember my first name. I was just glad to smell his aftershave up close and see his pearly teeth and blue eyes.

# # # # #

I had begun to fantasize about Link every night. I wasn't usually into older men, but I would make an exception for him. I was twenty, and he was twice that, but I had seen him in a tank top in the makeup chair and knew he took care of his body. I'd begun looking at his crotch and imagining his thick dick inside his trousers. I would idle away hours wondering if he wore boxers or briefs, if he'd ever let a guy suck him off, if his dick might be uncut. The guy was a flirt, and I was convinced he'd fucked every woman at the station from Buffy, the non-vampire slayer, to the manager. He was even flirty with the two other homos — Jorge, the makeup guy, and Randy, the producer. Not only did he wink, but he always made a point of touching them on the arm before he walked away. No wonder I caught Jorge with a boner the day Link was in his makeup chair with his fly undone. Jorge must have been in gay heaven getting a peek at Link's underwear.

After two months of watching Link's antics but really never interacting with him, I was sent on assignment by his side to film a segment about the iniquity on the downtown streets near the park. Link charmed the prostitutes and even got one to appear on camera with him for an interview. Of course, she said, "I walk up and down this street at night for exercise, and I don't see a problem. People are friendly." Just then a truck drove by and yelled, "Give him the Bunny Special." She smiled coyly, leaned forward and whispered something. Later, I found out the Bunny Special involved a finger in the bum right when her johns were about to shoot. According to Bunny, nine out of ten men loved it, but the one in ten who didn't like it often took off without paying.

"Thank you for speaking with us," Link said with the charm of George Clooney.

"No, thank *you*," Bunny said, effusive. "Come by any night to see how safe and entertaining these streets can be." Poor thing didn't realize her magenta tube top and black fishnets belied her wholesome "apple pie" spiel.

What Link failed to realize is that I had not turned the camera off when he slid under a tree to buy a bag of weed from a kid passing by. That ended up serving me better than any Oscar-winning documentary ever could have.

# # # # #

Link caught me beside my van watching the footage I'd just shot. "Whatta ya doing?" he asked nonchalantly.

"Watching you buy drugs from a teenager," I responded coolly. His face blanched. "Wanna see?"

"Uhh" was his only response.

"Relax. It's not like I'm going to show anyone." He visibly relaxed; then I threw in the zinger: "Hey, have you ever done it with a dude?"

That was the first time I saw his confidence and studly demeanor falter. After stammering a bit, he asked, "What do you want?"

"I don't know. Thought maybe I could see your place."

His cocky smile returned. This sonofabitch is smooth. He'd flirt with a nun and make her think she initiated it.

"Sure. I'll text you the address. See you in an hour."

# # # # #

When I arrived, he was freshly showered and dressed in jeans and a black sweater that hugged his thick torso beautifully. He was still wearing that damn smile, and I wanted to see him wearing nothing else.

"Come in, Ryan."

"It's Alex, big guy."

"I know," he responded as he raised the joint to his lips and took a big puff. "Want some?"

"Nah. Makes me too paranoid." I slid past him and our chests rubbed together. My cock stirred at that simple contact. I couldn't lose my confidence, or this wouldn't go the way I wanted.

"Relaxes me. Makes me go with the flow, do things I might not otherwise." He pushed the door closed with his foot. "Got my first blow job while I was smoking a joint." My interest was piqued. "He had a mouth like a hoover." It was my turn to smile. "See, I'm an … open-minded guy."

"Let's see how open minded." It was my turn to be cocky. I reached for his crotch and rubbed his dick and felt it thicken.

"You like?"

"Maybe." I unzipped his fly and reached in and pulled out his thick cock. Looking up at his smug smile, I unabashedly stroked his thick member a few times and then turned to walk into his posh living room. "Come," I instructed.

Dick flying free, he walked into the living room and put out his joint in an ashtray shaped like a hand.

"Strip," I ordered. He laughed nervously, but then grabbed his sweater insistently. "Slowly. Make it sexy, like you want to please me."

In slow motion, he peeled the sweater up and over his head. His cock, still protruding through his fly, was fully engorged and bounced playfully as he shed the sweater. Then he peeled off the tank top.

For the first time I could see that he had a spattering of chest and belly hair over that muscular frame. My own dick responded immediately, straining against my khaki pants. Link unbuttoned his jeans and pulled the fly wide, so I could see he was wearing no underwear. His blond bush was trim but covered a wide thatch from hip bone to hip bone.

"You want to suck my big cock?" he asked.

"All the way," I responded as I waved for him to remove the rest of his clothes.

While he finished undressing, I walked around the living room as if I was disinterested. The furniture was leather and chrome. Rather than heading for the bedroom, I was going to do him right here, and I knew just what position I was going to demand.

"Where's your bedroom?" I asked. Standing buck naked, and looking hotter than I'd imagined, he pointed. "Stay here."

I headed down the hallway and found his monochromatic bedroom. The wanker actually had a bust of himself next to some broadcasting awards on his chest of drawers. Rifling through his bedside table, I found exactly what I was expecting:

a drawer of toys and accoutrements. "What have we here?" I said as I pulled out a strap on. "This is going to be fun."

When I returned to the living room, Link was sitting in the middle of the leather couch with his arms spread across the back. His thick cock pointed heavenward. The fucker knew he looked hot, and that he turned me on.

I held up a moderate size butt plug. "Put this in your hole."

"Ugh, those are for my guests."

I tossed the butt plug and a bottle of lube onto his chest and then began unbuttoning my shirt. My cock could not wait to be freed; it was beginning to hurt.

"Uh, I'm not really into this," he said holding up the black butt plug.

"Okay, then you can put this one inside," I said as I held aloft the larger dildo attached to a strap on.

He groaned and then reached for the lube. By the time he'd lubed up, I was completely naked.

"Impressive," he said nodding to my cock. It was modest size in both length and girth, but it curved upwards toward my belly when hard.

I walked over and took the butt plug from his hand and rubbed a finger over the lube. I slid my moist finger into his ass.

"Whoa. Easy, champ."

To give him a little kindness I took his thick cock in my mouth and started sucking. He relaxed instantly and started to moan. My finger continued probing deeper, faster as he spread his legs wider for my assault on his tight hole.

"'Suck me," he said.

I pulled out my finger, loosed his cock from my mouth and then raised one of his legs over my shoulder. Anxious, he looked at me with imploring eyes and then grabbed the back of the couch with his hands. I shoved the butt plug into his tight hole with one strong push, and he gasped.

"You like when your girlfriends fuck you?" I asked.

"Sometimes," he replied tentatively.

"I think you should suck me now. Ever sucked a guy?"

"A couple times in college."

I grabbed his cock and stroked vigorously, and he started humping my hand. Then I stepped up on the couch and dangled my cock in his face. Without any instruction, he pulled my cock downward and put the head in his warm mouth.

"Deeper," I demanded, and he obeyed. I had a strong gag reflex and couldn't deep throat, so I wasn't going to make him do it, but he surprised me by sucking all the way to the base.

"Is that good?" he asked.

"Keep sucking, big boy."

I arched my back and stroked his cock, but the position was just too awkward. I let him suck for a few minutes before I dropped onto his lap and kissed him deeply. For a mostly straight guy, he kissed with élan as his cock throbbed against the crack of my ass.

"You're fucking hot," he said breathily. I had to confess I was glad he liked our encounter so far. I just hoped he'd be able to handle what was coming next.

I slid off his lap and was kneeling between his legs.

"You ready for me to fuck you?" he asked. Instead of responding, I lifted one of his beefy legs and pulled the butt plug out of his ass. "Oh fuck," he gasped as the butt plug ejected his hole.

"Get in doggie," I instructed. He just looked at me. "Do it."

"Look, Alex, I sometimes let a woman inside me, but I'm ... straight."

"Why do straight guys always pretend that they're not into ass play? You liked that butt plug in your hole, you like a woman using a strap on, so you'll fucking love my cock inside you."

"I don't think I can do this."

I stood and tossed the butt plug as if I was disgusted. Then I walked over and picked up the camera I'd used to film him buying pot from the teenager. The truth is that I would never have used it against him, but I liked feeling as if I had leverage and was in control. This was always my fantasy, but something I'd never experienced.

Finally, he stood and turned. Then he assumed the position, doggie on the couch.

I slid a condom on my rock hard cock and lubed it up. While I rubbed a generous amount of lube on his hole, I said, "Tell me to fuck you."

"Fuck me."

"Say it like you mean it. Tell me you want me to fuck your tight asshole hard."

"Fuck me, Alex. Come on slide that hard cock in my virgin hole. I want you to be the one, the only man to fuck my ass."

Wow he was good!

I placed the head of my stiffy against his tight hole and leaned forward. "Turn your head, so I can see you face." He obeyed and laid his head on his arm. As I slid inside, he grimaced, and I stopped about a third of the way inside. To my delight, he pressed his ass back until I was all the way inside him. Unable to resist, I immediately started to rock back and forth, fucking him.

He let out a sigh and then moaned, "Yeah, fuck that ass."

"Take it like a man, Link."

"Fuck me, Alex."

I got a little too vigorous too quickly and he squealed. Though I loved being in control, I had no desire to actually hurt the guy, so I eased up. He arched his back and shifted his ass in a circle for a minute. "Okay, now you can pound that hole."

I started to bounce up against him slowly to test the waters. He had a look of ecstasy, and I reached under him to find his cock rock hard. I stroked it aggressively as I started to work my cock farther out and back inside him. I could see his asshole stretched around my cock, and I knew I couldn't hold back long. I was fucking Link Masterson hard in his tight ass!

"I'm close," he said. "I want you to shoot in my ass."

I couldn't waste this opportunity, so I started pounding like a jackhammer, and his eyes rolled back in his head as he gasped, "Fuck yeah. Keep pounding me. Don't hold back. That's it. Ahh, that feels so good. You're going to make me shoot."

I could hear our bodies slamming together, and his body bounced with every thrust, and I couldn't delay it any longer, so I pulled out and shot my load onto his freshly fucked hole.

"I was close," he said, disappointed.

"Squat," I told him. He stood on the couch facing me and squatted down. "I'll fuck you with this dildo while I suck you off."

He seemed suspicious, but once I shoved that dildo up his hole and began sucking, he was entirely convinced. He moaned like a porn star as I pounded that dildo inside him. Soon I tasted his spunk as he shot globs of it inside my mouth. While he came, I pumped that dildo at full speed.

When he collapsed onto the couch, I thought, Good thing it's leather 'cause he's still got my load in his crack. Then Link pulled me in for a kiss. I took his flaccid penis in my hand and then felt remorse that I'd probably never get to experience this again.

"I'll delete the video from my camera," I volunteered.

He stood and walked toward the bathroom. Then he turned to me and said, "You want to spend the night?"

YES, SIR
By R. Talent

R. Talent is a freelance writer who is putting the final touches on his debut novel along with the series he hopes to develop from it.

"Stop all that yammering … like your old ass never had this big white dick before," Curtis growls.

He is angry when he fucks my mouth open like this, calling it his pussy and me his black cunt. He tells me to keep my mouth open, but my head throbs tremendously from the blood rushing into it in this virgin position. He doesn't care. He just wants me to take his prick and gag on it. He wants to scrape the back of my throat with it. He isn't happy that I can't breathe around it or that snot is furiously bubbling out of my nose.

All he knows is that he worked too damn hard to get me this way. To make sure that my mouth perfectly aligns with his prick. Adjusting and readjusting the rope from the ceiling.

He has me suspended by a single leg from it, arms tied behind my back with my free leg cuffed behind my thigh with this thing.

"It's to let the naked ass crack breath free from all those old man farts," he says.

The cool air rolling through its gorge is quite soothing in the cemented shed we are in. My jaw hurts immensely from its severe unhinging. Curtis is big that way. I sniffle and grovel for precious air, so that I take care of him to the best of my ability. Curtis doesn't allow that. He thinks its defiance. He thinks that I should be grateful that a hunk like him would even bother to waste his time with an old man like me. He is right. He reaches over and twists my ear hard to remind me of such an honor. I cry out, in both pain and in gratitude. He doesn't give a fuck about any of that. I am only there for his enjoyment. He rapes my mouth because he can. I take it because I have no other choice available. He screws my nipples for his sadistic pleasure. He crams his prick further down my mouth to meet my masochist need.

He likes listening to the loss of life puffing out of my lungs, the gurgling and such. It makes him feel like an almighty god knowing that he is the gatekeeper to my very existence. I snort more snot onto his hairy nards. He just does what he does, causing me to eventually blackout. I don't know how long I am out. I am still conscious enough to feel him pull out of me and reawaken my soul with the acrid flow of urine that falls out of my mouth and over my face, blinding me with it warm sting.

Curtis stands back, looks and laugh.

He is quite solid, five-eleven, two-hundred-fifty pounds. He isn't fat. He is muscular in the way an American football player is. He is not cut but is handsomely beefy in a way that's enjoyably masculine, a throwback to the natural way of hardworking men before gyms.

He makes me weak trying to look at him in his leather chaps and black boots to match, his arrogant certainty, his youth and his rugged redneck beauty compressed in all of eighteen years.

I am sixty. I will not tell you that I don't look anything like it. I have too much gray in my wool to lie like that. I do have a nice body due to those hardcore workouts videos on TV. I have a uniquely hairy face, hoop earrings and tattoo sleeves to show off with it.

Still, I am a lonely man.

Too young to give up on life, and yet considered too old to be such a willing submissive.

Again, he doesn't care.

He only curses that he didn't attach a funnel to my faggot mouth as he relieves himself across my face. "Good piss gone to waste," he bemoans.

The yellow river of his creation stops. It runs across my face through the top of my head down to a puddle on the hard floor beneath.

"But if I had," he says for his forgotten funnel, "I couldn't do this."

He rams his prick back into my gaping mouth still drowning in his piss. It forever surprises me with its mammoth girth. It isn't naturally expected of a white boy his size, his age. I seem to enjoy it endlessly just the same as it finds its joy in humiliating me so.

He has me gagging on it again in no time.

He doesn't know the meaning of the word slow. He only knows the adjectives fast and hard, fucking my mouth like it is good pussy. It's my motherfucking pussy, always and forever, old man! He reminds me to watch my teeth, to keep them tucked behind my thick lips. He cusses and moans, and I slobber and groan for more of the precious air he denies me. He thrusts more violently. I hear him grunt and grunt again. His prick swells enormous in my tightened mouth and then twitches as if it is possessed.

"Oh, God! Aw, shit! Aw, fuck! Yeah!"

He shoots a gallon of hot fire cum into my mouth that is just as abundant as his flowing piss.

I try to impress him by swallowing it all the best I can. It is showing my respect, my honor to take care of him. He doesn't care. His thick fingers find my dry butt hole as he pants.

He didn't mean to bust his nutt, he groans. He wanted to save that load for my ass.

I ignore him for once.

119

The fun he is having with my hole and knowing his drive, I know he'll be ready to go again in no time.

I lick his nards, tasting my sweet mucus on them taking him back in my mouth to clean him up.

Even as it goes soft, he is still hung as ever.

He has a hood and a big pair of nards that swing midway down his bulging thighs.

My eyes maybe on this, but my head is on my tender hole.

He threatens to take care of it for me, for him, fingering it roughly.

He pulls his prick out of my mouth and pulls away, going somewhere out of sight.

I hear his feet move around on the raw cement floor to the corner. I hear the clanking of a footstool come near me. He sets it up behind me along with tall box crate.

I am anxious.

My head hurts. My mouth is in influx. I feel my arms are getting tired behind my back, though. My leg hanging from the ceiling is in excruciating pain. My other leg bent double is cramping.

I have no time to cry behind all of this. He is ready.

He climbs the stepladder and slaps my ass hard. He pries open my ass cheeks and spits a wad on my parched hole. He fingers it some more, only going deeper and with unforgiving will. I grovel again, begging him to stop. It hurts. It all hurts. Like hell. I am afraid that he is out to fuck me without lube, and I know that will hurt even more. I know how to take him this way. But with all my bodily fluids rushing to the top of my head and being stripped of my natural wetness for him, I know I can't this time. I just can't. I can't!

He grabs my testicles and yanks them.

120

I cry out.

Again, he grabs my testicles and yanks them even harder.

And, again, I cry out.

"Stop your whining bitch," he says. He says some other stuff, but its sum total is that he doesn't want me to ever disrespect him ever again.

I feel the head of his prick nudge my opening. I brace my body for the unkind slaughter for him to simply thump his prick hard against my ass crack.

"Aw, fuck!"

Curtis throws his leg over mine onto the crate beside me and nudges his way right in. I wince and I groan and I moan and I struggle to get upright, making a futile attempt to tear free of my restrains. He laughs at my efforts, dipping enough of his flared tip into my puckered asshole to show he is serious in fucking me. That he is in control. It burns terribly. He then pulls out once he feels that I get the point that he is in charge, the only one in charge, and squirts something quite relieving throughout my crease. He can be a merciful god sometimes, I remember. I can feel by it diluted consistency that he has to be using his favorite jack off brew of baby oil and baby oil gel on me. He points down to my hole and slides into home with no brakes.

"Oh, God! Aw, shit! Aw, fuck!"

"Shut up bitch," he growls.

"Yes, sir."

"Say it again, cunt."

"Yes, sir."

"Again, cunt!"

"Yes, sir!"

"Good ... bitch."

121

He sinks his prick in even deeper, pass the second ring, pass the third. He holds it there inside of me as he pulls my roped ankle along for the ride. He wants me to get use to the enormous size of him berthing inside of me. He lets me know that his pig prick is in there for the long haul. But, right now, even with so many bodily places so tender, it feels goods with his hairy nards resting quietly on my hole. It feels like home. He gradually pulls back. I feel my stretched walls close around him as he pulls back up. He keeps the head in and pushes back down.

I yelp. I yammer.

He pumps me like this for awhile, testing me and my vulnerable reaction. Testing me and my ceiling restraint ever so often, throwing all of his incredible massive weight onto me. He outweighs me by a hundred pounds. I sometimes think that my leg is just going to snap off, and I'm just going to fall and bust my head on the floor. But that never happens.

He breathes intensely, immensely.

He tells me that my hole is sweet and tight, and that he just can't get enough of it.

I can't get enough of him either. His way is everything dear to me. The way he walks. The way he talks. The way he moves his sexy body about. And, of course, I am remiss to leave his prick out. It isn't so much its staggering size that gets me. It is that he knows how to work it as well as he does. It is the satisfaction of knowing when he is done. He is done. Leaving me exhausted and spent with a sore back hole that feels as if it takes forever to get right again.

"Aw, fuck! Shit!"

My rectum stretches and pulls.

"Shut that shit up!"

"Yes, sir."

He begins pounding. I begin to whimper.

122

"Stop all that crying, you hear, acting like your old black ass never had it tended to by this big white dick before."

"Yes, sir."

I shutter because he is absolutely right. He just doesn't understand that it feels like the very first time every single time he enters me with that thing.

"Take this dick."

"Yes, sir."

"Take it!"

"Yes, sir!"

"Take my dick, cunt!"

"Oh, God. Yes, sir!"

"There you go."

"Thank you, sir!"

"Grip my dick, bitch."

"Aw! Aww! Aww! Aww!"

"Grip it!"

"Yes, sir!"

"Grip it!"

"Yes, sir!"

"Grip it!"

"Yes, sir!"

"Put your ass into it, cunt."

"Yes, sir!"

"There you go. That's my sweet black cunt."

"Thank you, sir."

"Hungry old cunt hurts for this dick, doesn't it old motherfucker?"

"Aw! It hurts! It hurts for your dick!"

"That 'cause it suppose to."

Curtis leans forward again. He pumps like a freakish mad man on top of me straining my leg. He calls me his bitch, my hole his everything. His cunt. His pussy. His ass. His twat. His snatch. His snapper. His beaver. His joy. And I am left in suspension, pitiful and in pain, hung there to take it all.

"You like me roaming your guts, don't you?"

"Yes, sir."

"I'm going to fill your old black cunt with these white babies, you hear?"

"Yes, sir."

"Your old ass black is going to have some pretty white babies for me, aincha?"

"Oh, yes, sir! Yes!"

My muscles relax into euphoria at the thought of this, the thought of him dumping his milky white babies into my black hole. Pregnancy, I bask. Then, my body trembles at the sinister thought of him taking his belt to my ass forcing me to fart out every one of them.

"The beautiful births!" I cry. "Oh, sir, yes! Yes, sir. Pretty pretty babies, sir."

"You love dick, don't you?"

"I love your dick, sir."

"Your hungry ass always loved dick, huh?"

"Yes, sir. Oh, yes!"

"Even when your black-ass momma was taking it from your black-ass daddy, huh? Shoving that big ole pimp pipe in her pussy womb while you were sleeping in it, huh?"

"Yes, sir."

"You probably turned your baby back to just so that your baby ass could get a piece of it, huh?"

"Yes, sir."

"I bet your faggot ass used to ride it out back in the locker rooms in high school, huh?"

"Yes, sir."

"You probably were a big ole slut back then just like you are now. Just letting any ole dirty fucking somebody run a train on that sweet ass! Players, coaches, teachers, you name it."

"Yes, sir! Oh, god! Yes!"

"I bet my pappy and his pappy saw it, too. Probably wanted to rip you a new one for you thinking that you thought your sweet ass was better than anyone."

"Yes, sir."

"They raped this pussy good and thought this pussy was good, too. I bet they used to pass your ass around town. Let the married men get at your wet snatch, huh?"

"Yes, sir, most of them, sir. When Aunt Flo came to ..."

"Even between visits, too, huh, cunt?"

"Yes, sir. Oh! Aw! Aww! Aww!"

"You probably were getting double-fucked weren't you! Had two big dicks up in that hole! We probably could've won Vietnam if the soldiers and Vietcong weren't tearing for a piece of you."

"Yes, sir!"

"Robbing your cunt, cunt."

"Yes, sir. You're absolutely right, sir!"

"Making it easy for everybody with a dick to slide on in the way you get wet for it."

"Awwwww!"

After this wave of pleasure hits me, my body aches terribly from its restrains, the blood rushing to my head, and his heavy weight on top of me. I think this is too much. I am on the verge of passing out again. So I am floored when I find that this is just the beginning when he happens to just fall onto me, literally. His body topples mind upside down. He amazes me that his smooth chest is against mind. I think he wants to kiss me, but quickly remembers all that he has done to my face. The piss, the cum, straight into my mouth. He looks at me because he can't hump me in this way. He stays like this for a few seconds. It feels like forever looking into his eyes, as he swings up.

"Gimme that black ass black boy. "He fucks me again with my legs across his shoulder.

The former race man in me should be offended by the word boy, but I'm not. I convince myself in the moment that he is too young to be so conscious of old matters like these.

"Where's my Yes, Sir, cunt!"

"Yes, sir."

Even though I am hurting because of it, Curtis doesn't give any more regard to the restrain suspending me from the ceiling as it has proven that it can hold up quite well. He begins to fuck me without the balances of the stepladder or the crate and just uses me for everything. Each thrust he delivers pulls at my leg even more. It feels as if it's coming out of socket at the hip, out of place just like the rest of me. I labor in heavy breaths trying to shield the pain. He continues to fuck me as if we have the comfort of a bed there. I scream. I scream. I scream! I am not sure how long I can take this, his weight on top of me like this. I feel these giant beads of sweat roll over me like rotisserie meat. For how long, I am not sure. All I know for certain is that he is sweating profusely, and it pours off of him onto me. I feel it cut through mine, making its way down to my eyes that I can't wipe. I am soon blind from it all.

"Give it to me."

"Yes, sir!"

"Gimme that black ass, boy!"

"Yes, sir!"

He pumps and pumps and pumps. He cusses and pumps. He moans and pumps. He cusses and moans and pumps and cusses some more. He finds his stride on me like this, thrusting more violently to the point that the rope is rocking the rafter. I thrash my head, whipping it from side in an attempt to get the sweat out. I hear him grunt and grunt again. His prick swells enormously in my now well used ass, and then twitches again like he is possess.

"Oh, God! Aw, shit! Aw, fuck! Yeah, fuck! Yeah, shit! Oh, God!"

Curtis quickly falls onto of me again, just in time to shoot his warm-hot babies straight up in my ass. It burns just like my hole, but feels good when he done.

But it proves not to be my end as I feel my own dick twitch.

"Oh, fuck! Motherfucker! Fuck!"

I cry when I feel my body expels its own wormy babies between us in this continuous white ribbon that barrels over my head toward the floor.

Curtis and I share a special moment looking into each other's eyes. And then, he flips off me.

He leaves me there to hang there for an hour more. He comes back to undo me, but not without another heavy spray of piss over my chest.

"Good piss gone to waste," he bemoans as it comes down in a thin sheet over my neck and head and puddles back onto the floor.

I am more than spent, exhausted, and tired. And still, I find the strength to offer to pay for his schooling in the fall. He refuses. I try to sneak him some extra money from my pension, so he doesn't forget to come by more often. He doesn't except. He says he never will. He says that I'm the only man in the world that gives a young man like him the respect he deserves, and to that I say, "Yes, Sir."

SPANKING THE STEP
By Rob Rosen

Rob Rosen, author of the three novels, has been published in well-over 150 anthologies. Please visit him at www.therobrosen.com.

"Just go see him," said my mother on one of my recent visits home. "He's lonely."

"Then you go see him," I replied.

She frowned and shook her head. "Too soon."

I couldn't help but laugh at her remark. "You've been divorced from him for four years, Ma."

Her head kept right on shaking. "Way too soon. You go. You were always his favorite."

Which wasn't even close to being true. See, Alvin, my step-father, or The Step, as I liked to call him, didn't exactly see eye to eye with me when I was growing up. In fact, all we generally saw was hand to ass. My ass. When he spanked me. Which was often enough. Unfortunately for me, the guy grew up in a strict household and firmly believed in the concept of corporal punishment: he was spanked as a child; he turned out all right; so I was spanked. Case closed.

Needless to say, I hated the fucker. And so did my mother, though it took her a decade to realize it. Too bad for me. And my ass.

Anyway, I hadn't seen him since the divorce. We talked on the phone, from time to time, because, for some fucked up reason, we still considered him family. I mean, he did, after all, provide well for us for all those years. Did put food on the table and a roof over our heads. In fact, said roof still covered my mom's head. She got it in the divorce. All of it. Me, I just got a bunch of bad memories.

"Please," she said. "Just go see him. He sounds miserable every time he calls here."

"And we care about that why?" I asked. She replied with that same frown, head tilted down, and I knew my protestations were for naught. "Fine. Five minutes. Just to make sure he's not sticking his head in the oven."

She ran out of the room and returned quick as a wink, pie in hand. "If he is, hand him this. Three-fifty for thirty minutes, Ted."

I smirked and took the pie. "How can I be his favorite if I'm your only child, Ma?" I finally thought to ask as she ushered me out of the house.

"Process of elimination, Ted," she replied, walking me to my car. "I'm not high on his list since I took him for everything he had."

"And rightly so," I couldn't help but add, stepping inside the car.

"And rightly so," she echoed, shutting the door and waving at me as I drove off.

I waved back and forced a smile on my face. Then I sighed. Because this, I figured, wasn't going to be easy. Or fun. I mean, even on the phone we argued. He didn't approve of me, and I didn't approve of him. In his eyes, I was a long-haired hippy, even though my hair only came to my shoulders. But I was an artist, and he thought about artists about as highly as bums on the street. And those he generally ignored, not even a nickel tossed their way.

Of course, as I said, I thought about him in just about the same way. Guy was a fifties throw back, you see. He wanted supper on the table and a family that spoke only when spoken to. If even that. So what, you might ask, did my mother see in such a schmuck? Well, that's an easy one. See, guy was Stunning. Capital S. And well-deserved. The prick was Clark Gable and Cary Grant all rolled up in an athlete's chiseled body. All-state football, in fact. Naturally, he was the quarterback. And, naturally, I detested team sports. Go figure.

In any case, that's what she saw in him. It's what blinded her. Blinded her to the beatings. Blinded her to what he was like on the inside, which was deep and dark and brooding. Hot on the outside, frigid on the inside. And nary a thermostat to control it all. Poor me. Poor, little ass of mine.

In any case, I pulled up to his house a half an hour later. I smiled despite the circumstances. The Step, it appeared, had come way down in the world. In fact, the house was barely larger than a trailer, the lawn a mere swatch of untended grass, the car a relic, just like him. Not too surprisingly, this all delighted the fuck out of me.

So, with a spring in my step, I bounded up to the front door, pie in hand. Many knocks later, he answered, wearing cut-off sweats and nothing else. Not even a smile for yours truly. Or the pie. "The prodigal son returns home," he grumbled.

"Stepson," I reminded him. "Mom thought you were depressed and wanted me to check on you."

He eyed his home, his car, his lawn. "Depressed? Fuck, Ted, I'm happy as a clam." He stepped aside and let me in. All things considered, I was fine with just the witty repartee. Still, I walked inside, if only to be the better man.

Oh foolish me.

And, yes, he was still a site to see, still in fine form. Not a paunch or even a receding hairline. Grayer, perhaps, around the temples, frown lines more evident, crow's feet etching his handsome face, but all this just added to his good looks. I was still the geeky little kid, and he was still the handsome, old asshole. Which, of course, made it doubly as hard to be alone with him, especially in his current state of undress.

"The pie for me?" he asked, shutting the door behind us.

I tried as best I could to keep my eyes off his chest, at the etched groove between his pecs, at the thick nipples poking out from the swirl on graying chest hair. "Apple. Your favorite."

He snickered. "Bitch knows I hate apple."

I winced at the word. "She was just being nice."

The snicker went full-throttle. "Nice, huh? Since when? Did she buy that with my money?"

I gritted my teeth and prepared for a hasty exit. "She earned it, Alvin." I tried counting to ten, but only made it to five. "In spades."

He inched in toward me, setting the pie down on the coffee table. "Only thing that bitch earned was you. Two wastes of a life, if you ask me."

And then, for the first time since I'd known him, I hauled off and slapped him one, hard, on the chest, the red quickly rising from the point of contact before working its way to his face. He paused, clearly shaken, but quickly gained his senses. Meaning, the palm across my cheek felt like a sack of bricks.

I reeled, covered my face with my hand, and fought back the tears. But then I remembered that crying didn't work as a child, and it certainly wasn't going to work now. So I did the next best thing and ran forward, butting his chest with my head, pushing him in reverse. And that's the direction he went, exhaling loudly as he tripped, fell, and landed on all fours.

More angry than I'd ever been in my entire life, I dove for him, spanking his ass like he did mine as a child, belting it with every ounce of strength I had. "She." Spank. "Is." Spank. "Not." Spank. "A bitch!" I hollered, the entire house shaking at my sudden outburst. It and me both, my heart pounding so furiously that I thought it would burst.

Then silence as he rolled over, so red in the face it was a wonder he had any blood left in the rest of his body. Only, from the looks of it, he did. Meaning, those nasty sweats of his were suddenly tenting something fierce. He glanced down. From it to me. Was he shocked at my beating or from his boner? Honestly, I couldn't say. "Get out," he croaked, voice suddenly uneven, hand over his burgeoning prick, which only called more attention to it.

"Fucker," I said, kicking his shin before I spat down at him, the gob of spit sliding down his rapidly rising and falling chest.

He wiped it off and then suddenly dove for me. Only, I was quicker. Much younger and much quicker, in fact. I sidestepped him, and he landed on his belly, legs splayed, ass up. Like a target all in gray. Again I dove, anger still boiling at the surface, bubbling over, my hand coming down hard, again and again, seeking revenge for all those many years of his doing the same to me.

He grunted and rolled over, cock swaying from within his sweats. "Finally got some balls on you, kid, huh?"

I leaned down and slapped his face. "I never deserved your beatings, Alvin," I raged. "You deserved this one, though. And then some."

He paused, eyeing me, breathing hard now. "That make you feel better, Ted? Even the score some? Tit for tat? Eye for an eye? Spank for a spank?"

I gulped. There was an edge to his voice I'd never heard before. Not as a kid. Not in all those miserable years. Though, in truth, it did make me feel better. "That was a drop in the bucket, asshole."

He nodded and rubbed the spot on his face where I'd slapped him. Then slowly he turned and got on his knees again, ass out. "Fine, kid," he said, barely in a whisper. "Fill the bucket up then. Have at it. Have a field day with it, for all I care." He chuckled and spread his legs wider. "Fucking wimp. Will probably hurt you way worse than it does me."

I fell to my knees, face twisted in anger, hand up high before it came crashing down. And it did hurt, actually. And felt better than anything else in recent memory. It hurt and hurt and hurt as I spanked him, but with each wallop my soul felt just a little bit better, like a wound was finally healing inside.

Eventually, I fell backward, panting hard. He remained where he was, on all fours, also panting. "That all you got, Ted? You squirmed like a fish when I spanked you as a kid. I barely even flinched all these years later."

I rubbed my palm on my leg and fought to catch my breath. "I was bare-assed back then, Alvin. You've got padding."

His chuckle returned. Then he did something even more unexpected. "That all, kid? That all you need?" And with that, he reached behind and slid out of his ratty sweats.

I'd never seen his ass before. Never even saw him naked. Now there it was, white as a sheet, thick with muscle, hairy down the crack, asshole winking out, swirled in curly brown fuzz. His balls hung low, also hairy. And then jutting out in front of him was his massive cock, thick as my arm. "I ... I gotta go," I managed, though was unable to move.

"Chickenshit," he grumbled. "Now's your chance to get even, kid. Can't even do that right."

I paused and stared at his ass. Oddly, I'd fantasized about seeing it when I was younger. At him catching me jerking off and then lending a hand. True, I hated him, but it was hard to get beyond the fact of his beauty. And his ass was indeed beautiful. More so than I ever imagined. Perfect, in fact.

Alabaster and perfect. Until I slapped it again, the red quickly rising, darker as I repeated the motion, both cheeks getting their turn, both crimson in no time flat.

He grunted with each wallop, but otherwise stayed rock-solid in place. Which only angered me more. So I upped the ante on him, grabbing for the base of his balls before tugging on them, yanking them back. Far, farther still. Until, at last, he whimpered. And that sound was like a choir of angels to my ears. Again I pulled back and up, rubbing them on his ass, his cock pointing straight down now, hard as granite as I slapped it and sent it careening.

"Fuck, kid," he groaned. Again I gave it a thwack, his back arching now, until he was panting like the dog he was. The third smack made his knees buckle, the fourth made him try to move away.

"Did I hurt you, Alvin?" I asked, with obvious glee.

Again he grunted, but got back to his position, legs wide, cock and balls and ass now red. "Get real, kid."

I spanked his hole. "Fucker." Only this time his grunt turned to a groan. I spanked it again, his legs going wider, the groan louder. I got my face up to it and spit at the ring, saliva dripping down. Then I crammed two fingers up and in and back. This time he howled and fell forward, sprawled out beneath me, my fingers impaled inside of him. "Take it, Alvin," I barked in his ear. "Don't be such a pussy."

I knew that would do it. His back stiffened at the word. Then he unclenched his asshole and dropped his head down, grunting again as I worked a third finger in, feeling every smooth inch of his insides, cramming and jamming my way to his farthest recesses. And now the sweat was pouring down his broad back, his body heaving with each thrust of my fist. "Fuck," he coughed out, rocking into me now.

And at long last I knew I had the upper hand. Literally. And it was buried deep inside his ass. "Such a pussy, Alvin," I whispered in his ear. "With the little hippy kid's hand up your ass." He tried to squirm away, but I wrapped my free hand around him and held him in place. "What is it, Alvin? I thought you could take it? Poor, little hippy kid hurting you?"

He stopped squirming. "Get a grip, Ted," he replied, the chuckle returning, my anger right along with it.

"Will do, old man," I said. "Get back on your knees."

Huffing and puffing, he did as I said. And then I got a grip, like he asked. Held on to his pole and gave it a slow stroke as I retracted my fingers from his ass and then slid them back in. Stroked and withdrew and then slid. Stroked and withdrew and then slid. Until he was really moaning now, the come obviously working their way up from those mammoth balls of his. And then I suddenly stopped. "Don't," he yelped.

"Don't what, old man?" I asked, all innocent-like.

He flicked his head, the sweat pouring off. He knew what I was asking. Knew what he had to say. "Don't ... don't stop."

And now it was my turn to chuckle as I again stroked that Billy club of a prick of his, all that meat swelling in my hand, his asshole again wrapped around my fingers. His stellar body, slick with a thick layer of sweat now, rocked and swayed, as did those nuts of his while I picked up the pace, jacking him and fingering him, lightening fast.

Until I stopped again.

His sigh ran down the length of him and rumbled through me. "Fuck, kid. Don't."

"Don't what, old man?" I teased, again retracting my fingers from his hole in an audible pop. "I gotta go. House call is over."

He craned his neck around, eyes wide. "Not ... not yet."

I shook my head. "Not yet what?"

His eyes squinted shut, sweat dripping off his forehead. "Not yet ... please," he said, which finally yielded a smile on my face.

I crawled around him and sat in front, face to face now. "You want to come, Alvin?" I swatted his cheek with my upturned palm. "That it, Alvin? You want to come now?" He didn't reply; he just eyed me, not blinking for a second. "Say it, Alvin. Tell me you want me to get you off?" Again I slapped him, not too hard, but hard enough. Then I leaned in even closer. "Say it, Alvin."

His eyes squinted tight now. "Make me come, Ted. Please, make me come." And, oh, how it sounded. That plea from him. Finally.

I nodded. "Sure, Alvin. I'll make you come. No problem." He smirked, thinking he'd won. But he wasn't even close. "But me first."

"You first what?" he asked, head in a tilt, mouth in a sneer.

I stood up and unbuckled my pants. "I come first, Alvin. Then you."

He shrugged. "So go ahead and come."

I kicked off my sneakers and dropped my pants and my boxers, my cock springing to life, hard as a fucking tree limb. Then I got on my knees and grabbed his face in my hand, squeezing his jaw. "Oh, I will, Alvin. And you're gonna help." Again his eyes went wide. "I mean, if you want to come, too. Otherwise, I'll just go ..."

"No," he quickly said. "Don't, uh ... don't go yet." Now he really was pleading, which made my cock throb and bounce.

I let go of his face, my hand on the back of his head as I stuck my dick up to his lips. "Open wide then, old man."

He stared up at me. "Fuck you, kid," he said.

"What, like I just did to you with my fist? Nah, you just gotta suck me off, is all. Seems fair," I said. "I come and then so do you. I mean, you always tried to teach me about being fair, right? See how I learned my lesson?" I slapped the wide, helmeted head against his lips. "Open up, Alvin. Trains coming in the station. Choo choo."

His mouth opened, his face in a snarl as I slid my cock in his mouth and down his throat, every nerve ending in my body suddenly on fire. This was the humiliation I wanted for him. Not the spanking, not the fingers up his ass. This. Or what was soon to come.

A gagging tear streamed down his face as I rammed my cock down his tight throat. I retracted, and he coughed, face now wet with sweat, then shoved it back home, grabbing his head and forcing him down to the hilt. Again he gagged, spit dripping down his chin as I pummeled his face with my rod.

And then my knees started to buckle, balls rising, and I knew I was close. I pulled out and gave my prick a series of quick jacks, aiming the head for his mouth as I stared down. Then I grunted and shot, my entire body on fire as I watched those thick bands of come splatter all over his face, my hand still on the back of his head, keeping him where I wanted him as all that pungent come dripped and slid down his cheeks and chin and lips.

"You suck dick like a pro, Alvin," I rasped as I bent down, eye to eye with him. "You letter in that, too?"

He wiped the spunk from his face. "Fuck you, Ted." Slowly, he stood up, magnificent body creaking, cock still jutting out. "Now get me off and go."

I nodded. "A promise is a promise, Alvin," I said, standing up as I made my way to his couch. I sat down and patted my lap. "You know the drill, old man."

138

He walked over, still sneering at me, but did as I told him, lying down across my lap, ass up, his cock between my thighs. Then I let him have it again, one spank after the next, while he reached around and started jacking at his cock. The harder my palm came down, the faster he jacked, grunting again, groaning each time flesh met flesh. And when his ass was finally cherry red, his body quaked and he howled as he shot, the jizz hitting the carpet in a steady stream. With him still panting, I tossed him off of me and got up.

I stared at him as I got dressed, using his sweats to clean myself off. He sat there staring back, covered in sweat and come, cock amazingly still rigid. Then I headed for the door. "Enjoy your pie, Alvin," I said as I stepped outside.

"Don't be a stranger," he quickly tossed in.

I turned and looked at him, matching him sneer for sneer. "Get a grip, old man," I said and then slammed the door behind me. "Get a fucking grip."

COACH DADDY
By Jay Starre

Residing on English Bay in Vancouver, Canada, Jay Starre has pumped out steamy gay fiction for dozens of anthologies and has written two gay erotic novels. Contact Jay Starre on Facebook.

Scott prayed his sneaky plan would work. It might take time, even a few months, but Coach Walter was worth it. What a fucking Daddy hunk! Scott had fallen for the hulking Coach the first day he showed up for football training at his new college and set eyes on him.

He wanted Coach's cock, and his ass, and everything else about him. Truthfully, he wanted not just to get it on with the sexy older stud, but he also wanted to somehow dominate him. He wanted to turn the tables on Coach; he wanted to be the one in control.

He put his plan in motion and hoped for the best. Could he trick the older, wiser Coach? The seasoned football jocks called him "Coach Daddy," and there was no question about it, Scott wanted him for his own personal Daddy.

Would his plot work? Scott would do his devious best to see it did!

# # # # #

Coach Walter stood just inside his office facing the team's change room across the hallway. Massively built, he towered over the college football player standing before him. The young redhead was angry and spiteful.

"I think you should kick Scott off the team. He's arrogant, rough and snotty. He's not a team player."

"He's a great linebacker, and it's his job to be rough. But the arrogant and snotty part aren't necessary. I'll speak with him, Randy. In the mean time, cool down."

"Can you talk to the asshole now? He's still in the locker room."

Walter was an experienced coach. At twice the age of his young college players, he was not only their coach but their mentor. If he was tough, he had an agenda behind the gruff discipline he employed. He wanted the best for the young men, beyond merely winning at the game of football.

He'd spotted Scott Gerry's faults immediately but had also noted Randy's obsession with the handsome freshman. Scott was a real hottie, and at six-two and 240 pounds, a healthy hunk of young jock flesh.

Walter was sure there was more to the story beyond Randy's take on it. "OK. I'll talk to him. Now get the hell out of here."

After dismissing Randy, Walter crossed the hallway and headed into the locker room. It was late, and practice had ended more than an hour earlier. He'd be surprised if Scott was still there. He wandered down the empty aisles of the locker room in search of the blond linebacker. He heard subdued chatter coming from the far corner of the large room.

When he rounded a bank of lockers, the coach wasn't prepared for what he saw. He halted dead in his tracks and held his breath. He'd found Scott Gerry all right and another of his teammates. They were sprawled over a bench.

Naked and fucking.

Facing away from the coach, neither jock seemed to spot him as they writhed over the bench. He quickly slipped back around the corner where he was hidden from view. He could still watch if he leaned forward and peered around the lockers. With a wicked grin, he did just that.

Scott straddled the bench, pounding down into the other college jock with deep, rapid strokes. Walter wasn't sure who that was with his face blocked by Scott's broad back. The coach held back a snigger as it dawned on him why Randy sent him in search of Scott. Obviously he had witnessed the same thing.

Coach Walter was good at football and also good at getting into the minds of his young players. He understood Randy's motives. The redhead was jealous, hoping the coach would catch Scott in the act, as he had. Randy wished it was his ass getting pounded by Scott's dick!

The linebacker's pale butt strained and tensed as he plowed his fellow jock's willing ass. With his legs apart on either side of the bench, Scott's spread butt-crack was directly in Walter's line of sight. The hairless crevice was sleek with sweat and a sheen of dribbling lube as the linebacker fucked exuberantly. In the centre of that crack, a crinkled butt-hole clenched and gaped with amazing responsiveness.

At forty-two, Walter was not only an experienced coach, but also he was experienced in the sexual arena as well. Specifically, hot, raunchy jock-on-jock sex. The way Scott's asshole palpitated, yawning in and out, Walter recognized the little slot was ripe for a work-out of its own.

He watched for the next five minutes as the blond drilled his teammate to a frenzied climax. Walter gazed speculatively at the alabaster cheeks of Scott's butt as it pumped up and down. The chunky ass was stupendous, and equally so were the linebacker's massive thighs and broad back. Scott's lengthy cock slid in and out of well-lubed butt-hole with wet slurps, the jock under him grunting as he squirmed. Along with those nasty sounds of hot sex, the stench of raw jock wafted over to assail the coach's nostrils as he watched from the sidelines.

What a sweet stink!

The poor football player under Scott's muscular body flopped wildly, getting cock slammed up his butt harder and faster with every passing moment. Both jocks' balls were visible between their spread butt-cheeks, bobbing and banging. Scott's thick, juicy bone appeared and disappeared from behind, moving faster and faster. Lube now spurted from the violated hole as that cock drove home and then yanked back out.

When the linebacker abruptly tossed back his head and groaned with orgasm, Walter smiled and slipped away.

He'd learned patience in his years as Coach, unlike the redheaded Randy who'd rushed to betray his teammate with immature spite. He waited comfortably in his office with the door wide open where he could observe the locker room's exit. The first football player to come out was Danny Thompson. Walter grinned at him and nodded, while the flustered tackle nodded in return and hastened away. Guilty as sin! The jock had just been fucked up the ass.

He sat back and continued to wait.

Scott emerged and noticed the coach in his office staring at him. He waved and would have slipped by if Walter hadn't called him in.

"What's up, Coach?"

He stood in front of the coach just as he stood on the football field, feet wide apart in a bold and aggressive stance. He smiled winningly, although Walter could tell it was fake. The linebacker was not as sweet as that smile promised.

"How are you getting along with your teammates?"

Scott laughed. "Who cares? I'm here to play football. I gotta kick ass or I won't hold my spot on the team."

Walter looked over the freshman jock. At nineteen, he was a powerhouse and very confident. Some of that was bluster, and some of that confidence was due to the fact the kid was self-centered. Walter had his legs up on his desk, and wearing shorts, his big thighs and calves were bare. Scott's eyes were bold, wandering up and down the coach's body, checking out his legs and even checking out his crotch.

"On the field that's fine. But I want you to make an effort in the locker room. Try to get a little closer to your teammates."

He smiled as he spoke, his dark eyes hooded, and his white teeth flashing. Although he was more than twenty years older than the blond jock and could have been his father, Scott merely grinned back and nodded. He wasn't going to be intimidated.

The linebacker turned and strode out of the office. Walter watched the pump and roll of his beefy butt-cheeks with a keen eye. He laughed to himself as he contemplated his next move. The coach decided Scott Gerry was going to receive some private, and very special, coaching. Soon.

After a week, it was apparent Scott was making little or no effort to win friends among his teammates. Both Randy and Danny were in foul moods around the blond linebacker. Scott was bruising more than bodies on the field; he was bruising egos.

He made his move on a Friday night when he knew the young jocks would be in a headlong rush to shower and dress for a night on the town. He made his way through the naked football team in the locker room until he found the linebacker.

The blond had a teammate cornered. He was waving his substantial cock at him as he dried off, chatting up the flattered and horny football player.

The coach imagined he knew exactly what was going on. The big jock intended on scoring another conquest.

"Hit the steam room, Scott. I'll join you in a minute for a chat."

The blond was cut-off in mid-sentence as he hovered over his seated teammate, but he turned to the coach and nodded without any protest. He never argued, always following orders, even though he was an arrogant young jock to his teammates. Walter saw right through that façade. The football player thought he was playing his coach. Little did he know what he was up against!

Coach watched the hefty jock pad away barefoot and naked to the steam room beyond the showers. What an ass the punk had!

He strolled around the locker room, chatting with the players as they rushed to change and get out of there. He'd let Scott stew in the steam for a few minutes.

Finally, he made his way through the empty showers and to the steam room. By this time it should be cleared out, all except for his troublesome young linebacker. First he turned down the heat, not wanting to roast while they were occupied in there for more than the usual few minutes!

He slipped off his shorts, shoes and T-shirt to leave them on a bench beside the door but brought a towel with something extra hidden in the folds with him as he entered. With his back hiding his actions, he locked the door.

He turned and surveyed the room. Billowing steam dissipated slightly. Against the far wall, the blond was sitting on the tiled bench, his towel under his big butt, his muscular arms folded behind his neck. He looked at ease, and probably was. The punk jock was all too confident and full of himself.

Walter approached, his fat cock swinging above his hefty nut-sack. Scott's eyes betrayed him, zeroing in on that substantial package. The coach allowed his dick to swell, still in control of his own lust but wanting the football player to glimpse what was coming.

"I think you need an attitude adjustment, Scott."

He stood beside the jock at the end of the tiled bench he was sprawled out on. He looked down at him with his dark eyes, scanning the relaxed football player's sultry body. The thatch of yellow-blond hair on his head was mirrored by a pair of tufts at his armpits and one around his cock and balls. He was coated in steamy sweat, his big pecs hairless and dripping. His thighs were huge, spread wide on the bench below him so that his crack was open, his dangling ball-sack just covering the hole Walter knew waited there.

"Sure, Coach. Whatever you say," the blond murmured. His grin was crooked, more of a smirk than a real smile. His cock swelled slightly, and he grinned more broadly. He wasn't going to let his coach fluster him.

Walter stared down at the blond, a smile of his own matching the young jock's. A huge man who worked out in the gym daily, he outweighed even the bulky linebacker. He was the product of a black grandparent and white everything else. His skin was a pale sepia, but his features were broad and bold. A trimmed beard and goatee outlined his square jaw and dimpled chin. Dark brows and eyes, lush lips and straight white teeth created a devilish allure. Handsome as hell, he was mature, confident, and in charge.

He believed the college freshman had no chance against his own mature certainty.

"This is what I have to say, and you'd better think twice about how you respond." His deep bass whipped out, and the young football player actually blinked and looked a little surprised at the forceful directive.

With quiet deliberation, the hovering Coach pulled out the hidden bottle of lube from within the towel he'd carried into the steam room. As Scott stared at him quizzically, he upended it over one hand. A stream of slippery liquid coated his big fingers.

His hand snaked out, sliding up under the blond's nut-sack with bold purpose. Scott gasped out loud as he felt slippery fingers searching up into his parted crack, and gasped again when a pair of them found his asshole and poked into the steam-soaked slot.

Coach smiled, his dark eyes locked with the blond's blue ones as he forced his fingers deep into his palpitating butthole.

Scott's dick rose up like a rocket blasting off its launchpad. Stiff and drooling, it slammed against his rippled belly. Although his hands were still clasped behind his neck and he didn't move on the bench, his ass rose slightly as he inhaled a deep breath and relaxed his butthole around the pair of fingers shoving deep inside it. Even though a deep ache had to be throbbing in his fingered asshole, the jock's soft blue eyes stared back up into his coach's, and he actually smiled. The bold jock made a last ditch effort to win the brewing battle.

"Behind your back, the guys on the team call you Coach Daddy."

Walter laughed out loud, his fingers beginning a slow slide in and out of the blond's squishy, lubed and steam-dripping asshole. They did call him that, with good reason. Every year Walter picked out a likely and willing young jock from his college team and made him his special bum boy. He didn't fuck around with the players other than that. And he was discreet, never having been caught in the act. The title didn't bother him at all.

Their eyes were locked. Those fingers made squishy slurps as Walter twisted and probed Scott's asshole. The silence lasted for a few moments as their wills clashed. But there was the unspoken connection, the daddy-boy radar sense they both had. Walter wouldn't have made his move if he hadn't already known he had a damn good chance of succeeding.

Scott was ripe for the plucking, Walter felt.

"You like that, don't you, Boy?"

The young football player grunted as his coach's fingers slithered even deeper. Walter imagined he could read his mind. The jock felt as if he was drowning in the deep pools of Coach's dark eyes, and those fingers were feeling so painfully good. His body began to writhe, just slightly, as his cock jerked on his belly, oozing sticky pre-cum. He kept his hands clasped tightly behind his neck, now unable to move them as he succumbed to the power of the older man's seduction.

"Yes," Scott suddenly blurted out, the heat of passion rising up in his blue eyes. "Yes! Yes I like it! Finger my asshole, Coach Daddy!"

He grinned as he leaned over the jock, running his free hand over the slippery flesh of his massive torso. Young flesh, tender and sweet and willing. He loved it. It was his passion. Being the coach, the older man teaching the young and impressionable men of a football team was his life. He loved that.

But this was more, on a higher plane, and satisfied his own deep urges. From the look on the jock's face, half-defiant and half-yielding, he was flying high himself. If Scott was falling for his manly allures, there was no question he was also falling for the youth's equally intoxicating charms.

He stroked the smooth chest, tugging on the slippery nipples and eliciting a long moan. He dug around deeper in Scott's asshole, probing for the prostate and finding it. The jock grunted, and lifted his hips, squirming his big ass on the bench.

He ran his hand into an open armpit, stroking it gently and feeling the young, huge body quiver like a strung bow. His cock stiffened to full mast, thrusting against Scott's side, causing the sweating jock to moan even louder.

Walter bent farther down over the blond's face, planting fleshy lips over smaller ones. He thrust his tongue into the jock's mouth, forcing it open as he simultaneously forced his fingers all

149

the way up his quivering asshole. The blond squirmed, humping up into the heavy body of his coach, his mouth and asshole gaping as he yielded up his orifices to the dominating power of the older man.

They kissed passionately as the coach's big fingers fucked Scott's asshole. He twisted those fingers in circles, stretching out the tight slot, pressing against the tender rim and then pushing as deep as possible to stab at the aching prostate. He kissed just as deeply while he ran his free hand all over the jock's quaking torso. He pinched the taut nipples, tickled armpits and then dropped down to tease the throbbing boner. His hand slipped lower and massaged the blond's fat balls, tugging harshly on them as he drilled his asshole with fingers and his mouth with tongue.

Steam dripped from both their bodies, creating a slippery lubricant as they squirmed on the bench. The kiss lasted and lasted, Scott growing more agitated under the bulk of his coach as the fingers up his ass heated his guts to the blowing point. It was the young football player who broke the kiss with a loud gasp.

"Fuck me with your big cock, Coach Daddy! Give me some daddy-dick!"

Walter rose, sliding around to stand in front of Scott. His fingers maintained their deep penetration and possession of that steamy gut-hole. The coach's cock was a tower of purple passion, bobbing in front of him as he positioned himself between the blond's sprawled thighs. The linebacker trembled from head to toe, his biceps bulging as he continued to clasp the back of his neck as if his hands were bound there with leather or ropes.

"I'll give you cock, if that's what you want, Boy. I'm expecting some attitude adjustment along with the fuck, though. Understand?"

As he delivered that ultimatum, he reached over to the bench where he'd discarded his towel and the lube and snatched up the bottle again. While awaiting the gasping jock's answer, he squirted lube all over his massive prick.

He aimed it at the linebacker's asshole, where his fingers twisted and probed for emphasis. Scott groaned and wiggled his big butt on the bench. His eyes were glued to that giant column of fuck-meat. There was no question about where he wanted that cock to go.

"OK. Yes! I'll stop being such a fuckhead. I'll stop being a jerk to the rest of the team. I'll do whatever you want! Please, fuck my ass with that big daddy dick! Shove it up my ass!"

His voice was a quaking hiss. With his hands locked behind his neck, he looked helpless. He was helpless. He was entirely in his coach's capable hands. He was entirely under the spell of his coach's mind, body, and cock.

At least Walter believed that.

He grinned, his dick aching to test out the warm slot his fingers already explored. The hole was tight, but accommodating. The young linebacker would make one hell of a sweet fuck.

He slid his fingers out of the jock's trembling asshole. He stared down at in the dim light. He could see the pink orifice dripping steam and sweat and lube. It was flushed and swollen, gaping outwards with heated desire. He leaned forward and pressed the flared cap of his prick against the swollen center.

Scott moaned and raised his thighs high in the air. He was wide open for the cock that began to press into him.

"Ohhh- yesss- give me your cock- all of that big daddy dick- please- ohhhh- so nice!"

The linebacker blubbered as cock-head pushed past his convulsing ass-lips. They parted and then clamped, then yielded again as Walter kept on pushing. Relentlessly, the coach forced his way into that churning butt pit. The jock squirmed and moaned, his hefty thighs shaking, his butt jiggling and steam dripping from his every orifice.

He looked as if he was in heaven.

The coach was in a paradise of his own. The conquest, the sweet young man at his command, and the feel of a squishy asshole surrendering to his stiff cock coalesced into an emotional pleasure that transfused every fiber of his being. He slid his cock home, his fat balls pressing up against slippery, hairless ass crack.

"Now I'm going to fuck your hot jock-hole. I'm going to fuck it until you blow a load all over your own belly. Open up and take Coach Daddy's dick."

Scott merely grunted, definitely feeling all that cock up his ass. The column of stiff flesh was deep in his guts, pulsing with molten heat. He squirmed, clasping his neck and shaking all over. His own tool ached and twitched on his belly. It seemed to Walter the young linebacker knew he was going to shoot without even having to touch his dick. His surrender appeared total.

Walter believed he had completely overpowered the young jock, the will of a big, dark coach impossible to gainsay. Walter thought he could see the flickering glow of irresistible desire and something more in those blue eyes, perhaps the realization that he'd always wanted Coach's attention and now he was getting it. Perhaps the arrogant jock had been acting the punk just to get this special treatment, this cock up the ass and this sweet discipline, hole stretching as huge meat rode inside it. Scott probably didn't know what he'd wanted, until now, Walter imagined.

The big coach began pumping. Withdrawing slowly, feeling the ass-lips cling and stretch as his purple pole slid out, he grinned down at the young jock. When the flared head of his dick was poised at the blond's aching butt-rim and about to slip out, he slowly began to feed it back to that warm butt-hole.

Scott hissed and squirmed as cock filled him. His dick oozed pre-cum all over his sweat-soaked belly.

The coach smiled as he stared down into wide blue eyes. "This is what those other jocks felt when you fucked them up the ass. They loved your hard shank thrusting up their tender quims. Didn't they? Now you're getting the same. Cock up your ass, Boy! You won't be such a big shot from now on, just a pussy-boy who loves cock any way he can get it."

He moaned an incoherent reply. Walter continued grinning down at him, pumping steadily in and out, feeling his body respond with deeper submission as each stroke reamed him out. The jock's dick grew stiffer and drooled steadily. His mouth remained open, his tongue out licking at his lips, his eyes on the coach's big chest and powerful shoulders.

The punk-jock looked as if he was drowning in the deep, steady fuck.

Walter's cock was bathed in steamy ass-gut and lube. The hole rippled and pulsed, stretched and clamped with the jock's churning emotions. He was feeling the young football player from the inside out. He took command and began to drill him. Harder, faster and deeper, slamming his nuts against the slippery ass.

Scott grunted and panted, jiggling and jerking on the bench. His asshole was obviously on fire. His prostate must have been aching unbearably. His cock was so stiff it looked about to explode. As the coach's big dick reamed him faster and faster, it was apparent the pleasure in his asshole was flooding in a torrent of unbearable heat up to his dick.

It was odd, but Walter almost felt as if that asshole was fucking him, rather than the other way around. It seethed wildly, clamping, yielding, wrapping his pounding prick in a heated embrace that had the big Coach fucking harder and harder. To his own surprise, it was as if he was running downhill and couldn't stop himself if he tried. That only made him fuck deeper and harder.

That's when Scott gripped the back of his neck, arched his back and yelped like a kicked dog.

"I'm cumming! I'm shooting with Coach Daddy's big cock up my Boy-ass!"

The linebacker's cock leaped on his belly, purple and strained. The sudden spray of jizz went everywhere, all over his belly and chest, and even up to his chin and cheeks. He snorted out wild laughter. The release was so powerful he flopped around like he was flying and about to take off. The look in his eyes was of pure, unadorned and honest satisfaction.

Walter witnessed the young linebacker's orgasm with righteous pleasure. He had Scott now. A cum like that would not be soon forgotten. His own dick was on fire. The linebacker's asshole clamped over it like a vice. Walter shoved deep a few times, then pulled out just in time to let loose.

"I'm coating you with Daddy-cum. All- over- your- sweet- jock- ass!"

Walter spewed all over the blond's hefty white butt-cheeks and exposed crack. Scott squirmed as that goo painted him, his own nut-blow coming in rapid spurts to coat his stomach in sticky white stuff. He shook and moaned as Coach Walter enveloped him in a sticky embrace.

He cradled the linebacker in his burly arms until both men had calmed down, their hearts and lungs returning to normal. It was the young jock who ventured to speak first.

"Is this gonna happen just once? Or will there be more?"

The plaintiveness in Scott's voice seemed honest. Walter smiled as he ran his tongue over the blond's cheek line before stabbing it deep into his hot mouth. They kissed for a few minutes until the randy young linebacker's cock began to stiffen again between their bellies.

Coach broke the kiss and rose. "Do as your told, and you'll get plenty of dick up the ass. Maybe even more than that."

Walter abandoned Scott on the bench in the steam room. He was satisfied with his reaction, but only time would tell if the arrogant jock had really changed.

After that steamy fuck, Coach noted how Scott's eyes followed him like a hungry puppy whenever he saw him. The linebacker played well on the field and followed instructions to the letter as he always had. Walter was pleased to notice the blond was no longer preying on his teammates. He was even friendly to them.

He was in his office with his feet up on the desk when he spotted the linebacker leaving the locker room across the hall. "Get your butt in here!"

Scott actually scurried inside, shutting the door behind him and facing him with a hungry look that told him all he needed to know. "Am I doing OK, Coach? Am I doing what you wanted?"

He grinned and nodded. "You're doing just fine. I'm pleased. I guess you'd like a little reward, now wouldn't you?"

He spread his feet apart on the desk and reached down to stroke the bulge in his shorts. Scott's eyes brightened, and he smiled from ear to ear. The linebacker kicked off his shoes and tore off his pants and underwear in a lightning move that displayed his athletic prowess. He was naked from the waist down when he leaped over the desk and dove for Walter's crotch.

"Can I have your dick, Coach Daddy?"

He was laughing at the linebacker's unbridled enthusiasm, but stopped laughing as Scott fished out his cock and gulped it down with a hungry mouth. Moist lips, a slathering tongue and vacuuming cheeks had him writhing in his seat.

"You can have my dick. And I'll take your ass after that."

Coach Walter sighed as Scott slurped noisily over his cock. The jock's beefy white butt humped on the desk in front of him, thighs parted and deep crack open. There was no question about it, he would fuck the freshman ass, all season long.

But as the blond linebacker's mouth bobbed and his big butt humped, Walter wondered if maybe there was more.

Maybe this year he would keep his Boy a little longer. Yes, a little longer. Well, maybe a lot longer.

That's when a pair of freshman fingers slid under his nut sack and toward his asshole. Hmmmm. That felt good.

# # # # #

Scott chowed down on Coach Daddy's big brown cock with unbridled enthusiasm. He was in heaven as he perched on Walter's desk and buried his cute face in the coach's lap.

His plan had worked! He'd paid Randy to report him to the coach that very first evening, while he also paid off Danny Thompson to let him fuck his ass good, while the coach himself had fallen into his trap and watched silently from behind the lockers. Under him, getting his butt pounded, Danny had spotted the big coach although he pretended not to see him. He'd told Scott as soon as Coach left. He'd continued to bribe the pair to act hurt and jealous for a few weeks afterward. They'd done it willingly, especially since he'd pounded their butts good with his stiff cock as a reward for their acting. All according to plan.

He'd pretended to be an asshole, which wasn't too hard, then pretended to be a nice guy. And Coach had swallowed his act!

It hadn't been an act in the steam room, though. He had played all his cards then. He sucked in Coach's fingers with his talented asshole, and offered up everything, with suitable humility. Coach Daddy had succumbed to his charms without a hitch.

Now Coach Daddy was his! Hopefully, he'd never guess how he'd been manipulated by the young freshman. Hopefully, he'd enjoy Coach Daddy dick for a long time to come. And he would, if he continued to play his cards right.

He wriggled his big football butt around in the air as he sucked noisily. Coach Daddy would love that, a total sucker for hefty, white young ass like his. He also slid his fingers between Coach's big dark thighs and under his balls. The Coach grinned and spread his legs.

Scott's fingers found hole. Coach hole.

What would happen next was anyone's guess. Could he sucker the big Coach into giving up his ass? A fingertip tickled that warm slot. Coach's eyes grew soft and almost dreamy.

Yes. If he played his cards right, he'd have Coach ass before the season was over!

BIKER BOSS TURNS BITCH
By Jay Starre

Bronco had won the pool game and arrived to claim his prize.

The garage door was open on the warm summer night, and there was one man waiting inside for him. At least six foot and six inches tall already, his black biker boots added more than an inch to that towering height. He was busy polishing the gleaming cherry-red paint on his motorcycle.

"Hey dude, I'm here to claim my winnings."

He didn't bother stopping what he was doing or turn around right away, but there was a tensing in his broad shoulders that the shrewd young biker noted. Members of opposing gangs, they knew each other only by reputation and the odd time they'd both been at the same bar.

They had been at the same bar only two days earlier. Bronco had beat one of the rival gang members at pool, and the poor fucker couldn't pay up. They were both drunk, but that didn't make it any less serious. It was a substantial wager. Before the night degenerated into a deadly brawl, the gang leaders stepped in and offered a compromise. In two days, he could claim his winnings from the boss of the gang himself. Even when a drunken Bronco dared to demand more than money for his compensation, the other gang chose not to argue.

RJ hadn't turned around to face the young biker yet, and Bronco had time to look him over. His black tank top revealed broad, bulging shoulders and long arms roped with muscle. He was surprisingly symmetrical for such a tall and muscular dude. His back narrowed at the waist before his hips widened to a full butt beneath snug jeans. He was a little bow-legged, from years of riding a bike most likely, but his legs looked powerful.

Bronco contemplated that solid butt. He had come here for one thing, and one thing only. That ass.

The tall gang boss finally turned around and faced him. By the easy smile on his face, you would never know he was about to turn bitch for the young rival gang member. Bronco, so sure of himself most of the time, felt a little disconcerted. Was RJ going to welch on the deal?

The big biker had a number of vivid tattoos splashed across his bare arms, a shaved head, big nose, and a grizzled short beard around a mouth as big as his nose. He stared quietly out of ice-blue eyes at Bronco as the interloper stood just outside the garage door and waited to be invited in. There were rules to these things.

At forty, he was twice Bronco's age. Tough as hell and the instigator of some harsh shit, he probably deserved whatever Bronco had in mind for him.

"So? Are we cool? Are you going to give it up for me like you promised?"

It came out a little on the strident side, as if he had something to prove. But then the truth hit him — seeing as how this gang boss had a rep to uphold, Bronco held all the cards. RJ didn't welch on his agreements. Ever.

Bronco was young, foolish and impulsive. He knew it, and he was proud of it. His confidence came back in a rush, along with a stiffening of his cock under his jeans. He grinned back, flashing his white teeth and winking.

RJ's cold eyes grew a little narrower and his smile a little more brittle. He finally spoke.

"Don't fuck with me, punk. Come on in and do what you gotta. I can take whatever you can dish out. Trust me."

So that was how it was going to be. He would play the tough guy. Bronco hardly cared. He had plenty of nasty shit in mind, and the older, self-assured biker boss would take it. Like it or not, or pretend not to, who the hell cared?

He strode into the Boss's den, the garage full of tools and motorcycle parts and shit like that, and immediately felt the passionate intimacy of the place. He was on RJ's turf. But now, he was going to play the alpha dog, not the other way around.

"Should you close the garage door?"

"Why? The closest neighbor is more than a mile down the road. Nothing out there but raccoons and owls to watch us tonight."

Bronco didn't mind that at all. If someone was lurking in the bushes, let them watch. He'd put on a show to curl their hair. "All right, dude. Let's not waste any more time then. Get naked, but leave your boots on. "

The cold grin didn't change even though the pale brows rose slightly. He was obviously assessing the kinky motives Bronco might be entertaining, but the young interloper didn't worry about that. Let him think whatever he wanted. Tonight was all about his own pleasure.

He dropped the leather bag he'd brought with him on the floor and removed his leather jacket as he watched RJ strip. The long arms rose as he pulled off his tank top, revealing a smooth, lean torso. It was splashed with colorful tattoos like his arms. He had pierced nipples, too. Bronco smiled as he thought of what he might do to those plump pierced nubs. A moment later, his grin grew even bigger when RJ unbuckled his big leather belt and opened his fly to reveal the lengthy snake beneath.

"Nice. Very nice," he murmured appreciatively.

RJ's expressive brows rose again. "Why don't you come on over here and suck on it? It gets a lot longer when a pair of pretty plump lips like yours wrap around it."

Stifling laughter, he chose not to answer. The dude just couldn't help trying to be the boss. Let him try. That wasn't the deal, and Bronco was fully intending on getting his money's worth.

His comment about Bronco's pretty lips were right on the money though. He had a bow-shaped mouth with bright pink lips. And they stood out prominently on his clean-shaven face, especially since his nose and eyes were on the petite side, and his complexion was like ivory porcelain.

As Bronco finished removing his own clothing, it was apparent that not only was his face clean-shaven, but so was the rest of his body. All of it. From smooth scalp to ankles, he had no hair at all, except his blond eyebrows. He took pain-staking care to shave from head to toe every few days. He liked the sensual experience of the razor running over his body, and he liked the result.

He and RJ had some obvious similarities, and dissimilarities. RJ was also smooth, although he had a patch of fair hair at his crotch and under his pits, and that clipped grizzled beard. The biker boss boasted a number of bright tattoos and pierced nipples while Bronco's pale skin was without any blemish or markings.

Bronco was tall, too, but still several inches shy of the towering RJ. He was muscular as well, like the biker boss, but he was not nearly as lean. A smooth layer of fat gave him bulk and padded both his big chest and round bubble-butt. They both had blue eyes, but Bronco's were very pale and a little dreamy while RJ's were bright and hard.

Placed side-by-side, you would have to bet on RJ as the sure winner in any type of contest. But not this evening.

Right now, their cocks were showing their differences. RJ's lengthy snake hung down between his naked thighs quietly, although the flared head curved outward just enough to show it was growing aroused. Bronco's fat meat was at full mast, bobbing up toward his navel and drooling pre-cum. His nasty imagination was already at work as he looked over the booted but otherwise naked biker in front of him.

Leaving his leather bag with its nasty contents behind but within reach, he strode forward. He was dressed in nothing but his own black biker boots just like RJ. A big man himself, he experienced a rush of exhilaration when he stood next to the towering biker boss. Rarely did someone make him feel small. The thought of dominating this gigantic older man was such a turn-on, he felt his cock spurt out a juicy dribble of pre-cum and smear the mushroom cap with its sticky goo.

"First things first," he said as he gazed up into those piercing blue eyes and grinned. One hand whipped out and seized that snake-dick while the other reached up to seize the gleaming silver ring embedded in RJ's dark brown nipple.

He tugged on that ring just hard enough to cause the big biker to jerk slightly and emit a startled gasp. He squeezed the long shank just hard enough to cause it to swell under his grip. Those actions weren't really a surprise for the hulking biker boss, but what Bronco did next was.

He dropped to his knees on the cement floor and crammed the snaking cock into his mouth, gulping half of it up with a smack of his bowed lips. The feel of that soft tube suddenly growing thick and beginning to pulse in his mouth was exactly what he was looking for. The thing got longer, as earlier promised, and longer. He gurgled over it, letting spit drool out over the shank as he aimed the head at his throat and opened up for it.

The hand on RJ's nipple continued to tug while the other hand moved lower to seize and pull on the biker's hefty set of nuts. The balls dangled low between his lean thighs as he spread his booted feet and let out a big grunt, testament to the rough treatment both nipple and nuts were suffering, off-set by the equally intense pleasure of Bronco's slippery suck.

Obviously in an effort to counter the kneeling rival's control of his tender parts, RJ reached down to grab Bronco's smooth scalp and press it forward into his crotch. The pressure forced his cock-head to slide past tonsils and into the throat beyond.

That suited Bronco's purposes. He sucked harder, which only made the snake-dick grow. The head slithered into his throat while the shank throbbed between his smacking lips. Even though it steadily lengthened, Bronco managed to suck it in right down to the base.

And he was barely getting started. On his knees between the biker boss's boots, he arched his back and spread his knees, opening up his deep ass-crack. He released his squeezing grip on the tall biker's nuts to reach back with that hand and pull his crack further apart. He wriggled his plump can and looked up at RJ, whose sparkling orbs couldn't help focusing on that open divide and the puckered hole in the center.

There was a method to his madness. Let the big boss see his ass and the tight hole, let him look and let him long for it, but deny it to him. He wasn't going to fuck it, no matter how much he might want to. Unless, of course, for his own pleasure Bronco himself chose to get fucked. But that was enough of that. He pulled off the foot of cock with a drooling smack of his lips. "Turn around and bend over your bike."

RJ's rippled abs fluttered wildly, revealing how affected he was by the deep-throating, and he momentarily hesitated as his massive cock bobbed in Bronco's face. The kneeling biker stared up at the standing one and smiled. He could read the turmoil in his expression. With his hands still on the back of Bronco's smooth scalp, it was clear he wanted nothing more than to force those pretty lips back over his aching, spit-gobbed cock.

But a deal was a deal, and the older biker yielded. He released Bronco's head and slowly turned around. His cherry-red motorcycle was right behind him, and it was easy enough to lean over it and plant his hands on the bright red leather seat.

Of course, he didn't know what to expect next, although he was certain the young alpha dog behind him planned on fucking him up the ass, sooner or later. When tongue snaked up along his ass-crack, he shuddered involuntarily and allowed his shiny black boots to slide farther apart.

"Yeah. Spread your legs and open that big butt for my tongue. I am going to eat you out, and you are going to love it. Come on, bitch, spread 'em and give up that hole."

He didn't shout or demand, in fact he spoke calmly and deliberately. He was in control, and anything he wanted he would get. RJ was in no position to argue. His honor and the honor of his gang was at stake.

And he was quite happy to be humiliating the tall biker. Although he was the one on his knees, and he was the one licking ass, it was RJ whose hole was getting violated. It was all about his own pleasure, but he knew RJ was going to get plenty of pleasure from his talented tongue. His hole would be wet and juicy and hungry for more. He would get more.

That ass was solid as marble and utterly smooth. Bronco ran his hands over the large mounds as he licked up and down the hairless crack. When his tongue ran over the snug hole, RJ shuddered and pushed back slightly, which had the young biker grinning even as he licked.

He took his time running his fat tongue up and down in long strokes while he kneaded the full butt-cheeks and pulled them open for his mouth. He even rubbed his smooth scalp in the crack briefly before returning to the slow licking.

Finally, he settled on the hole itself and began stroking it. His tongue lapped back and forth over the snug entrance as RJ struggled to maintain a grip on his tight sphincter. It was a losing battle and shortly the big biker let out a groan and shoved backwards, his ass-lips pushing outward to flutter against that stroking tongue.

The moment he surrendered, Bronco clamped his lips over the pouting hole and began sucking like mad. The velvety butt-lips quivered wildly as they pushed outward toward the violent suction. Once he had the hole turned inside out, he stuck his tongue in it.

He literally forced his tongue past the gooey rim and into the seething interior. RJ's loud gasps were music to his ears. It was time for the next step in the biker boss's degradation.

He pulled off the fluttering hole with a slurp and sat back on his boots to gaze at his handiwork. The hole was bright pink now, a flaming rose blossom between the solid white ass-cheeks. He grinned as he rose to his feet and turned away to fetch his leather bag. Over his shoulder he called out to the tall biker in that same calm voice.

"Stay where you are. Now that I have your hole warmed up, time to stretch it out some."

Let him stew on that. Bronco had some nasty shit in mind and all the biker boss could do was go along with it. He pulled out the items he intended on using first and returned to the bent over biker with them in hand.

RJ hadn't even bothered turning around, which was a blatant display of the strength of his willpower. It would take more than some cock-sucking, nipple and ball yanking and ass eating to break his nerve.

Bronco grinned as he contemplated the toy in his hand and how likely it was to affect those nerves of steel. It should make him squirm at least. He reached out and planted the open spout of the bottle of Rude-Lube against the spit-gobbed asshole and squeezed. A stream of slippery goo squirted deep into the hole, which had RJ's hefty ass jiggling with surprise.

He squirted more and more. He didn't stop squeezing the bottle until the translucent stuff began to ooze back out and slither down the biker's pale crack to coat his dangling balls. It was quite thick stuff, but very slippery and perfectly suited to what Bronco had in mind.

He closed the lid and tossed the bottle back onto his open bag behind them. He began to feed RJ the toy in his hands.

It was shaped in a banana-like curve, with the head in the form of a flared cock-head. The long shaft was covered in round bumps. A dark navy blue, the base had a black button implanted in it. The button's use would be clear later.

The flared head settled between RJ's gooey ass-lips and immediately found the entrance Bronco had opened up with his voracious sucking and tonguing. Still grinning, he stared down at that pink hole and the navy-blue cock-head as he slowly pushed inward.

RJ couldn't help himself. He let out an explosive grunt as the knob slid past his sphincter and popped inside him. The gooey lube spurted outwardly around it. At least there was plenty of it to ease the way.

But Bronco was just getting started. The head had disappeared and the bumpy shaft with that wicked curve in it was about to follow. With slow and steady deliberation, he pushed the blunt knob deeper. As the bumps over the shaft rubbed against RJ's tender ass-lips, his butt jerked, and his thighs shook. He took his time, pulling out a little, then pushing back in, allowing the bent-over biker to feel that large head massaging his gut while the bumps on the curved shaft teased his sphincter.

More and more disappeared. The curve was an ingenious design, allowing the toy to slide upward and inward without obstruction. Finally, the entire thing was up RJ's convulsing asshole. Only the base with its black button remained visible between the oozing pink lips.

"Now I want you to lie down on that bench."

RJ obeyed without uttering a single word. Walking carefully with legs wide apart, he strode over to the nearby work-out bench. Bronco was right behind, his hand up between the biker's solid butt-cheeks holding that dildo in place. He could only smile as he contemplated how that felt for the big biker.

RJ straddled the bench and lay back over it as ordered, his icy-blue gaze as direct as ever as he stared up at Bronco and planted his boots on either side of the bench. Bronco stared back, unaffected by that glare.

"And now you are going to eat my ass. Open wide."

Quick on his feet, he whipped a boot over the sprawled biker and settled down over his face while still maintaining a hold on the dildo planted up his ass.

Bronco had a very fleshy ass. Each cheek was exceedingly plump while still being firm, swelling out from his waist like twin watermelons. He squatted right over RJ's mouth and nose, the big butt cheeks surrounding the biker and holding him in place as Bronco leaned forward enough to stare down into his spread crotch. RJ's lengthy cock was fully stiff and lay on his rippled belly like a snake ready to strike.

Bronco ignored it for the moment as he focused on the area between RJ's thighs where the curved dildo was still implanted. He could see the dark end of it protruding slightly from the swollen lips and imagined how all that bumpy rubber and big knob felt up his ass. It was about to feel even better.

He pressed in the button. The base immediately begin to quiver and hum. It was a vibrator and the button had started it up!

"Get your tongue to work. Eat some ass, bitch," he ordered.

As soon as those vibrations began, RJ's big body jerked and his boots came up off the ground. Bronco pushed in the button again which increased the tempo of the vibrator. RJ's feet thrust into the air and he held them there, his thighs trembling and his boots bobbing as that curved vibrator went to work up his gut.

He began to suck and lick at Bronco's ass-crack, using his hands to pull the hefty mounds apart and probe deep between them. The young biker bit his lip and groaned. The scratchy feel of RJ's grizzled beard rubbing around in his sensitive ass-crack as he sought out the snug hole buried there caused a wave of shivering sensations to pulse up into his crotch and gut. He imagined RJ experienced similarly pulsing sensations as that vibrator hummed inside his asshole.

He rubbed his ass over that big nose and mouth, humping the tongue that lapped away at his smooth butt valley and worked its way toward his hole. He held the vibrator in RJ's oozing asshole and continued to punch in the button to increase the speed of the pulse, watching with glee as the biker's boots jerked in the air and he spread them wider apart.

RJ's smooth ass crack was wide open with his boots in the air and spread apart. He had a perfect view of the buried dildo as the navy blue base vibrated madly against his fingertips. The humming pulse traveled up his wrist and arm to his chest then back down his spine along his back and into his own asshole. RJ had found the hole and was busy as hell digging around in it.

It seemed the more Bronco increased the pace of the vibrator up his ass, the more RJ's boots jerked and his tongue danced up the young biker's tender asshole. His big hands squeezed the plump cheeks of Bronco's ass and the big nose rubbed around in the deep crack while the busy tongue twisted up into his gut.

He found himself groaning and sweating as he humped that tongue, his asshole yielding to the assault and gaping wide to take all that was being offered. He couldn't help himself and pushed in the button on the vibrator to its highest frequency.

RJ's black biker boots danced in the air and his smooth butt-cheeks jiggled crazily. The vibrations from the base of the dildo rocketed up Bronco's arm and throughout his body. The tongue up his ass gored him.

The sprawled biker boss's cock had lengthened to its greatest extent yet. It writhed on his belly like a true snake, pink and swollen. Bronco's own fat cock bobbed between his thighs, equally stiff and about to blow.

It was too soon. He had more planned for the unlucky biker. He let out a big grunt and rose up from his perch over RJ's face. At the same time, he yanked out the curved dildo. Lube squirted out along with the dark tool, then oozed in a viscous stream from the abandoned slot.

RJ's boots dropped back to the ground as he gasped for air. For the moment Bronco ignored him as he returned to his leather bag to fetch his second nasty tool of the night. Pulling it out, he snatched up the discarded bottle of Rude-Lube and carried them both over to the waiting biker still sprawled out on the weight-training bench.

"Time to really stuff that ass of yours. I can't wait to see how much of this baby you can take."

Smirking, he displayed the toy in his hand to an obviously appalled RJ whose mouth fell open and eyes grew wide. The look on his face was quickly masked by one of cold indifference.

"Do your worst, punk. I can take it."

But Bronco wasn't fooled. The way the tall biker had squirmed and jerked with that vibrator up his butt was more honest than that lofty denial. He sat down at the foot of the bench, feeling his spit-wet crack slide over the smooth leather and recalling that big nose and mouth so recently buried there. He would have them there again soon enough.

"Lift your legs and grab hold of your boots. This giant thing is going up your butt."

It was truly giant. Bright red just like RJ's precious motorcycle, the dildo was shaped like a kind of traffic cone, with three ripples of increasing size descending from the conical tip to the square base.

As soon as RJ raised his legs and grabbed his ankles, Bronco aimed the open spout of the lube at his exposed hole. He squeezed out a stream of slippery goo, not relenting until a stream of it began to squirt back out around the bottle's end. He set it down and then placed the tip of that fire-engine red dildo directly against RJ's pink asshole.

The lube oozed from the hole as he began to push inward. RJ knew what was good for him and pulled back on his ankles to open up his crack and hole as much as possible. Bronco had to grin at that. The big biker gripping his own boots and holding his ass open for him was a real treat for the eyes.

The sight of that massive rubber toy poised to violate his pink hole was a real treat, too. He wondered how much he'd be able to feed him and shivered at the prospect of burying it all up that oozing slot.

He started out by merely dipping into it, massaging the tender rim with the tapered red tip and pushing just past the lips. As he felt the sphincter yielding, he pushed a little deeper, then deeper. Glancing up he noted the look of intense focus on RJ's face. The nostrils of his big nose flared, his blue eyes squinted, and his mouth gaped open as he sucked in deep breaths. He was ready for it.

It was then Bronco knew for certain that the biker boss would never give in to whining or begging, or useless protests. He would take it, no matter what. He realized that didn't bother him at all. He meant to get off, regardless of how RJ felt about it. If he took it like a man, no big deal.

One thing he knew though. RJ was going to feel it.

With a big grin on his face, he began to tease the gooey hole. He punched inward with the tip, burying it almost to the first ripple, then yanking it out. The hole made satisfying squishes, and lube spurted out. He liked that.

He shoved a little deeper, yanked out, then deeper yet. Suddenly, the first ripple disappeared beyond the straining pink lips, and RJ let out a huge grunt. Better! He yanked it right back out, laughing as the abandoned hole pouted outward and emitted another squishy spurt.

He really liked that. He drove the red dildo past that first ripple again, then yanked it back out, slammed it in again, and yanked it out. This time the hole expelled a gasp of air along with the spurt of lube.

He laughed out loud as he repeated the action, only this time ramming well past that first ripple and into the thicker part of the second ripple. RJ's body jerked, and he gritted his teeth as he pulled farther back on his ankles and writhed on the bench. Bronco pulled out the dildo with another satisfying spurt then shoved it back in, deeper yet.

Sweat rolled down RJ's face over his big nose and fat lips. He grunted every time the dildo rammed into him, and jerked when it was yanked out. His hole spurted out lube and air every time the fat toy came out of it.

The slamming punishment worked its magic on the gooey slot. Before he knew it, Bronco was ramming the toy past the second ripple. He was sweating as much as RJ, and grunting almost as much.

Interestingly, that snake-dick remained stiff as hell on the tall biker's belly between his raised legs. Bronco's cock was hard and aching, too. He decided it was time to get some more oral.

Ramming the dildo deep beyond the second ripple and holding it there, he got up and twisted around, facing the foot of the bench and scooting back to sit on top of the sprawled biker. RJ's raised legs were forced back beneath Bronco as he sat down over the biker's face once more.

"Eat ass and suck cock, bitch. You know you want to."

Whether that was true or not, the biker boss immediately started rooting around deep in Bronco's ass with his tongue and lips. The big nose rubbed back and forth in his crack and the fat tongue swabbed out his pouting hole with wet thoroughness.

He sat back on RJ's bent-back thighs and that mouth and nose, and began an earnest attempt to force the entire dildo up the tall biker's quivering pink asshole. It was already buried well beyond the second ripple. The giant part of the third strained the stretched lips. He could feel the hole yielding though, as it had so far to everything he'd forced on it.

As lips and tongue stroked his own hole, he used both hands on the square base of the giant dildo to push it in and out, a touch deeper each time. Lube coated the crack and his hands and continued to spurt out of the hole.

When he got close to forcing most of it in, he decided to up the ante. Holding the toy with one hand, he used the other to reach under his smooth belly and shove back on his cock. RJ's open mouth swallowed it up.

"Fuck yeah! Take my fat cock to the balls and this fat dildo to the root!"

It worked. As the crown of his cock drove down into RJ's gullet, the remainder of the dildo slid into his ass.

"Hell yeah! Fuck yeah! Oh fuck yeah ... oh hell yeah!"

He shouted with glee as he felt that tight throat massaging his cock head and those fat lips caressing his shaft. The ruby-red base of the dildo was all that remained to be seen as the rest of it was buried deep inside the poor biker's gut.

RJ thrashed about on the bench, while still maintaining a grip on his own boots and still sucking on Bronco's fat cock. But he was trapped under Bronco's hefty ass and there was no escaping the buried toy. All he could do was squirm around all that rubber and all that cock and ass.

Bronco lay down over the heaving biker, relenting enough to let his cock slide from his throat and give him a chance to snort in air — even though it was ass-crack air! The young biker sprawled out over the older one and rode him. He fucked his face while he rubbed RJ's big smooth ass with his hands. Gleefully, he watched him squirm and push outward with his ass-lips in an unsuccessful effort to dislodge the huge toy buried up his ass.

Sweat coated them both. Equally smooth, their shaved skin created a slippery glide between them as they slid back and forth in a writhing embrace. RJ's snake-dick rubbed against Bronco's smooth belly and remained rock solid. If he was suffering from the abuse, his cock certainly wasn't showing it.

Feeling the firm length of that snake-dick against his belly, Bronco knew what he needed now. His hole had been thoroughly massaged and teased by RJ's tongue and lips. It required some deeper satisfaction. He got up and straddled RJ's belly facing the foot of the bench. He grabbed the bottle of lube off the floor beside them and squirted a stream all over that snake-dick, took it in hand, and aimed it at his hole.

Arching his back and willing his hole to open up as he held the flared knob in place, he slowly began to sit on it. "Yeah! Hell yeah," he cried out as the slippery crown popped inside him.

He took his time at first, feeding the snake-dick to his hungry hole in small increments as he straddled RJ. Even though the aching pleasure was awesome, he didn't forget about the biker beneath him. He used the palm of one hand to slam against the protruding red base of that buried dildo, eliciting yelps and grunts from his trapped victim.

It wasn't long before he was taking almost all of that lengthy tool up his ass. He continued to slam his hand down over the base of the dildo buried in RJ's ass as his own plump ass-cheeks bounced up and down over the biker's crotch.

RJ continued to hold onto his boots and grunt, wriggling mightily but making no real effort to buck him off. With all that squirming, he only managed to ram his cock in and out of Bronco's tight ass.

The young biker's round ass-cheeks bounced and jiggled as he rode that cock. He craned his head around and got a look at the sprawled gang boss. He could see from the look on his face he was putting on a good show. His blue eyes were riveted to the sight of Bronco's smooth butt rising and falling over his stiff cock.

That stiff cock was so far up inside Bronco, he felt like it was banging against his lungs. It felt fucking fantastic. He drove his hips up and down over it, fucking the snake-dick with his tight, lube-dripping hole with ever-increasing ferocity. He squeezed and milked the rigid meat with his talented asshole until he finally achieved what he wanted.

He felt the stiff pole begin to pulse inside him. RJ was coming. He was coming with a big dildo up his ass and a tight ass riding his cock. He bounced harder and faster, milking every last drop out of the biker boss's churning balls.

Even though he got a real charge out of forcing RJ to shoot a load up his ass, he wasn't ready to blow his own nut quite yet. It was time for the finale. He rose from his perch on top of RJ, that snake-dick slithering from his squishy hole. On shaky legs, he ordered RJ to get up, too.

"Climb on your bike. You know what I want."

With that humongous cherry-red plug still buried in his ass, he obeyed.

The tall biker straddled his bike and lay down over it. The seat was made of bright red leather to match the gleaming cherry-red paint job. The full cheeks of his ass rose up from the seat with that matching ruby-red dildo planted in the deep crack. His bulging shoulders and long arms were splashed with colorful tattoos, but his shaved head, broad back, round ass and powerful thighs were creamy white in sharp contrast. Sweat coated his entire body in a glistening sheen.

Bronco straddled the bike right behind the prone gang boss. Staring down at that gorgeous ass he began to pump his slippery cock. "Wriggle that big butt for me, bitch. Show me how much you want my load."

RJ heaved and squirmed, humping the seat of his own bike. It was an awesome sight. Jerking faster and faster, his plump cock swelling up to the bursting point, he finally blew. He shot a huge load over that heaving ass, coating it with a sticky mess.

As soon as he'd urged out the final drops, he bent down and licked off his own nut-juice. The taste of cum and sweat mingled as his broad tongue roamed over the smooth expanse of that heaving butt. As a final gesture of dismissal, he planted the palm of his hand on the base of the big dildo and shoved hard against it. RJ grunted and jerked.

He left the big biker like that, with the red plug protruding from his battered asshole and spread over his bike.

It was a night to remember.

BENDING OVER BRIAN
By R. W. Clinger

SESSION 1 — UNDERNEATH IT ALL

I have Brian Catrell under my control at hello and know it. He is putty in my Alpha Boy palms, and I can mold him into anything I want. When he answers his apartment's front door and consumes my twenty-three-year-old good looks, it is all over for him. Unsurprised, the man studies me from head to toe, doing a long and steady once-over of my six-two frame, an obvious subject of his sexual interest right from the very start: coal black hair, wide eyebrows, onyx-colored eyes, Greek-sloped nose, pinkish lips, dimple in the center of my pretty boy chin, rugby player shoulders, jock-chest, tapered waist, titanic-sized package between my legs and under khakis, and thick thighs.

As we shake hands, I carry out a mental review of his personal file between my temples: librarian at Plimpton City Library for the past three decades, forty-seven years old, parents deceased, two siblings, a hoarder, sometimes depressed, smokes marijuana, lonely, no children, no significant other, homosexual, a silent partner of Drinks, a sixties-themed club on the east side of the city. His four-by-eight color photograph inside my file is a replica of how he looks now: bottled-blond hair, Southern blue eyes, five-eleven frame, 200 pounds of thin build, pert nose, steel-rimmed glasses, soul patch under his lower lip, dressed in a cotton dress shirt from a secondhand store, jeans, and hemp sandals. I determine quite clearly that he's the last American hippie on the planet.

"Come in, Mr. Mei," he says, nodding his handsome head, and stepping to his right for my entrance.

"Thanks. Be sure to call me Christopher," I respond, and walk into his life as his personal coach for the next few months, or however long he needs me.

Plimpton City, New York, along Lake Erie is the next Greenwich Village, Key West, Provincetown, or Palm Springs. The gays are taking over: professors, doctors, lawyers, brokers, bankers, and high-end real estate agents, and others. Toss in a few mechanics, bearish construction workers, a collection of blue collar monkeys with great bods, and … it is the perfect place to live.

Brian's apartment is not like any of my other clients'. Boxes of vintage queer magazines cover the floor, numerous Hefty bags of dildos, a gazillion XXX DVD cases are everywhere, and other sex toys are scattered about the premises: hand cuffs, leather straps, masks, ball gags, robes, feathers, satin scarves, and a variety of lubes.

He offers me a strong drink, which I politely decline; I never drink on the job. Across from him, I sit in a leather chair with ripped arms, open my notepad, click my Mel Blanc for use, and now tell him, "Start at the beginning, Brian."

"A very good place to start," he replies and winks at me.

For the next hour, we discuss his problems in full detail, which include: he's a recluse and needs to get out and meet new acquaintances, friends, and men. People he can socialize with. Young men he can kiss, lick, or fuck. Men he can have one-night stands with, find boyfriendhood, or something more serious like a partnership.

I tell him he's going to overcome this social problems, that we'll take baby steps to help him through this issue and …

Honestly, I don't know what comes over me, but the naughty young man — that boyishly horny and simple unprofessional who likes the company of hippie men that are almost twice my age, surfaces — and I begin to play with him, exactly the way I shouldn't play with him. What comes over me? Why does this happen in his presence? Why do I begin to flirt with him, eyeing him up and down and cause him to feel uncomfortable? Why do I spread my legs and fix the goods inside my khakis? Why do I unbutton the top two buttons of my shirt for his pleasure? So his eyes can study a sliver of my suntanned and hairless chest, a bulging pec, a pointed nipple — whatever he can consume for his man-pleasure.

"Baby steps," I repeat, and pass him a list of objectives and goals to reach before our next session. Now, I ask, "May I use your bathroom, Brian?"

He escorts me to the bathroom around his pornography stacked all over the floor. We weave right, left, back to the right through his apartment, and finally stand at the bathroom door. Here, I step inside the aqua-blue porcelain world, perform a healthy piss alone, wash my hands in his dirty sink, and find myself in the living room area again, next to the battered leather chair, his personal file, and my notes.

The look on his face is of hunger as he visually consumes my center. Wide-eyed and interested, he chants, "Christopher, your zipper is down."

Actually, I know it is, purposely wanting to tease him, being a naughty boy in full control of his sexual yearning yet again. Acting surprised, I peer down at my center and see the gap of cotton and a view of my veined cock and its accessorizing pubic triangle.

"No underwear?" he inquires, licking his lips, seated across from me on a Swedish sofa that has seen better days.

"Never," I admit, apologize for my carelessness in dressing, and zip up. "Boxers and briefs always tend to get in the way."

He points to my zipping up action and admits, "You don't have to do that on my account." He becomes hypnotized by my planned sport, and the now-hidden treasures behind their cotton. He adds, "As you know, Christopher, I have a weakness for a young man's flesh."

"I do realize that. But, as your life coach, I insist we keep our relationship purely professional, and without any undulations whatsoever."

"Of course," he replies, rather sad that I will not allow him to touch, smell, or taste the professional product between my muscular thighs, among my other body parts.

Within minutes, I end our first session. In doing so, I tell him to carry out the goals I have outlined for him, to have a very good day, and that I will gladly see him in a week.

(Personal Notes: Brian Cantrell, client #83728-BJ, desires me, inside and out. All he wants to do is pull my clothes off and mess around with my skin. Something tells me he wants to shove my ten-inch dick down the back of his throat, or push it into his ass. I have driven him into a state of sexual delight. He wants to gag on my ooze. He wants to be pounded over his battered sofa. He wants to … Unfortunately, Brian can't have me as of yet. My game/coaching/gig/therapy continues. Our sessions ensue. We will meet again.)

SESSION 2 — INSIDE HIS MOUTH

I agree to meet him at Plimpton City Park where we will carry out our weekly session. Here, the summertime evening is quite warm, rather pleasant, and offers a stunning blue-purple-red twilight. My client wears a pair of running shorts, Adidas shoes, and a Nike T-shirt. He claims he has spent the last half hour running around the park, but there isn't a drop of sweat on the man's entire body. In due time, I will surely discover why he lies to me, but for now, I let it go.

We sit in the shade at a picnic table. I leave my notebook and Mel Blanc in my Honda Civic, providing a relaxed session for my client. Here, we discuss his goals: did he reach/maintain any (or all) in the past week?; how much progress does he feel he has made in the last seven days?; can he create one goal and meet it by our next session?

He tells me he tried to pick up a guy in the grocery store; the guy gave him his cell number, but he hasn't called him back as of yet.

I reinforce the idea and action that he will eventually be able to return a call to the man in the future because of our helpful sessions.

Brian agrees.

I inquire if he has considered cyber dating.

Brian admits that he hasn't. "I'm just not ready for that yet."

He says, since our first session he is feeling much better, though, more outgoing, and has even spent an evening at Drinks.

I provide him with a new list of goals, which entail: walks around his neighborhood, harmless flirting with a man/men, more communication within his surroundings, ask a man/men out, try a one-night stand, and continue spending evenings at Drinks.

Brian agrees, nodding his head, still seated across from me. Now, he decides to change the subject, and inquires, "You're only twenty-three, right?"

"Yes."

"You work for Everyday Life Coaching in the city, right?"

"Yes. A non-profit organization to help women and men through everyday problems."

We talk for the next half hour about my life: sociology degree obtained at Ruben College; mental illness internship carried out at the Howell House for eighteen months; two older brothers; my father lives in Miami; mother deceased; I live in a

Tudor on Espee Way on the other side of town. I feel safe about telling my client these details because all of this information can be found on the Internet with very little searching.

I lose Brian. His mind is elsewhere, and he daydreams about undressing me, applying his lips to my chest, fondling the package between my legs with his right hand, spreading my bottom with his fingertips and diving his extended tongue into its warm and cozy cavern for his ultimate pleasure. I have this power over the man that ... seems ridiculous but exists between us. I actually get off on the fact that he's a mere token I can play with in the palm of my hand at any moment. A pet. A toy. Something that makes me grow hard under the picnic table, and causes me to cross a professional line between client and life coach.

"Brian," I chant, and snap two fingers together in front of his face, waking him from his elsewhere state.

"Your shaft ... It's all I've been thinking about," he admits, taking in my black eyes and surprised look, I'm sure.

I'm horny. The hippie is totally my type of older man. The realization of my bond with him is quite simple: I call the shots and can have him at any moment I want. He's a sport for me, amusing fun, and at my sexual beck and call if I want him. He likes everything about me: my pretty boy looks, muscular build, intelligence, and the fact that I have a youthful cock and set of balls for his intimate use. We both know that I govern his hunger, having a silenced power over his sexual frustration. The client can be mine within seconds; a treat for my man-needs; a resource to shoot a pent load onto, or into. The man is my gadget of man-fun, whenever I want or need him, honestly.

Brian doesn't surprise me when he says, "Let's go for a short walk in the woods."

"Of course. If you're more comfortable with the session by doing this ... I understand."

We rise from the picnic table, and I follow him to a narrow trail called ASH. The woods are dense and offer much shade here. There is no wind. Sounds of pesky birds and playful chipmunks mingle around us. We walk side by side, close to each other. Our shoulders gently brush to and fro with each step. Eventually, I ask him, "What do you want from me?"

He's honest, to the point, and rattles off, "I want to have your cock in my mouth."

"Why?"

"I don't know. It's just what I want."

"You have to know why, though. Tell me." My comment proves I have power over him, control of our time spent together, and ...

He can't help himself any longer. His appetite for me surfaces to its maximum potential, and he immediately pushes my back against the trunk of an oak tree. The older gentleman falls to his knees, my khaki's buttons are ripped open, and their material is yanked down to my knees. Of course he doesn't find underwear beneath. Now, he goes for my semi-deflated tool with his open mouth. His lips separate and two inches of my floppy mass are sucked inside. His right hand finds the dangling balls between my perspiration-covered thighs, and his fingertips gently squeeze their orbs, which provide me with pleasure.

My six inches of limp mass turns into ten firm inches with the librarian's help. Quick and steady sucks proceed on the shaft. Brian's mouth becomes wicked on the stick, which leaves me breathless as he rushes his head to and fro at my middle. Truth is, he does all the work, attempting to get me off. The guy falls helplessly under my spell and begins to moan and groan with utter bliss. Dozens of sucks ensue in a repeated manner, which continue for the next three ... seven ... eleven minutes inside the woods. Here, we are alone, just the two of us, united in the naughtiest act among birch, maple, and sycamore trees.

Bumblebees, robins, and summertime dragon flies meander around our connection.

His mouthy motion causes me to lose my breath against the oak trunk. I heave once … twice … three times into his mouth. My ten-incher slides down the back of his throat and gags the older man. Perspiration builds on my forehead and torso as my orgasm heightens. I end up plowing the man's face with all my force, unable to hold back my heedless motion. Swift and concurrent movement occurs to his mouth. I listen to the man gag by my touch, lost and bemused. A rush of sounds escape the librarian and …

I push his head away from my meaty device and warn him in a chaotic whisper, "Shooting, pal." Within seconds, I hold the base of my pole by its balls and aim its capped head at the librarian's right cheek. What occurs next is nothing unexpected. A last grunt of euphoria is heard from my lips and a gush of white, sticky blow erupts from its head. The goo clings to my client's right cheek and hangs against his neck. Feeling hungry, post-spray and empty of my man-ooze, I briskly tell him to stand up from his knees. Once the guy listens to me, facing me in the public woods, my appetite takes over, and I lick every last drop of my seed off his cheek and neck.

"Savor it," Brian coaches, smiling at me as I go to town on his flesh with my tongue, lapping the bittersweet drug into my system.

His evening session comes to an abrupt end, though. Teenage voices are heard in the distant, working their way closer to us on Ash Trail. The young boys discuss football, detailing field plays, and are only a hundred feet away.

Spent and out of breath, I yank up my khakis, button them, and dash into the woods, heading back to my Civic. What happens with Brian Catrell is unknown; I won't learn of his public park escape until our third session, which is scheduled for the following week at his office in the public library.

(Personal Notes: I have Brian exactly where I want him. Begging for my skin. Wanting it. Needing it. Desiring nothing less than our bodies to mix together with sweat and semen. The man is clay for me, and I can mold him into a hungry and relentless older man who wants nothing less than my flesh against his lips, fingertips, and cock. Brian is under my power, a puppet for my use, a weakling of an older man — just for me. He'll continue his sessions for sex; I know this. History repeats itself and ... these older men always want sex from me: ass-riding, dick-sucking, and cream-blowing fun. Don't they? Always. Of course. This is how I cure them. This is how they become social and face their problems. This is my personal goal to better the queer society of today.)

SESSION 3 — OVER HIS DESK

August 23. Almost the end of summer. I meet Brian at six o'clock in the evening at his office, which is a private room filled with books, papers, files, and other office machinery. He stares at me from across his desk, robustly smiles, and says, "I've missed your cock."

"These sessions are not about me. You need to start to make small, but accurate changes in your life."

"I want to lick your ass," he admits, out of the blue, shocking me. "You're so young and handsome ... and everything I crave. You're a drug to me. Something I can't get out of my system and want more of." He smells of vodka and cigarettes. When was the last time he shaved? Has he accomplished any of his goals that we agreed on during our last session in the park? His smile grows and he whispers, "I want to eat your ass out. This is what our sessions have come to, Christopher. Are you up for a good rump-munching, my friend?"

I'm not his friend, although I can be. I've had clients like him before: older men who fall under the power of my Alpha

Boy skin; sex-driven men in their middle lives who feel sexually helpless while in my presence; police officers, mechanics, military war heroes, and librarians who inadvertently collapse because of my youthful sexiness and ...

Something that seems erotically strange and overpowering enters my client's eyes. He spreads his arm over his desk in a swift motion and it is cleared off, clean as a whistle in seconds, free of everything. Files, paper, books, pens, pencils, a coffee mug, and a calculator fly off the plane of mahogany and plummet to the floor. A wickedness of sexual longing encompasses the man's grin. Shockingly, he quickly rises from his seat, leans over the desk, and lunges at the collar on my Brooks Brother shirt. I'm yanked forward by the shirt, glide across the desk on my stomach, told to take a whiff of the man's slacks-covered goods, which smell like dried urine, perspiration, and ancient goo.

"Hold on there, buddy," Brian utters. He rushes around the desk with the speed of a superhuman, rips my Cole shoes off, drags my chinos off my body without even undoing their leather belt, and decides to have his way with my bottom.

It's exactly what I want him to do. I have purposely devised this string of sessions with the older man to fulfill my sexual demands. Of course, this is unethical according to my education in human studies, but what the hell, right? Every twenty-three-year-old has to get his kicks, even if it's with a client.

My legs are spread open, and his wet and warm tongue laps at my rump's solid orbs. Licks continue for the next minute or two. I let out a moan of pleasure, delighted with the cordial affair over his desk. In truth, a boner sports between my legs and rubs against the desk's fine grain of wood, which is an aphrodisiac for me to the fullest comprehension.

To my utter surprise, a smack sounds within his library office. The noise is redolent and rather shocking to hear. A snap of sorts as his right hand meets my right ass-orb.

"Going in," the librarian whispers above me. He spreads my legs a little wider with some rough care, dives his mouth to my man-opening, and darts the tip of his moist tongue in my center, obeying his yearning. Consecutive darts ensue, one after the next. A dozen ... two dozen ... three dozen or more wet my crack as he pleasures himself overtop me. Fingers pull my bulbous bottom apart and he buries his entire face inside my jockish rump. Moans, murmurs, and mumbles escape the man's mouth, overjoyed with his ass-fest during his Session 3.

Pleasure is discovered yet again for me, just as I expect. During his rump-buffet, my waist is pulled to the edge of the desk, which allows access to my stiff cock. Within seconds, the bookworm reaches for my ten inches that point to the hardwood floor, using his right palm and fingers. As more seconds continue to tick by during his session, the man begins to milk me like a farm animal while he proceeds to lather my taut crevice with his ravenous mouth.

"Mr. Catrell," escapes my lips as a whisper during his milking and ass-nibbling. My fingers dig into the desk's wood as his duo-performance quickens. Earth-shifting euphoria is discovered during his cock-friction and behind-action. The man's studious hand rides up and down on my tool, which sends me into a spiral of utter bliss. His movement on my stick is swift and unyielding. And, his mouth against my hole is climax-reaching for me. Huffs exit my lips. Moans surface from my lungs. I gag on my rough exhalations. Deep satisfaction is discovered because of his desk-gig. No longer can I keep my load pent. No longer can I hold my load in and ... and ... and ... I release spew out of my steel bar, ejaculate life coaching-cream from its firm length and spray the side of Brian's desk, his office floor, and our feet.

Like our connection in Plimpton City Park, we conclude our union rather abruptly. My client's session comes to a halting end, with very little care for himself to release his own load. He simply rises from my rump, gives it two smacks, and says, "Got you off ... Exactly what you wanted me to do with your skin."

I'm sort of blown away by this admission and want to ask him about it. My question is never shared, though, since my cell phone rings. Quickly, I rise from the desk, yank up my chinos, study the incoming call, and realize it is one of my clients, a suicidal young woman on Baener Street. I decide rather immediately to help the client out, excuse myself from Brian's session, and admit to him on my way out of his office, "We'll meet in two weeks. I'll call you tomorrow to arrange it."

(Personal Notes: Never underestimate the sexual urges and social skills of a middle-aged man. In fact, I have learned they desire sex more than younger men. This is what I determine regarding Brian Catrell. Using his skin. Teasing him. He wants more of me, but doesn't know when he can have me. I rather enjoy his struggle, pent desires, and attraction for me. My next goal is simple, of course. Leave him stew. Let him soak in our intimate moments together until ... he can't take his sexual frustration any longer and demands an immediate session with me. This is how I can help cure him. If he can fend off my youthful skin for as long as possible, he can begin to reach out in life and start dating men ... he can meet the perfect man and share a relationship with him ... he can leave his apartment and enjoy Drinks a few nights out of the week. This will make him a better man who is positive, raise his self-esteem, and ... cause him to believe he can have any man he wants for his sexual needs, including me.)

SESSION 4 — UNDER MY MAN-CARE

I prompt Brian to work for our next session; this is part of his life care. I ignore him for the next twelve ... fourteen ... seventeen days. He watches me in the city. He follows me to the grocery store, movies, the book store on Pendgraff Street, the drug store, and the convenience store where I sometimes by lottery tickets. The librarian is always behind me. I am watched, craved, desired, and needed. Brian becomes powerless, lusts for me, and learns to have a sense of control in his life. He e-mails me, which I ignore. He calls me, which I ignore. He sends a letter to me via snail mail, which I send back to him unopened. He calls my secretary a dozen or more times, insisting to set up an appointment/session to see me; Luanne is instructed to note his calls/concerns, but never to give into a scheduled meeting. Brian is healing, slowly but surely, and doesn't even realize it.

Our fourth session happens in the middle of the night. September-something. Rain plummets the city. Thunder wreaks havoc overhead. Lightning dances outside the windows, long into the night. I'm awakened at approximately three o'clock in the morning: banging ensues on my Tudor's front door and Brian hollers through its wood, "Christopher! ... I need to talk to you! ... Christopher!"

I don't call the police on him, although I can because of his unannounced intrusion in the dark hours. Instead, I expect this unplanned session; it's part of his care, and my job. I let him inside the Tudor, study his dripping-wet body from the night's tempest, and say, "I'll get you a towel."

Minutes later, he undresses in the foyer, down to his Hanes briefs, and uses Martha Stewart cotton to dry off with. Now, he provides a greedy grin of sexual longing for me, and says, "I can't get you out of my head."

This is his session, just as I predict it will occur according to my past trials and tribulations with clients harboring the same social issues: we sit on either ends of my Belgium sofa and discuss his concerns in full; he tells me he is starting to want to leave his apartment for socializing at Drinks; dating a man/men, or carrying out relationships is not out of his equation; he admits that he has flirted unconditionally with a few men at Drinks; Brian confesses he sucked a guy's cock in the bar's bathroom; tomorrow evening he has a date with a college student named Tab and ...

"Progress," I utter, listening to him, taking mental notes.

"But," he admits, starry-eyed and looking hungry for my skin — something.

"But what?"

"I need more of your coaching."

"I perceive this," I share, and add information regarding his e-mails, calls, the single letter, and his texts, all of which I have so intently and easily ignored to better him, remedying his acute problem of social deprivation.

"I want you to fuck me," he admits. "Our final session."

"Final session?" I ask, raising an eyebrow, interested in his demand to conclude our meetings. "What do you mean?"

"I want to feel your cock in my ass. The end of your coaching. The last bond between us until … I meet the right guy. A climax to our encounters. The last of your naked medicine."

"Social healing," I confess, perhaps correcting his verbiage. "Let me clarify this. You're ready to leave your apartment, meet a variety of men, sexually socialize, and eventually find a partner. Do I understand this clearly?"

He nods his handsome head and confesses, "You've controlled me long enough. I understand your Alpha Boy gig … your therapy. It was all to better me, even if I didn't comprehend it at first."

"It was."

"And now I want to have my final session with you."

"My dick in your ass. This is what you want, right?"

"Exactly," he replies, smiling from ear to ear, obviously cured.

"Your payment for being a productive patient, Brian."

He hungrily keeps the grin on his face, and replies, "Call it what you want."

# # # # #

Not even three minutes later, we are both completely naked and he is sprawled over my Berber carpet inside my living room, belly down. I have a condom affixed to the ten inches of dong between my legs, and warn him in a rather civil manner, "Brian, it's going to hurt."

"I want it to hurt. Medicine doesn't always go down smooth."

"Indeed it doesn't," I admit, spread his legs apart, bend over him, and enter three inches of my stick inside his middle-aged man-hole with an immediate push.

The librarian groans on the floor and begs for more of my protein slab.

Like an over-achieving life coach, I give him what he wants, and lodge three more inches of my ten into his core.

He gags from my poker. What escapes his mouth is rather shocking for me, "All of it, Christopher ... Shove all of it into me. End this relationship between us. Set the both of us free."

Progress is devised. I shove all ten inches into the client, slide eight out, force ten back in, and begin to ride his ass in a steadfast and pounding motion, which catapults the librarian into a position of pure delight.

Friction builds between us. On my knees, I bang his bottom with all my weight, pull away, and bang him again. Two ... four ... six ... eight ... all ten inches of my post drives him into full recovery. I fuck him like I haven't fucked a man in weeks ... months ... or even years. I bang the social maladroitness out of the man and devise a cure for him. I bang ... bang ... bang his bottom with my ten-inch rod until he has tears in his eyes, until he loses oxygen, and claws at the Berber with his fingernails.

"Faster," he begs, underneath my working body. "Fuck me harder ... and faster," he murmurs.

Bolt after powerful bolt occurs to his manly hole. I bash his behind with my weight, release my club from his cavern, and bash him again ... again ... again. Perspiration flies off my torso and stings his spine. A hollow but intrepid sound escapes the man under my forceful weight. Each hump to his behind causes the client to murmur another indecipherable plea of enjoyment.

Of course, I cannot keep my man-cargo banked for much longer. The friction between our two bodies becomes unyielding and causes an unstoppable orgasm to occur within my system. Following a swift and curable set of ass-humps to the older man's body, I confess down to him, "Ready to burst."

"Do it!" he exclaims over his right shoulder, delirious and healed under my buffed and naked care. "Spray it all over me."

I listen. What life coach wouldn't, right? With a rather forceful tug, I remove my shaft from his man-tunnel, continue to kneel over the man, rip the condom off my wanker, lose it on the living room floor, and begin to rotate my flag in a north and south motion with my right hand. Hips thrust into my fist and fingers, providing me with an unstoppable feeling of elation that whips throughout my torso. Fast and faster jolts occur to my centered limb with my right hand. And, I call down to the man on his belly, "Firing, Brian."

Spew spirals out of my veined timber and covers his back, shoulders, and his ass. White goo collects against his skin as I pull away from him and stand. Here, inside my living room, I become spent, post-sexed, and numb. My orgasm is swift and torso-gripping. Breath is lost. Dizziness occurs. Quickly, our shared cock-to-ass session ends, just as we both desire.

"The best fuck ever," the librarian admits on the floor, happy with his prize, my tenderness, and approach to his mental state of healing.

I demand from him, "You're coaching is finalized. If you need me in the future, I'll be here for you. You know how to reach me. You're cured as far as I can tell. Put your clothes on and leave, Mr. Catrell. I feel you don't need my services any longer." It sounds terribly unemotional exiting my mouth, but it comes with the job. Points need to be made. Therapy for the man has expired for the time being. Our connection must end here and now, until he desires my assistance again, if he needs to, of course.

"Cured," he whispers, naked and ooze-covered on the Berber.

"Yes, cured," I agree, unemotionally walk away from him, find my way upstairs, into my shower for a quick spray-down, and head to bed, knowing he escapes my Tudor, and our meetings, for good.

(Personal Notes: We both get what we want, I know. Brian can now return to a male society and enjoy the company of men: naked or clothed. No longer will he be a hermit or socially inept inside his apartment. Men and boys will be at his beck and call, thanks to my Alpha Boy approach. I have cured another man/patient/client. I believe Brian will find the right man or men to spend the rest of his life with. I believe I have fulfilled his desire, and my own, on both a sexual level and a professional one. Bottom line: the librarian is healed, which allows me to help others. At 736 Sutton Street in downtown Plimpton City is another man, two years older than Brian Catrell. My notes include that he desires young men, he's been single for the last ten years, and he has a low self-esteem and doesn't date anymore. His name is Michael Henderson, a poet, my next client, my pet, my toy ... I'll help him the same way I have helped the librarian, of course.)

THE MEN OF M.A.N. (MARSBASE ALPHA: NEWEARTH)
By Logan Zachary

In the year 2060, a nuclear accident occurred on earth and set off an explosive, radioactive reaction, polluting half of the world's surface. An outpost of men traveled to Mars to set up a colony: a MarsBase.

Nine years later, the first base on Mars was operational. It was called Alpha: NewEarth. The residents were settling in, and this is one of their stories...

Star Date 2069: MarsBase Alpha: NewEarth

"Why do I have to take off all of my clothes? The medical scanner can read my life systems through my uniform," Captain Alex Peters asked, as he stepped into the clear plastic medical tube.

"The scanner gets a more accurate reading if there isn't anything impeding the results," Dr. Michael Cavanaugh said, as he pushed a series of buttons on the panel. An image of Alex appeared on the screen as numbers scrolled by too fast to be read on a counter.

"My cruiser landed hard, but I've fallen out of my bunk harder."

"When your twenty-five-year-old body has fallen out of your bed, you've always landed on your ass. When you fell out of space, you crashed head first, which may have scrambled your brain up a little more."

"Hard head, hard ass." Captain Alex unzipped his shirt along his sleeve and removed it. A thick pelt of hair covered his chiseled body. "Are you happy now?" He threw his uniform top at him.

"Once you've been debriefed, I'll be satisfied." Dr. Cavanaugh typed on the keyboard and waited. He attended college with Alex's dad back on earth and had looked after Alex ever since the accident building the MarsBase took the father's life.

"When you see my hairy ass and my other assets, I know you will be happy." Alex blew him a kiss as he kicked off his shoes and removed his socks. "Your communicator isn't on, is it? I don't want you transmitting my naked body across the MarsBase."

"You'll never know. Strip." Dr. Cavanaugh pointed to his pants.

Alex unzipped down the side of his right pant leg. "Why they put the fly down the side instead of where it is needed, is beyond me."

"Worried about being a fashion victim?" The doctor clicked his tongue.

Alex stepped out of his pants. His long muscular legs were as hairy as the rest of him. He balled up his pants and threw them at the doctor. The plastic tube reflected his hairy ass, framed in the white jock strap he still wore. His deep crease funneled the dark hair that crossed two perfect orbs, the buns of titanium.

The medical monitor flashed as the numbers changed rapidly. A warning beep sounded, and Dr. Cavanaugh looked at the readout. "What the ..."

An icon of Alex's heart appeared, and the beat was seen as a white line, which streaked across the screen in an irregular rate.

"Sinus rhythm interruption ... beep ... Sinus rhythm interruption ... beeeeeeeeeeep ..."

The white line flattened across the screen.

Dr. Cavanaugh looked into the plastic tube and saw Alex close his eyes and sway from side to side. He jumped off the platform, raced to the back of the tube and opened the door.

Alex's body fell into his arms as the medical lab went black.

"Lights."

Nothing.

"Back up lights."

Nothing.

Dr. Cavanaugh picked up Alex and carried his unconscious form to where he thought a cot was. "Emergency lights." His voice rose as his feet felt his way. He held Alex close to his body. He knew his patient was breathing, faint but even. His furry body felt warm to the touch as his fingers combed through the hair on him.

His feet hit the hospital bed, and he set his charge down gently. Why had Alex passed out? Dr. Cavanaugh felt the pulse at his neck. It felt strong and steady, despite the scanner's readings.

Amber lights slowly started to glow and fill the room with a yellow light. An electric hum vibrated through the clinic as the air filtration system started up again, cooling off the stale space.

The door slid open as a young male nurse rushed in. "The power was interrupted across the base ... oh shit, what happened?" He rushed over to the bed, pulled out the vitals scanner and placed it across Alex's chest. He pulled out a pair of scissors from his pocket and moved down to Alex's jock. He cut the elastic band and leg loops.

Dr. Cavanaugh watched as the supportive pouch was removed, and Alex's cock and balls flopped free. He pulled a blanket over his waist. A monitor on his desk flashed and beeped. "Commander Dylan Frazier: unconscious, Lieutenant Robert Riley: unconscious, Lieutenant Justin ..." name after name was read unconscious.

"What the heck is going on?" the male nurse looked at Alex. He pressed a button on the panel and watched as a bar graph rose and fell.

Alex flinched, his hand jerked, as he gasped and sat up. "What's going on?"

Alarms and lights flashed warnings throughout the base. Dr. Cavanaugh frantically pressed a bunch of buttons across the console. "Everyone on the base is unconscious, except us."

"Can MarsBase continue to operate without anyone?" Nurse Cooper asked, fear easily read in his eyes.

"We have eight hours max, and then the systems will start shutting down." Alex tried to sit on the edge of the bed, and realized he was naked. He pulled the blanket over his lap, covering his rapidly growing flesh.

"Who'll take charge?" Cooper asked

"I will," Alex said, as he readied himself to jump off the cot.

A disturbance formed in the corner of bay seven. A swirl of light and matter buzzed and quickly materialized into a humanoid shape. Straps of form fitting leather surrounded his legs and arms, what looked like metal ribs covered his vest, tight shorts hugged his hips, and boots that ended just below his knee shined black and smooth.

He had long flowing blond hair that made him look like Thor. Chiseled muscles that made the leather squeak as it stretched at his every move.

Cooper found a hospital robe and handed it to Alex.

Alex wrapped it around his back and slipped his arms through the openings. He pulled it closed in front and tied the belt. Standing on wobbly legs, he curled his bare toes on the cold floor. "What does this guy want?" flashed through his brain.

"Greetings and salutations," the big man raised his hands up as he approached.

"Hello, we weren't expecting visitors."

The man smiled, but the warmth didn't enter his eyes. They remained cold and black. "I heard a distress call and decided to come over and explore."

Alex doubted the commander had enough time to send off any messages, but he didn't say anything. "Our crew has blacked out, and we're the only three awake."

"And why is that?" the guest asked.

"I'm not sure, but I was only out for a few minutes. I only recently awoke."

"How strange," the golden man said. He stood a few feet away from the trio. "So who is the leader here?" His gaze switched from one man to the next. His stare stayed on Dr. Cavanaugh.

Alex rested his hands on his hips and wished the robe was longer. He wondered if his business was hanging out of the bottom. At that thought, he felt his penis leap under the material and threaten to rise. This close to the visitor, he was able to smell sun and forest on his skin, sweat and leather, male and something more, primitive.

The air filtration system removed everything from the base's air, humidity, positive and negative ions, scents, and smells.

The visitor noticed the flare of Alex's nostrils and moved closer.

Nurse Cooper slipped behind Alex and avoided eye contact.

Dr. Cavanaugh stood his ground and continued to read the scanning monitors. All the vital signs of the residents on the MarsBase showed healthy and alive, but unconscious. He wondered when they would awaken.

Alex shifted his weight, and one leg slipped out of the robe's slit.

The guest's eyes drank in the sight of the muscular, hairy, tight leg.

Alex caught the shift in attention. Ahh, something he'd have to remember. "We're fine, so thank you for checking on us, but I don't think we would like to waste any more of your time."

"No waste at all. Just trying to be neighborly."

"Well, we have it from here, so you may return to where you came from."

"It sounds like I've worn out my welcome, and so soon." He shook his head, and the long mane of hair cascaded around his head like rays of sunshine.

Dr. Cavanaugh stopped looking at the monitors and stared at the intruder. "Who are you, and what do you want?"

Their guest laughed. "Hasn't your computer figured out who I am?"

A synthesized voice spoke "Captain Steve Barker, space pirate and profiteer. He has sold more men into slavery and hijacked more alien technology to keep four galaxies going. His barbaric treatment of women and animals has been legendary for crimes against nature and beasts. He has ..."

"Yeah, yeah, yeah, we get it. So let's get things moving." He pulled out a weapon from his hip and aimed it at Dr. Cavanaugh. "Let's start with you." He fired, and a red beam of light shot out of it. The beam went through him and hit the panel on one wall. Sparks and fire sprayed across the room.

Dr. Cavanaugh looked down at the hole in him as the beam continued through. "Impressive, cold fusion tech from Sector 5. Not allowed in our galaxy, but what else would we have expected from you?"

Captain Barker stopped shooting. He stepped forward and waved his hand at the doctor. His holographic image distorted and reconfigured as soon as the hand passed.

"Santorum!" Captain Barker swore.

"I'm only solid when the need arises," Dr. Cavanaugh admitted and blinked out.

Cooper and Alex pushed the gurney between them at Captain Barker. The edge knocked the weapon from his hand, as it slid across the floor; the automated floor sweeper captured it and whisked it away.

Alex's hairy, bare ass flashed as he and Cooper escaped to the lab portion of the infirmary.

Cooper dove for the tranq gun on the bedside tray.

Alex didn't see any place for shelter or protection, so he spun around and faced Captain Barker.

Barker stopped and smiled. "I like a little fight in my captives; it makes their surrender even sweeter."

Alex saw that Cooper had the tranquilizer ready, he pulled on the side of the robe and showed more hip and leg. The thick pubic bush peeked out.

Captain Barker licked his lips. "So tender, so pale, so innocent, so easy to bruise."

Cooper jumped up and raised his arm over his head. He brought the tranq down, but as soon as the tip touched bare skin, Barker slashed at him and knocked Cooper's slender body against the wall. His head hit the panel and slowly he slid down to the floor.

Barker spun and faced Alex.

Alex raised his hands in surrender. "Please." His robe opened wider and his semi-erect dick swung free. His low hangers rolled back and forth.

Barker moved closer and sneered. "You thought you would be able to control me, save the base, and rescue your friends. You." He laughed and stopped as he towered over Alex. His hot breath blew into his face and spittle landed on his lips.

"What are you going to do?" Alex's belt released, and his robe opened wide. He thrust his hips forward, and his erection bounced up and down gently.

Barker reached down between his legs and grabbed his balls and twisted.

Alex rose up onto his toes and moved with his captor. "I'll give you anything you want. Just don't hurt me." He reached forward and ran his hand underneath his vest and felt the ripple of muscles beneath.

"Pinch my nipples," he commanded.

Alex's fingers found the pierced nubs and twisted. He cranked as hard as he could, but Barker didn't even flinch.

He thrust his pelvis at him and unzipped his pants. His massive cock flopped out of its confines and slapped against Alex's chest.

Alex reached down to stroke the thick member.

Captain Barker pushed down on his shoulders and forced Alex's face to his groin. Musky sweaty balls, urine, and old spunk clung to his flesh. He grabbed his raging hard-on and forced it into Alex's mouth. His cock slipped down his throat, choking him. His hairy balls pressed into his chin. The coarse bristles cut his tender skin.

"Drain them dry."

Tears rolled down Alex cheeks as well as spit, pre-cum and sweat. Captain Barker thrust deeper down his throat and blocked his airway.

Alex's nails dug into his solid ass and tried to push his head away just enough to get a breath of oxygen.

Barker pushed him away and pulled his mouth back onto his cock.

He had only a second to inhale a lungful of life saving oxygen. More juices flowed out of his mouth and over his chin. The slimy flow ran down his hairy chest and matted his fur to his skin.

Alex dug between his flashy butt cheeks and slipped a finger into his crack. The tip burrowed harder and deeper and found that sensitive hole. The end darted in and out.

Captain Barker paused and held his body stiff.

Alex penetrated him again, deeper this time. He pulled it out quickly and shoved it back in.

Barker pushed his ass back onto his hand and rode his finger. His throbbing, dripping cock forgotten with the new sensation.

Alex sensed his excitement, inserted two fingers and twisted.

A low guttural moan escaped from him, and he pressed down harder on Alex's hand.

Alex pulled out of him and slipped three fingers into Captain Barker.

He threw his head back and savored the pleasure, forgetting all about Alex's pain and his complete control.

"Do you know how good a hot, wet tongue would feel deep inside you?" Alex asked.

Flipping his long hair back, he looked into Alex's eyes. "Lick it, lick it now, but ...." His hand grabbed Alex's neck and squeezed so hard his captive saw stars, "I'll break your neck with one squeeze, if I have to."

Alex licked his lips and waited as Captain Barker turned and bent over. Barker spread his ass cheeks, and Alex dove in, tongue first. He tasted tangy man sweat and funk. His lips made a seal and sucked, drawing on the tight pucker and stuck his tongue in and out of his hole. Slippery and dripping, his tip circled the tight muscle and worked its magic to relax. Slowly, the pointed end wiggled its way around the sphincter and in. He sucked and thrust, filling the opening.

Captain Barker threw his head back and howled. He pushed his ass back onto Alex's face and opened his hole wide for deeper penetration.

Alex pulled his ass cheeks apart as wide as he could to get the best access. His tongue did tricks that stimulated every nerve ending in his hairy hole. The hole was so smooth and sweet.

Captain Barker's cock and balls swung between his legs and sprinkled pre-cum across the floor.

Alex reached around his muscular torso and found the massive cock. He pulled on Barker's penis as he thrust into his ass. More liquid poured out of his cock as his tongue licked deeper. He circled the opening and reached between his legs to capture the hairy orbs that dangled. He rolled them around and around in his palm.

Captain Barker's body relaxed and absorbed the attention.

Alex stopped and kissed his muscular cheek. "I have an idea that you will love."

"What?"

"If you lie on your back and let me stand between your legs, I can be deeper inside you and work your beautiful cock at the same time."

Captain Barker looked over his shoulder and narrowed his eyes.

Alex inserted the finger again and tapped his prostate.

Captain Barker flipped over instantly.

Alex moved between his legs and lifted them over his shoulder. He felt the power in those thighs; one sneeze would crush him like a bug. He stroked his cock, getting it ready to plow into his captor. He found a tube of lube and greased his rod.

The fat mushroom end found his opening and slipped in easily. As his belly hit Barker's taint, he grabbed between his legs, found his cock, and applied the unused lube from his hand. His grasp slipped up and down as he pistoned into him.

Captain Barker arched his back and encouraged deeper, deeper. "Faster, harder, faster."

Alex increased his speed on the greased crease and tightened his hold on the throbbing dick. Pre-cum mixed with the lube and poured over both men.

Alex could feel the load in his balls rising closer to the surface. He didn't know how much longer he could go. "Take that," he said with each thrust.

Barker gasped and said, "Oh yeah."

Alex jacked his cock faster and slammed into him deeper. His dick found the prostate and started the nuclear meltdown. Hot cum flowed over his hand as it shot out of Captain Barker's dick. As the spunk flowed, Alex's cock released and filled Barker's ass. Another wave hit his prostate and sent more cum out of his cock.

Barker closed his eyes as the pleasure burned across his body. Wave after wave of pure energy flowed between the two men. Alex collapsed on top of Barker's body.

Both men lay in each other's embrace as the pulsating joy slowly calmed back down. Each nerve screamed at any sudden movement.

Alex pushed up, his cock still deep inside Barker. "How was that?"

Barker opened his eyes. "Amazing."

Cooper popped up, "How about this?" He thrust the tranquilizer into Barker's chest.

Captain Barker sprang up with Alex still inside, but he didn't get far, before his body went limp.

"What is that ancient saying? The bigger they are, the harder they fall?" Copper helped Alex extract himself from his captor.

"Oh, but he was fine." Alex looked down at his sleeping captive. "Let's secure him and figure out what happened."

Dr. Cavanaugh reappeared. "The air filtration system is working, and the crew will awaken shortly. Nice job Alex, I can see you taking over command of this MarsBase sooner than ever."

"Cooper helped."

"Everyone needs a right hand man." Dr. Cavanaugh motioned to Captain Barker. "Why don't we put him in suspended animation, and then you can shower."

They dragged Captain Barker to the chamber and sealed him in.

Alex stood dripping on the floor as they looked at the suspended captor.

Cooper handed him a new, clean robe, just as the alarms started again. Red lights flashed as the computer monitor scrolled and blinked.

"Alex, I'm afraid you'll have to save us again naked and without a shower," Dr. Cavanaugh said.

Alex and Cooper took off running.

TEASING MR. TUTTLE — A NOVELLA
By R. W. Clinger

PART 1 — HUNTER UNBOUND

That hot little motherfucker of nineteen was teasing me, wasn't he? Hunter Craig from Allentown, Pennsylvania. The soccer player, guitar player, jogger, movie buff, and Joyce Carol Oates fanatic. I knew he was teasing me. The way he looked at me. The way he followed me. The way he stalked me. The way he found his way into my office and waited for me, wanting to discuss the most ridiculous things: the weather, my ties, where I liked to eat dinner, and my singlehood as a gay, adult man who taught a variety of English classes at West End College, next to the Falls and Lake Erie. He was half my age, but he didn't care. He was a tormenter who was driving me mad. And he really didn't give a fuck about doing it, did he?

That beautiful young man teased me because I was gay. He somehow discovered I liked to suck a man's cock, among other masculine body parts. He had control over me and believed he was more powerful than I. An Alpha Boy. Nineteen and dangerous. Curious of my world. An instigator of my semi-insanity. The controller of the nine-inch cock between my legs.

Bottom line: Hunter hunted me.

When he didn't sit in the third row back, to the far left side of Room 304, his visual beauty teased me within my mind: five-eleven frame, bulky for a soccer player with a muscular chest, rigid jaw, 190 pounds, thick black hair with long sideburns, a pierced eyebrow, challenging green eyes, and a tapered waist. I wondered if he had a hairy chest or not. I wanted to know if his nipples were more red than pink. How massive was his dick? I desired nothing less than to discover if the shaft between his legs was ten inches long and veined and ...

What did he see in an older man such as me? I was his puppet and he knew it. Something he enjoyed playing with, immensely, almost rudely. Did he really like my salt and pepper hair, gold-rimmed glasses, lean six-two frame, crystal blue eyes, and 200 pounds? Was Hunter a fan of my aged hands, which already showed a few wrinkles at forty-nine? Was he comfortable admiring the crow's feet around my eyes? Did he mind my slow walk and very few words of conversation? Was the young man aware that I was almost an antique who enjoyed shopping for antiques? Did he even realize that I had lost of a number of lovers in my youth, some of which died from AIDS in the eighties? Was he privy to the fact that sometimes I had a creak at the nape of my back, or achy legs after my long days of carrying out my lectures at the college?

I wondered. Of course, I wondered.

What sane professor wouldn't?

I taught that handsome prick how to write in Composition 201, a sophomore class at West End College. We met three days a week from eleven in the morning until one in the afternoon: Monday, Wednesday, and Thursday. The elements of writing were discussed: time, place, characterization, theme, narrative, dialogue, symbolism, irony, foreshadowing, climax, and others.

And Hunter wanted to teach me the elements of him: drinking, smoking pot, how he wanted me to touch his biceps and chest with my fingertips, pinching his nipples, the act of having his cock inside my mouth, and having his rod in my ass.

# # # # #

October was warm; I remember that. The temperature was sky-reaching. Students were dressed in shorts and skimpy shirts that read WEST END COLLEGE — MERTH, NEW YORK.

Hunter arrived in my class wearing a skin-tight wife beater the color of ivory elephant tusks. A horizontal red and blue stripe zigzagged across his center, covering most of his pumped pecs. I recall teaching that particular class about adding atmosphere to a fictional piece. His eyes never left mine. He never blinked. I was a magnet, and he was attracted to me in the oddest manner; an action between us that I simply adored again and again.

During the end of my lecture, I remember: he pulled the right strap of his wife beater to the center of his chiseled chest and exposed his plump pec and firm nipple just for my pleasure. I was stunned to see him accomplish that. I was blown away. How seductive that little prick was, showing off his skin to me, proving to me that his chest was completely hairless, or freshly shaven. What a tease he was, causing me to stutter and lose track of my notes/thoughts/lecture. Damn him.

It happened a second time in my classroom, approximately three days later. Hunter walked into Room 304 and placed a red delicious apple on the corner of my desk, which caused me to feel sinful. With his back to those students who entered the room and filled the seats, he lifted up his navy-colored tee and showed off his rippled torso. A ladder-like structure was chiseled into his stomach's skin. His puckered navel was hairless, and the soccer player's skin was smooth and soft looking, spray-tanned and ...

"Thank you, Hunter," is all I could muster.

"You're very welcome, Mr. Tuttle," the young man responded, dropped the bottom of his T-shirt, and eventually returned to his seat.

Nothing else was said between us that day. When I taught the twenty-three students, including Hunter, I purposely looked away from him, for fear that an erection would build under my pressed Docker's.

# # # # #

October 10. How did he learn about my birthday? Certainly not from Facebook, which I chose not to use, believing it slaughter to human nature. Did he secretly woo the dean, Mrs. China Dawn, and thieve my personal file and review its contents, learning many things about me? My attendance at Pitt for four years. My obtained master's degree at Edin University in Ohio. My two years in the Peace Corps. My published novella called *Frost Unbound*. The bookstore I once owned called Pandom Books on Histon Street in downtown Buffalo, New York, some twenty years ago. Did he ...

A birthday present awaited me in Room 304 upon my arrival. It was wrapped in my favorite color: forest green. A white bow garnished its top. A tiny card leaned into the gift. On the front of the card were my initials: CAT, which stood for Caden Adam Tuttle.

I discovered the card with two fingers, opened it, and read Hunter's script:

C:

Enjoy me. Happy Birthday.

H.

Inside the wrapped present were ten photos of the young man, each more prolific than the one before it: Hunter smiling into the camera; Hunter licking a lollipop; Hunter kissing his own bicep; Hunter pinching one of his nipples; a bare-chested Hunter with whipped cream sprayed between his mounded pecs; Hunter showing off the crack of his hairless ass; Hunter presenting one of his ass cheeks; Hunter sporting his navel and the V-area of his thick and dark patch of pubic tangles above his hidden cock; Hunter exposing his dick to me, which was limp and long and cut and veined and most beautiful; Hunter with a ten-inch erection; the tip of Hunter's spike coated with his own goo.

I sported my own erection when viewing the photographs, embarrassing myself. Quickly, I boxed up the glossy prints, gathered the envelope and card and bow, and shoved the grouping under a stack of students' essays. Next, I took a sip of my cold coffee, which sat on the right side of my desk, swallowed it down, closed my eyes, and listened to the students enter the room, one by one, taking their seats, all of them perhaps unprepared for a quiz on rising action.

"Mr. Tuttle? ... Mr. Tuttle?" Hunter stood across from my desk, waking me from my daydreaming moment alone before the quiz.

I opened my eyes, smiled at him, imagined the young prick out of his clothes, perfectly beautiful, and with an erection between his legs, which I guessed was ten inches long, perhaps even longer. "Yes?" slipped out of my mouth as a whisper.

He leaned over my desk and mumbled, "Happy birthday, Mr. Tuttle. I hope you're doing something groovy with your evening."

"Thank you, Mr. Craig," I replied, wanting to fake a smile with him, but couldn't bring myself to do so, since he seemed to melt my heart and have almost complete control over me.

My first mistake with that young man was rather simple: I shouldn't have kept the ten photographs and promptly returned them to him.

My second mistake with Hunter was just as simple as the first: he flunked my quiz that day, but I passed him anyway; shame on me.

I admit today: I was a weak man, and Hunter Craig was ... model-like, a beautiful motherfucker in my eyes. Every professor had his weakness, and mine just happened to be in Composition 201, Room 304.

I confess here and now: Hunter had me, and he knew he had me. He caught me, realizing my weakness, my sin, and my endearing passion for younger men. The student played me, if the truth be known. He was calling the shots. I was his pet, toy … something.

What would he accomplish next with me?

I wondered. Of course, I wondered.

What sane professor wouldn't?

PART 2 — HUNTER'S GAME

October 13. I knew he followed me home after my day at the college. His black Mustang was seen numerous times in my rearview mirror: turning left on Messner Avenue; making a right onto Smithfield; stopping at the light on the corners of Bent and Stowe. He followed me all the way home, keeping a satisfactory distance behind me.

Did Hunter think I saw him? Did he care? What kind of young man was he that he felt comfortable following an older man such as me? An almost-fifty year old gentleman who may have had the slightest crush on his chiseled physique, charming smile that reminded me of a boy's, and those challenging green eyes that I wanted to dive into and drown, so easily.

What did Hunter Craig want with me?

Better yet: What did I want with him?

# # # # #

Inside and protected at 271 Shade Street in downtown Merth, I was being watched. Hunter watched the house … and me. I felt him outside, spying on my every move, teasing me, and obeying his thirst for me. How intrigued we were of each other. How uncivilized. How … exciting, if the truth be told in this tale of queer men.

I swear, when I went to bed that night, Hunter had found his way into the house. I assumed one of the sliding windows on the east side of the Tudor wasn't locked and he climbed through it and found himself inside. Was it my mind playing tricks on me or not? Did he really find his way upstairs, outside my bedroom, and stand there for an hour ... two hours ... almost three hours, and watch me sleep, thinking of those naughty sex games that nineteen-year-olds like to think about?

No one was there, of course. A silly professor just believed the black-haired young man was outside his bedroom door. I was playing tricks on myself; shame on me. Sleep came, I followed it, and fell into its cozy dreams until a sun-bleached dawn.

More gifts arrived inside my office at West End College. The naughtiest gifts: handcuffs, a ten-inch dildo, a whip, a studded-leather collar, a nipple clamp, a butt plug, numerous cock rings, and other sexual toys that I found exhilarating; the perfect gifts for a man such as me.

Did that cock of nineteen, one of my prized students, someone who had caused erections to form within my Docker's ... did he know I liked to be tied up? Was he at all familiar with the concept that I enjoyed being bitten? Had he spoken to one of my ex-lovers and discovered that I enjoyed a good ass-slap or bitten shoulder? Or, was he merely guessing my sexual delights and knew nothing of my wild bed antics? I didn't know, but guessed that someday ... I would eventually find out.

The next day, Hunter decided to stay after class to discuss a paper on theme with me. He was disappointed in his grade, a B-, and thought he should have received an A. I was pretty clear that his sentence structure wasn't strong enough for him to earn an A.

He changed the subject; how clever. Hunter said my office was too hot, and he stripped out of his T-shirt, dropping it to the floor. There, I studied his lined abs, plump pecs, firm nipples, and his desirable waist. I knew instinctively he was trying to control me, perhaps bargaining a higher grade from me.

Shame on me for giving in, of course. What kind of horrible professor was I? Could I so easily be swayed by a jock's youthful skin to raise his grade from a B- to an A by the mere act of that young man removing his skin-tight shirt? Was it even considered ethical to do that? Could I have been fired?

I wondered. Of course, I wondered.

What sane professor wouldn't?

And the next day ... he followed my BMW X3 SAV to Ashtabula, Ohio, where an old friend and mentor of mine resided. One of my own school teachers from Shotendale High School: the one and only Mr. Randall Hobbias; my prized twelfth grade advanced English teacher whom I looked up to and wanted to become.

Hunter followed me in his sleek and black Mustang. Every left turn. Every right turn. Every hill. The young man was experienced behind his wheel, a NASCAR driver of sorts, which caused a bit of tingling emotion to occur between my legs that I found rather delightful, yet uncomfortable.

Never did we make eye contact on that day trip. Never did I confront him, although I knew he followed me throughout that entire day. Never did we collide ... as I often wanted to collide with him, of course.

And the next day ... somehow that young bitch of a man found his way into my Tudor and used my shower. I knew he purposely drained my bottle of Prell and tossed my bar of used Irish Spring into the bathroom's garbage can. Proof existed that he had showered and dried off with my towel, since it was damp and hung limp on the stainless steel bar behind the bathroom door, exactly where I had kept it nicely hung each and every day. My razor was missing from the shower, too; I was sure the little shit thieved it from the shower and showcased it in a glass box back at his apartment, titling the box: PRECIOUS THINGS STOLEN FROM MR. TUTTLE.

I wasn't afraid of Hunter Craig. In fact, I adored him, and enjoyed his mysterious games of guy-play. Often, I wanted to confront him regarding his bizarre antics: stealing things from my house, following me, showering in my personal bathroom, stripping out of his clothes in my office at the college, and other wildly unclear events. If I did confront him, though, his game would end, which I really didn't want to happen. I liked being the center of his attention, preyed upon, secretly watched, and the person he provided gifts to. I was his toy, a pet of sorts. Maybe I was the man he wanted to bed. Did he wish to digest every inch of my adult skin? Hunter wanted me, I was pretty sure, and had control over me, undoubtedly.

Someday I would give into his needs/cravings. I was a very weak man, if you want to know the truth. I would break down by his spell, and he would have me ... all to himself, greedily.

I created a list of questions and answers for my personal use regarding the nineteen-year-old. I designed and pondered the list in my office at the college, staying after my classes. The list's information entailed:

Q: What does Hunter want with me?

A: Sex. Games. Control over me.

Q: Does he know that I can't cross a line of ethics because of my position at the college?

A: He doesn't really give a crank about me. What he cares about is his cock and wanting to shove it into one of my holes.

Q: What will happen if I ignore him?

A: A man is never happy until he wins his game. Hunter will continue his task until he has me.

Q: If I fall for him, how long will he decide to keep me?

A: Young men like Hunter never have intentions of keeping older men like me.

Q: Am I just a task on his college bucket list to nail with his cock?

A: Better that than not having my ass touched at all.

# # # # #

It was still hot for October. Summer-like temperatures rose to their fullest potential. The sun baked us like grapes. I came home from the college and took a long nap in my upstairs bedroom. There, tucked within a folded dream, Hunter was swimming laps in my pool, skinny dipping. The young man glided to and fro in the blue-green water. His ass was bulbous and bleached white, unexposed from the forgotten summertime sun in August. He was graceful under the water, froglike, and rather beautiful. The man's biceps and back were all muscle. His shoulders gleamed underneath the water, and his legs were long and strong, kicking rather dramatically in the liquid.

I woke from the dream to my cellular phone ringing, which sat on the night stand to the right side of my bed. I discovered the phone, tried to study the incoming number, really couldn't see it because I was half-asleep, pressed one of its many buttons, and groggily said, "Hello."

No one was there. Nothing. Silence. Hunter was playing a trick on me that I sleepily absorbed. Some ludicrous game that young college men tend to get-off on: teasing Mr. Tuttle to their fullest potential. Spirited antics that seemed rather juvenile but ballsy. I pressed another button on the phone to turn it off, tossed it on the queen-size bed at my side, closed my eyes, yawned, and helplessly drifted back into my nap.

PART 3 — HUNTED: MR. TUTTLE

William Pike, my best queer friend of three decades, fetched me from my Tudor later that evening and demanded we share a cup of coffee at Darwin's Coffee House on Shore Road in downtown Merth. William was exceptionally handsome for forty-three and could have easily passed as a Bradley Cooper look-alike. His blue eyes were just as intoxicating as the actor's, and his beaming-white smile exemplified true happiness. William was also a professor at West End College, practicing in world literature. His studies of interest included the Peloponnesian War and Caesar's lovers. The man was a genius in my opinion, rather fun to be around, and adored.

Of course, he was sporty and arrived in his over-the-top Mercedes-Benz SLK-Class. William, I knew, enjoyed his expensive toys, even if he couldn't really afford them. Perhaps that is why he often visited his wealthy Aunt Charlie in Pittsburgh, a steel mill tycoon's widow, who had more money than God, and loved her only nephew to the fullest.

Darwin's Coffee House was a queer man's paradise. Racy, adorable young baristas waited on us. William was infatuated with one of the men; a twenty-something ginger headed god named Calvin. Both flirted heavily with each other, and the pair giggled like little boys in conversation, shared winks, and Calvin eventually gave William his cell phone number, and a free latte.

We drank our light, Madagascar lattes at the front of the house and observed passersby in the evening hour. There, we absorbed the brown and black hues of the business, the smell of chocolate, pumpernickel rolls, and freshly sliced blackberry tea bread. And there, we started to chat, mostly of Hunter Craig and his mischievous antics.

"Tell me about this little student-chap who is sexually torturing you, Tuttle," William supplied, beaming with his irresistible actor's smile, adding a modest wink.

Almost daily I had provided my best friend with Hunter tales. "He's horrible. Insane. Dramatic. And he makes me hard."

William tilted his head back and heartily shared a laugh with me. "Young men are teases. What do you plan on doing about Mr. Craig?"

"I'm in no position to do anything regarding the young man. He's my student. I vow not to cross a line with him, even if he is the sexiest creature on the planet," I declared, enjoying yet another sip of my coffee, and the October evening at hand, mixed with his company.

He laughed at me: sharp, steady, and blatant. "You're lying to yourself. I know you well, Mr. Tuttle. You'll be fucking Hunter before Thanksgiving. I believe you just may be teasing him as much as he is teasing you."

I dramatically shifted my head east and west and objected. "The boy has control over me. He's very smart that way."

"An Alpha Boy … that's what they're called. They like to have power over older men, particularly when it comes to sex."

"He's only nineteen," I prattled. "How can a boy his age have sexual authority over me?"

William giggled. "Ask yourself that, mate. I think Hunter is doing one over you. You're putty in his palms, and soon enough he'll have his dick inside you."

Our coffee event expired, and William dropped me off on Shade Street. There, I kissed his cheek, told him goodbye, and thanked him for our evening together.

"Keep your rump protected, Tuttle. That boy wants it."

"I'll try my hardest," I supplied, and vanished into my Tudor.

Half of me expected Hunter to be hidden somewhere in the house; that wasn't the case, though. After checking every room, playing a game of hide-and-seek with the young man, I found the Tudor empty of his presence.

Of course, I checked the fenced-in backyard which overlooked Lake Erie. Perhaps the young man was hiding behind one of the old oaks or slouched in the sleeping garage-sized greenhouse. Truth was, the lawn was bare as well as the greenhouse. The boy's succulent and youthful goods were not seen, which left me alone on my premises, spirited with the thoughts of Hunter Craig's beautiful body mixing with my own, intentionally.

# # # # #

October 20. That night I had a vigorous dream of Hunter and my body colliding:

The young student found his way into the Tudor through an open window, stripped out of his clothes somewhere in the dining room, discovered his way upstairs, and stepped into my bedroom.

There, I was naked, motionless on my sheets with an upright nine-inch spike between my legs. I smiled at the hunter, winked, and said, "Give me your best lick, pal. Show me what you've got."

Again, I studied the man on the other side of the dimly lit room: hairless chest with popping nipples, five-eleven frame, bulky for a soccer player, rigid jaw, 190 pounds, thick black hair with long sideburns, his pierced eyebrow, challenging green eyes, tapered waist, thick spirals of coal-black hair above his ten-inch spike, droopy balls covered in tangles of the same colored hair, and chiseled thighs.

Hunter climbed onto the bed and nestled himself between my sweltering legs. His lips met the tip of my cut cock, and his tongue twirled around its mushroom-shaped head.

"Down," I whispered, and pressed the back of his head southward, prompting the man to lodge my fat cock into his narrow throat.

It happened with such zeal: Hunter blew me in rapid motion, swift with his movement. The student's head rose and fell with a prominent effect. A steady gagging sound escaped his mouth. Shifting bolts filled his face with abrupt motion. The Alpha Boy sucked me with a sufficient speed and unstoppable hunger. He choked on my stick, but kept up his work. North and south motion continued on my throbbing stem. Gurgles escaped the man's mouth. Sweat dripped from his forehead and filled my navel.

I came inside his mouth. Cream rushed out of my flag and filled the back of his throat. My ooze attempted to drown the man. Sticky goop lathered his throat and dripped out the corners of his mouth. Hunter gagged on my load and swallowed as much of it inside his system. A string of the wad hung from his bottom lip when he lifted off my spent pole and …

I woke in the middle of the night with a stinging shaft between my legs. A bubble of cock-sap hung at its tip, which I wiped away with my right index finger. I fed myself the bittersweet treat, obeying my own hunger. Awake on my queen-size bed, I began to stroke myself off: speedily, with much skill, willed to blow my load. And there, nestled on the sheets, my balls flung to and fro, slapping against my ass, excited and into my fleshy gig. Five handy strokes turned into twenty. My breathing intensified. Visions of Hunter Craig blowing me filled every crevice and corner of my hyperactive mind. I moaned with pleasure and gritted my teeth, deeply satisfied with my self-performance. My fists rocked up and down, steadily … and spirals of Hunter-induced seed rocketed out of my hose. The glue decorated my hairless abs as a wash of euphoria spread throughout my entire body, from head to toe, and I became spent. There, I drifted off to sleep with sticky abs, a cream-filled navel, and jizm-lathered private parts; a smile of complete gratification covered my face.

The following day, I taught about symbolism: the motion or movement in literature that accentuates disconnected descriptions of feelings and thoughts. The piece we discussed as a class consisted of James Baldwin's novel *Giovanni's Room*. Such comments entailed: Joey's room in Brooklyn as reclusive; Giovanni's prison cell as suffocation, like a kiss; David's longing and guilt for Giovanni; a stopwatch mentioned in the novel is ...

Hunter was in the class, but his attention to my lecture was elsewhere. Nor, was he involved in the conversation with the other students about the novel, which was carried out after my lecture. Instead, he seemed to stare at me with a dazzled and hungry look about his face. If I didn't know any better, that expression clearly stated that he was in love with me. The student blinked a few times and smiled at me. And discreetly, he blew me a kiss, teasing me again, which made me feel hard between my legs, ready for whatever could happen between a professor and his liked student, honestly.

As some blonde-headed cheerleader type girl of eighteen rambled on and on about disliking the symbolism in the novel, I imagined Hunter alone with me inside Room 304.

Within the folds of my mind, between my temples:

There, he ripped my shirt off and tossed it to the white tile floor. And there, he unbuckled my belt, dropped my khakis to my ankles, and fingered my black briefs, fondling my cotton-covered cock and balls, obviously satisfying himself. My desk was immediately cleaned off; one of his arms splayed across its flat surface and knocked papers, pens, and textbooks to the floor. I was pressed against the desk, falling backwards. My chest was lathered with his tongue, and my nipples were fondly bitten. Hunter rolled his fingertips over my rigid abs, along my sides, and pressed his palms against the spot between my identical pecs. There, he opened his mouth and ...

Following class, Hunter decided to stay late. He locked the door to Room 304, peeled his shirt off and dropped it to the white tile. The gorgeous prick sported a beautiful chest that was model-fantastic, and sauntered up to my desk.

I was not dreaming. That moment inside my classroom was not my mind playing games on me. Hunter was truly there, positioned at the left side of my desk with his crotch in my face. Those seconds with the nineteen-year-old sophomore were real, not a figment of my imagination or pretentious lust. Hunter was there — real.

Perhaps confused about the class's syllabus or his homework regarding his analysis of *Giovanni's Room*, the young man unzipped his blue-and-white plaid shorts and yanked out his dick. Within seconds, he presented his ten inches of cut shaft in his two palms as if it were a loaf of bread. Hunter stared down at me, grinned wildly, perhaps crazily, and said, "Go ahead and touch it if you want … It doesn't bite."

Yes, I did want to touch his veined and beautiful cock. In fact, I wanted to lick its firm length, suck on its rounded head, and consume all ten inches of the beast down the back of my throat. Truth was, I desired nothing more than to have his flag inside my bottom: all ten inches of its inflated protein shoved deep into my tight core where it could easily puncture my functioning organs.

"Hunter," escaped my lips in a whisper. "What are you doing?"

He moved the tip of his spike closer to my lips; I'm sure he felt me breathing on the meat. The young man chanted down to me, "Give it a taste, Mr. Tuttle. You're dying to eat me up."

I was; shame on him for knowing that. Every time I saw Hunter Craig … I wanted his strapping good looks to collide with my own, among other facets of male-with-male action. Yes, I wanted him badly, in every way possible, mixing an older man with his youthful flesh.

At that very second between reality and the action of lust between masculine partners, I pulled my face away from his offered tool, quickly shook my head, and explained, "Not here,

Hunter. This is my place of work. It would be highly unprofessional of me to carry out such naughty things with you in this classroom."

Before he could respond to my rejection, before he could press me over the desk in Room 304 and have his horny way with my hungry ass, processing his Alpha Boy behavior ... I gathered up my textbooks, notes, and coffee mug from the desk's surface. I stood and walked out of the room, escaping his sexy side, abandoning the boy, and his bliss. Silent. Daunted. Sexually enlightened. Into the young man, wholly.

PART 4 — HUNTER EXPOSED

October 31. Halloween. Friday evening. Trick-or-treaters floated around Merth in their costumes: ghosts, goblins, fairies, princesses, hunters, zombies, aliens, cartoon characters, comic book characters, wolves, and vampires. Hunter arrived in a Nixon mask and banged on my front door three times. I answered the door in a pair of running shorts, snug T-shirt, and a pair of Hanes bootie socks. Upon opening the door, he said "Trick-or-treat." The zipper on his jeans was pulled down and his beef flopped out; his two balls were still hidden inside his denim.

"Are you the trick or the treat?" I asked, grinning from ear to ear.

"It depends what you want me to be, Mr. Tuttle."

"Mr. Tuttle wants you to come into the house, so you stop exposing yourself to my neighbors."

"No one can see my shaft except for you," he informed, tapping his Nixon-dick with two fingertips.

I laughed, welcoming him inside my Tudor, closing and locking the door behind him, selfishly swept by his sex-spell yet again. What was a professor to do when he was interested in one of his hot students?

"It's windy out there," he confessed, removing the Nixon mask from his handsome face.

It was windy. Autumn had finally crept upon Merth. The temperature had severely dropped in the past week. Leaves were starting to change color and drop from their trees. It was the time of year to cuddle with another man to keep warm, whether he be a student or not ... whatever it took.

Hunter dropped the mask to the living room floor, kept his wanker out of its jeans, and asked, "You want a show tonight?"

"What kind of show?" I stood next to my Swedish sofa and enjoyed the young man's visit. What other forty-nine year old man had that divine opportunity to share such an intimate moment with an eye-catching jock inside his living room? Not many, I believed. None, in fact, that I knew of.

"An autumn show. One of my best. You don't have to pay me for it."

"What does that entail, Hunter?"

He shook the goods between his legs with his right hand and laughed. "A jackoff show. I'm sure you want one."

"How do you know that?"

"I know a lot about older men. The way they desire me. The way they look at me. The way I have the ability to get what I want from them."

"What do you want from me?" I inquired, admiring his seven inches of soft shaft, his zipper and a thin follicle of pubic hair that fell out of his denim hole for my pleasure.

"You know what I want from you, Mr. Tuttle," he said, winking at me.

"You're a tease. Why do you want me when you can have a million other guys with your good looks?"

"You fit my bill. Other guys don't make me hard like you do. Plus, I enjoy this game I have going on with you."

"What kind of game is that, Mr. Craig?"

"Why don't I show you?"

I didn't object. Why would I? Hunter was what I desired in a younger man: my longing cured, everything I was not, the perfect medicine for me to feel younger, more handsome, and exuberantly charming ... a drug for my aged needs.

He unbuttoned his jeans and dropped them to the living room floor. He tugged his T-shirt over his head and added it to his jeans on the floor. The student spread his feet and grabbed the tool between his legs with both palms. Quick and steady jolts occurred to his beef as he pumped life into his private part — a full ten inches of veined niceness. Stroke after stroke ensued. The young man grunted as he bucked his fists. Sweat flung off his forehead and spiraled toward me. Another set of grunts escaped the man, which filled the living room. He arched his back, breathed heavily, and continued to manipulate his meat for the next minute ... three minutes ... five minutes, until he eventually stopped and grinned at me.

"You're teasing me again," I said, observing his game of Alpha Boy tactics.

He laughed, "Someone has to. You don't want your dick to shrivel up and fall off, right?"

"Now, you're being a smartass."

"Better than a dumbass," he replied, and gave his nipples a tug with two fingertips, one after the other.

Hunter toyed with his cock, strumming its excess skin with his right hand, jacking the tool up and down with feisty motion, and sporting a wide grin across his adorable face that told me I was a lucky man to have someone so handsome and so young to be in my presence; something I certainly didn't disagree with.

227

I recall the wind beating against the window and children screaming outside on the streets, enjoying their evening of trick-or-treating. A storm had found its way down from Canada and was ready to take over Merth (and surrounding cities) with a tedious game of its own.

My student helped himself to the sofa within the living room. I remember now how he played with himself: tenderly spanking his meat with swift strokes; massaging his balls with a cupped, left hand; wetting his right nipple with two fingertips and pulling at it.

I stood on the opposite side of the room and watched him toy with his body parts. Once, a gasp of excitement exited my lips and I glowed with deep satisfaction. The crank beneath my shorts came to life and leaked inside their cotton. My chest rose and fell with bliss, anticipating Hunter's explosion; the continuation of his naughty game.

"My God," exited my lips as I watched the man spread his legs and show off his pink and tight hole for my pleasure. There, seated on the sofa, two fingertips brushed against his cavern's tightness. One digit entered his bottom, he moaned, and eventually pulled the digit out. Again and again, that fingertip entered his rump, pulled free, and entered again. I was left awestruck, uncomfortable, and at a loss for words, so very stiff between my legs, perhaps over-excited.

While his right hand tugged on his beef in a hyper manner, Hunter's left hand was busy on his own asshole. Together, the hands worked in synchronized motion: up and down; left and right. The soccer player murmured rather confusing sounds on the Swedish sofa. Feisty hip-thrusts occurred, a gasp for breath, a long whine, and my hunter turned a shade of bright red in his face.

"Watch me shoot my load, Mr. Tuttle," he eventually found the strength to whisper across the room to me.

"I'm all eyes, guy ... Do your thing." Honestly, I was stinging hard between my legs and wanted to play with my own stick. Instead, I chose to be a voyeur and nothing more, relishing that spine-numbing and euphoric time within my living room with him.

Following a rash of east and west fingertip-plunges into his bottom, and a mixture of groans and murmurs within the room, Hunter pulled the finger away from his prized canal and applied his second fist to the upright and solid staff between his thighs. There, he began to use both of his palms on his joint: speedy north and south toying on his cock's excess skin; mouth hung ajar; winded and sweating.

"Shoot your wad," I coached, intoxicated by his action on the sofa, and pleasured to the fullest.

It took a matter of seconds for the young man to blow his load. After a string of huffs and puffs mixed with swift, up and down jolts to his throbber, he exclaimed with clenched teeth, "Firing, Mr. Tuttle."

What transpired was nothing less than amazing for me. He gave his hips a last bolt into his busy fists, which was then followed by a simple groan of jubilation, and twirls of spew erupted from his rod and spun into his semi-opened mouth. More man-liquid flew out of his spigot, shot into mid-air, and fell to his plated stomach. In doing so, he left out more groans and assisted his shoot-fest with a collection of humps, happy to release his cream, becoming spent.

"Eat it all up," I suggested from my reading chair in the living room. "Don't miss a single drop, Hunter. Some men would pay for your blow."

He grinned wildly at me, into our engagement. "Who's calling the shots now?" he asked, which totally caught me off guard.

"What can I say, I like it when a guy eats his own shoot."

Hunter kept that attractive grin smeared over his jock-cute face and replied, "Want to help me, pal?"

"I like to watch. Go for it."

He listened. Why wouldn't he? The man on the sofa rolled his right hand up and along his chest and gathered goo on his fingers. Once the fingers met his mouth, he licked every single one of them until they were clean. In a matter of seconds, the soccer player was completely tidy of his sticky mess, happy with his feeding, and burped, which caused us both to laugh with playful enjoyment.

Ten minutes later, he decided to climb off the sofa and dress.

"Leaving so soon?" I asked, intrigued with his behavior.

While he stepped into his jeans, he supplied, "You've had plenty of candy for one night, sir."

"You really don't have to run off if you don't want to."

He shook his head, determined about his exit. "I have soccer first thing in the morning. Two games. I need some rest."

"I have a spare room. You can rest here." I sounded desperate, almost begging him to spend the night with me; shame on me for being so forward.

"Trust me, I like your offer, Mr. Tuttle. I just need to sleep in my own bed tonight, so I'm well-rested for tomorrow."

I agreed, understanding his predicament, and dropped the topic. We hugged before he left, but didn't kiss. Then, I offered him a good night's rest, a gentle pat on his strong back, and escorted him out my front door, telling him goodbye.

# # # # #

That night, tucked into my own bed under a goose-feathered blanket, I barely slept. One name kept slipping between the folds of my mind: Hunter Craig. And scenes captured the space between my temples: the soccer player intoxicatingly staring at me in Room 304; Hunter spying on me, following me around the city in his Mustang; the many gifts the young man had shared with me; the way he enjoyed teasing me, always catching me off guard; his untimely visits to my Tudor, sexually obeying his thirst for my skin.

I tossed and turned most of the night away. Once, I found myself pacing the upstairs hallway, captured by insomnia. I even tried to drink warm milk, counted sheep while studying my bedroom ceiling, and started to read, which I believed would cause me to grow sleepy. None of those tactics worked, though. Instead, I stared into the darkness of my room and whispered that single name again and again, until dawn: Hunter Craig.

PART 5 – HUNTERLUST

"You watched him jerk off?" William asked, sipping two fingers of an expensive whiskey over ice at a boy-bar called Tangelo's.

"I did. He showed up at the Tudor unannounced, undressed, did his deed with his cock, and then he left," I admitted, took a swig of my Rolling Rock, and absorbed Tangelo's: two X-shaped bars, silver walls, rainbow lights abound, and semi-naked male bodies dancing or having public sex in the corners.

William laughed at me, or rather at the situation at hand regarding Hunter. "He's quite the handful, my friend. I would be overjoyed to have someone like him in my life."

"He confuses me."

"He wants to confuse you. It's how he controls you."

"Another Alpha Boy trait, I presume."

"Now you're learning," William replied, consumed another sip of his whiskey, and ogled the beefy and shirtless boys around the bar.

As I sat and sipped my beer, my head rolled with confusion. Hunter was locked within my thoughts. His Alpha Boy tactics had certainly manipulated me on various levels: emotionally, psychologically, and physically. The young man was like a jockish sprite to me: playful and whimsical, always toying with me. He truly did have a certain power over me, influencing my unstoppable desires like a puppet master. He was manipulatively evil in that aspect; a tyrant of my fragile condition. If he wanted me, why hadn't he had me as of yet? I would have gladly stripped out of my clothes and spent the night with him. Hell, I practically begged him to do a sleepover on Halloween night with me, but he kindly rejected my proposal. If the Alpha Boy desired my older skin, why was he taking so long to take advantage of it? That is what I wanted to know, truthfully.

A young man pulled me out of my thoughts at the bar, licked my left earlobe, and whispered into my ear, "Do you want to dance with me?"

I blinked, discovered consciousness again, turned my head to the stranger, and consumed his Hollywood looks: curly blond hair, unpredictable green eyes, tenderly sloped nose, goatee, California suntan, silver hoops in both ears. The guy had his right palm on one of my inner thighs, which moved up to my cock, and it obviously wanted to play.

William leaned into my other ear, giggled like a twelve-year-old boy, and chanted, "Go for it. You're not getting any younger, Mr. Tuttle. Don't waste the night away with me."

The handsome stranger already had me hard. His left palm secured over my private parts didn't help much, of course. Within seconds, I consumed another swig of my long-neck, swallowed the beer down, turned my attention to the

Hollywood actor next to me, and said, "I only dance to Lady Gaga."

His name was Scott Randall and he said I could take his shirt off and squeeze his bronze nipples with my fingertips, but only if I wanted to. Of course, I took him up on his offer, unbuttoned his cotton shirt, reached inside, and discovered his rigid chest with both palms and all of my fingers. There, while dancing to "Edge of Glory," I fingered his nipples, squeezing them. And there, having our hips connected and his palms on my sides, he leaned into me and dove his tongue down the back of my throat. One of his hands eventually removed itself from my side and fell into my jeans. Within seconds, Scott Randall found exactly what he was looking for: a curly, pubic triangle of salt-and-pepper hair and nine throbbing inches of Mr. Tuttle.

I was half-tempted to accept Scott's offer to leave the bar and end up back at his apartment, which he shared with three other Hollywood-types: Branden, Michael, and Vinnie. Of course, I would have fucked him, adoring his twenty-two-year-old body on his full-size bed, obeying my thirst. Truth was, Hunter infiltrated my mind like a disease, and I couldn't remove him. Cordially, I declined Mr. Hollywood's offer to spend the night (and a possible morning) with him. Instead, following our dance, I kissed his cheek, apologized for wasting his time, and watched him vanish from my life, just as quickly as he had arrived.

To my surprise, not even ten minutes later, I consumed the rest of my beer at William's side, and Hunter entered Tangelo's. My student was dressed in a sky-blue tank that made his chest look like steel, and a pair of Diesel jeans. Rawhide sandals decorated his feet, and an ear-to-ear smile graced his Alpha Boy face.

Hunter pulled up beside me at the bar and dove his tongue into my mouth. The kiss was relentless and mind-blowing. His right hand discovered the mound of cock between my legs, which he provided with a quick rub. When the kiss ended, he pulled away from me, ordered himself a Budweiser from the bartender, and demanded two shots of whiskey for me, calling the drinks his treat, perhaps willing me to become drunk and rather easy for more of his spirited play.

After his order, he stared solidly into my eyes and said, "You've been kissing another guy. I can taste him on your lips."

William laughed on my other side; I was stuck between them at the bar.

"What can I say, Hunter … you have some competition. You're not the only man in my life."

"Game on," Hunter said, winked at me, and applied another kiss to my mouth, which caused the planets to separate and fall into the universe.

Hunterlust was discovered yet again. The young man's kiss was similar to the sexual tension between Brick and Skipper in *A Cat on a Hot Tin Roof.* The kiss was earth-shaking, spine-clenching, and a catalyst to break down the barrier between a student and his teacher. The kiss was dramatically cleansing, a baptismal affair between men that could easily spark an unlimited sexual connection and long-term relationship.

When the soccer player finally pulled away from me and wiped the back of his hand across his succulent mouth, he said, "I had every desire to track you down tonight."

"How did you find me?" I inquired, enjoying another shot of whiskey that was placed in front me.

Hunter paid for our drinks, winked at me, and said, "I always have you on my radar, Mr. Tuttle. Merth isn't that big. Don't even think you can get away from me."

"You're lying."

"I could be."

"I despise liars," I admitted.

"You adore me," he challenged.

I could say nothing more; the smile on my face acknowledged his rightness.

William was whisked away to the dance floor by a ginger head; his utter weakness when it came to young men. The ginger head looked like a thirty-year-old porn star from head to toe: massive chest, clear complexion, six-two frame, 200 pounds of steel, fall-into green eyes. XXX star took my best friend into his arms and decided to have his way with William, not that my cohort disapproved.

My attention was drawn back to Hunter at my side. How awkward it was of me to think: I want you to tie me up, spank me, and do the naughtiest things to my ass. Those words never escaped the region of my mind, though. Instead, I asked, "When are you going to fuck me, Hunter? What's this game of yours really about?"

He almost choked on his beer. The grin that he shared with me exemplified utter shock. The student then laughed, took another swig of his beer, and confessed, "Are you over my gig, Mr. Tuttle?"

"I'm not."

"Then why did you ask that?"

"Because you make me hard. Because I want you inside my scholar ass, and I want to wear your shoot on my chest."

Again, he almost choked on another swig of beer. Once the choking passed, he inquired, "Are you drunk?"

"A little. I've been doing shots for the last hour."

"That will do it."

"So when do you intend to fuck me?" I boldly asked, cutting to the chase of our relationship. "You know I'm not getting any younger, right?"

"No more shots for you, my friend," he said, cupping my chin with one of his rounded palms, perhaps continuing his adventure to seduce me.

"I'm perfectly fine and know how to handle my alcohol." It was the truth. I enjoyed my whiskey to the fullest and rarely got drunk.

To my left, on the dance floor, the XXX star smooched with William. Both of them were now bare-chested. Outlines of hard cocks decorated their denim jeans. The two men, I guessed, were going to spend the night together at ginger head's abode.

"Older and wiser, aren't you, Mr. Tuttle?"

"Absolutely," I replied and decided to lean into Hunter and supply his lips with a kiss.

He pulled away from me, shook his head. "I call the shots, man. I'm not your game."

"Whatever," I chanted, kissed him again, and felt numb all over, beginning my end to that evening's fun.

William and his XXX star stayed at the bar when I decided to leave, feeling tired and needing some sleep.

Hunter said he wanted to have another drink before he called it a night. We parted with a goodbye, a hug, and the soccer player whispered into my left ear, "If you want to spend the night with me, you can. You know where I live."

I did know where he lived and was quite tempted to take him up on his offer, of course. How couldn't an English professor of forty-nine want to spend a night with a sexy, steel-plated soccer player of nineteen? I would have been a fool to pass up his proposal. Any sane man my age would have jumped on his invitation and the sophomore's ten-inch spike.

Honestly, half of me wanted to see his apartment, since I had never visited it before. I was quite sure the place was uninhabitable and littered with everyday Hunter things: garbage overflowing, jock-clothes strewn over the floor, and dirty dishes piled in the kitchen sink. Hunter, I imagined, was not at all a tidy creature in his apartment; not that that condition would have changed my feelings for him, of course. Untidy or tidy, he still caused me to grow hard with excitement for him; lust of an older man for his Alpha Boy.

"I'll think about it," I told him, escaped his side, and wrapped up my interesting evening at Tangelo's, striding away.

PART 6 — UNDER HUNTER

Perhaps the whiskey shots assisted my sleep that night. I made the drive home, slipped out of my clothes, took a quick shower, and climbed into my queen-size bed in the buff. There, I immediately dozed off, welcomed a night of black and dreamless sleep, and lightly snored.

What time of the night was I awakened by Hunter Craig's intrusion into the Tudor? Three o'clock in the morning? Four o'clock? I wasn't sure. I merely sat straight up in my bed, felt sweat on my forehead and bare chest, and listened to the strange sound of footsteps downstairs. Half of me was terribly frightened, believing it was not Hunter breaking in through one of the dining room's unlocked windows. The other half of me instinctively knew it was the college student, teasing me yet again, since he had broken into the Tudor numerous times before.

There, half-concealed by two blankets on the bed, I listened to the intruder climb the stairs to the second floor. And there, I watched a naked and already hard Hunter enter my bedroom, a mere shadow within the moon's November light.

"Hunter," I whispered his name in the unlimited darkness, and studied his chiseled, but semi-illuminated, body for the umpteenth time: cut abs, V-shaped torso, nipple-hard pecs, full head of dark hair, chiseled face, somewhat iridescent green eyes, and ten inches of upright staff between his bulky thighs, which was ready to be kissed, licked, sucked, or plunged into my bottom — whatever the young man had in mind to carry out with me.

"Mr. Tuttle," he whispered, and positioned two fingertips at the top of his shaft. My student pulled the tool away from his torso, released it, and prompted the device to snap against his sculpted abs, being provocative with me yet again.

"You broke into my house. That's against the law. I should call the cops on you."

"You wanted me to break in. Don't lie to yourself."

Silence. Darkness. Stillness.

"Mr. Tuttle," he eventually said. "You didn't find your way to my apartment."

"Why should I have when you just happened to find your way here?"

Silence. Darkness. Stillness.

"Do you want me?" he asked, a whisper in the night.

"What do you think?"

"I think you always wanted me. I think you were afraid to touch me. I think ..."

"Shut up and come here," I broke off his sentence. "Do what you want with me, young man."

I didn't have to tell the soccer player twice. He moved up to the edge of the bed, climbed aboard, and made his way between my legs. His right hand cupped my balls, and he gave them a little squeeze. His other hand found one of my inner thighs and he grazed fingertips along its smooth skin. Within seconds, he bent over me with his head and extended his tongue, which he applied to the tip of my cock, but quickly pulled away thereafter.

I moaned, "You're playing me again."

"Teasing Mr. Tuttle," he cajoled, and decided to lick the tip of my hose again while fondling my balls.

He had me exactly where he wanted me. The student rolled his tongue against my concave navel, up and along ever ab that lined my stomach, and drove the wet tool over both of my firm nipples. His mouth met my neck and sucked at its veins like a vampire. While doing so, his right hand (or was it his left, I wasn't sure?) toyed with my balls and shaft, rolling his fingers and palms over their smooth and hairy skin.

I was helpless under his connection. The man continued to lick my chest in an aggressive manner. My nipples were swirled with his saliva. My cut abs were garnished with his spittle. My navel was lapped with his extended tongue. And then, seconds after seconds passing, a whirlwind of satisfying emotion, he dove his mouth over my nine-inch hub and began to gag himself with hyper movement.

The blowjob lasted for the next five … nine … thirteen minutes. My balls were tugged on. My ass-slit was rubbed by two of his fingertips. My thighs were pushed apart, so he had easy access for all of my man-gadgets that offered both of us gratification.

I huffed on the bed as he orally took advantage of me. Hunter was wild with my stick inside his throat. His head bobbed up and down in chaotic likeness. He groaned and moaned, attempting to get me off. My student was diligent with his study of my body, into his professor-sport, and wanted me to fire my load.

"Stop," I whined, feeling an eruption begin to take place between my legs. Honestly, I held my load back, though, and desired more sexual amusement from him. "You have to stop, Hunter ... or I'll shoot."

Listening to me, he came off for oxygen, heavily breathed, and then decided to eat my bottom.

My legs were lifted, and his mouth met my rear for the very first time. I murmured his full name three times, arched my back for his easy access, and pushed on the back of his head, shoving his face into my core out of mere hunger.

Hunter was busy with his lips and tongue on my rump. The guy was a superstar between my legs and darted his sliver of slippery appendage inside my center. Again, he pushed my legs apart. Again and again his tongue lapped at my middle, pushed inside, yanked out, and slid back inside.

I growled from his touch. My consciousness was blurred. I became dizzy on the bed, out of breath, and fully into his mouth-engagement.

Was Hunter fucking my bottom with his face? I believed so. Slurps and gurgles escaped the man at my backside. His fingertips pulled my opening apart. His tour was long and tedious, a fun-filled ride between an Alpha Boy and his English professor.

His tongue was eventually replaced with his condom-covered ten inches of student shaft. Hunter found plastic within my bedroom, retrieving it from one of the night stands. (How many times did he trespass into the Tudor and learn where I kept all of my belongings? Too many times to count.) Once his shaft was plastic-coated, it found its way into my buttocks. One inch caused a light scream to escape my mouth. Two inches broke open my center for his thumper's easy access. Three inches punctured my core with a sinister passion. Four inches banged into my bottom, pulled out, and banged inside again. Five inches caused me to lose oxygen. Six inches made me tremble. Seven inches prompted me to lose track of my surroundings. (Where was I? What was happening to me?) Eight inches bucked my bottom with skill and pulverized my insides. Nine inches were agonizing, readily banged my asshole, and smacked against my rear. Ten inches ...

"My God!" I exclaimed under his weight, open for his services — whatever the young man of nineteen had to chaotically offer me.

Pain skied throughout my frame and caused my toes to curl. I huffed and puffed with ardor, locked under his muscular weight. My shaft bounced against my abs and navel with his every thrust. The room spun and spun, unstoppable motion which made me feel delirious. I bit my lower lip as the scholar's plummeting continued. His movement was swift, and my ass was durable. An unlimited connection occurred between us. I yelped, and he groaned. Synchronized sounds filled my bedroom. Our temperatures rose in the November cold. Again and again, my butt was bashed by his man-implement, and again and again, I let out barks of desired pain.

Hunter grappled my flag with his right hand; his left hand kept a sturdy grip on my right ankle. The man throttled my cock's skin up and down and sent me into a point of elation. I did attempt to buck my hips upward, but his dick-ride was far too much to handle, and I couldn't really move. Vibrations of bliss rippled throughout my aged structure, and I gritted my teeth. Wave after wave of homosexual longing cascaded through all of my nine inches. The soccer player caused a bubble of goo to leak out of my pole's tippy top, which rolled down and over one of its veins, decorating the dick's skin and his palm.

I came in a matter of minutes, followed by his hand-jive. A volcanic eruption of ooze shot out of my spike and lathered the man's abs and pecs. My sap clung to his skin in long, white lines. As that process of pure exhilaration was carried out, I bayed within the bedroom, under my student's care, hypnotized by his play.

Successive bumps continued to flood within my bottom. The man built up a refined tempo with our bodies as they mingled. Hunter's breathing intensified, grew louder, and eventually, he confessed, "Over, Mr. Tuttle ... I can't keep my juice in any longer."

"Shoot it!" I fired up at him, excited about what was about to come next.

Within seconds, he pulled his throbbing junk from my taut behind and ripped off its plastic coating; the condom went flying over his right shoulder and was lost inside the bedroom until dawn. A right-fisted grip took over his rod with speed, which thrust up and down. Hunter's body went into a spasm of sorts as his fist worked heatedly on his shaft and his hips swung to and fro. Growls filled the room, mixed with his jumbled murmurs. The man's action was sloppy but quite self-pleasing.

"Shoot it!" I called up to my student a second time. "Don't hold back!"

My instruction was the key for his orgasm, I believed. Following my outburst, the soccer player's body shivered in its upright position. Cream twirled out of his bolt, arched over my private parts, and sizzled against my heated torso. His thick man-glaze puddled between my pecs, along my abs, and even nailed me in the chin.

We showered together; I remember that now. After our entwined embrace on the queen-size bed ... after our heavy kissing ... after our laughter and how we suddenly gave into our needs, we escaped the bedroom and fled down the hallway within the Tudor. Inside the bathroom's confines, I started a warm shower for us, which we crawled into. And there, under the heated spray, having our chests locked firmly together ... having our still-stiff cocks kiss and our balls mingling ... having our arms entrapped around each other's bodies, we stayed silent under the falling water for the longest time, allowing the spray's temperature to drop and wrinkles to form on our fingertips.

He spent the night with me after our shared time in the shower. Hunter spooned me throughout the night. Before falling asleep, nestled against my back, spooning me, he whispered, "Mr. Tuttle, can I ask you a question?"

"Yes," simply escaped my lips, unprepared for his post-midnight inquiry."

"Do you like me?"

"I do. What would make you think I didn't like you, Hunter?"

"A lot of men don't like me."

"I'm not like those other men."

"You could be," he said.

"Never," I chanted, and snuggled my bottom closer to his naked and soft middle, enjoying my time with him.

"You promise?"

"I promise," I shared.

"Then you do like me," he said with a softness wrapped around his voice, finished our conversation, and drifted off to sleep.

PART 7 – HUNTED SECRETS

Our relationship discouraged labels. We weren't lovers or boyfriends or fuck buddies. We weren't acquaintances, either. Both of us were drawn to each other by sex and the likeness of each other's skin. And during those short but brisk intermissions from our separate lives, before our flesh frequently touched, he seduced me, loving the game he played with me.

I didn't fall in love with him right away, I admit today. Instead, I longed for the sex with him: against one of my Tudor's interior walls; along the floor in the hallway; kneeling on the living room floor; over the kitchen table. Our sex was healthy and continuous, rapture shared between us, unstoppable episodes of a young man's desire melting an older man's skin with just the slightest hungry look of molten bliss.

That sleepy November hedged into December. The snow along the lake started to fly and build. The storms became ridiculous and unbearable to move around in. West End College closed early for the holiday. Christmas was three weeks away and ... Hunter wanted to temporarily move in with me, until the thaw.

I objected, of course. A man such as myself enjoyed his space and time alone. I didn't want a roommate or a romance. I merely wanted sex from the soccer player. And he, too, only wanted sex from me. Having our parts connected in a pounding or receiving action was mutual ground for us; an elementary agreement between a professor and his student. Of course, he couldn't move in with me, and didn't. I refused him a long-term stay, but never did I refuse his cock. I established the simplest understanding with the young man: He could come and go as he pleased to enjoy sex with me. My body was available for his needs. He could spend nights with me, but he couldn't have his own drawer inside my bedroom, nor could he claim that he lived with me. I wouldn't have it that way. I didn't.

Hunter understood.

Any young man his age would have.

# # # # #

December 7. William demanded to see me at his house on Sassalina Drive. His abode was sprawling in size, all one level, no basement, and showcased an in-ground pool out back that was used for summertime parties.

He sat me down inside his Martha Stewart kitchen and served me Earl Gray tea with a slice of lemon. Bakery purchased sugar cookies were optional, which I passed.

"What is this about, William? What is the drama you need to share with me?"

"It concerns your bedfellow, of course."

"Hunter?"

"Yes." The look in his eyes was serious, affecting, and rather important. I had seen it at various times in our relationship when he had significant things to tell me regarding our lives.

"What is it? Tell me. You know there are no secrets between us."

He pushed a piece of paper in front of me, which was covered in a stranger's script. All the information and details on the single sheet of paper was a blur to me, wordy mumbo jumbo that I couldn't decipher. It was like reading Greek without knowing the language. "What does this tell us?" I eventually asked, straight-faced and no longer thirsty for the hot tea.

"Hunter has seven other older men in his life, Caden. The kid uses all of them in different ways. You're just another name on his list."

I felt that what William was saying to me wasn't true. His confession ended up being true after he clarified the notes on the single piece of yellow paper with me:

Marlin Dexter, age forty-six, was a lawyer in Rochester. No children. Wife of seventeen years. Graduate of Temple with his degree in law. William added: "Hunter doesn't need a lawyer, but he likes to fuck one."

Umberto Pasanna, age fifty-three, owned various hair salons in the tri-state area. The young soccer player had to have his hair washed and cut somewhere, right? Perhaps following his appointments, he ended up under Umberto.

Peter Style, age forty-seven, was a police officer in Erie. Peter pulled Hunter over for speeding in his Mustang. The two men agreed to work out the discrepancy at a bar called

Undermen in downtown Erie. William highly suggested that the cop and my student were now lovers.

Jack Springfield, age fifty-two, was a broker, retired from Wall Street and had an arrangement of boys who took care of his sexual needs. Jack obviously took pleasure in a certain soccer player from Merth, New York.

Sinclair Veezon, age sixty-one, the oldest man of the lot, lived in Berlin, Germany and owned a pharmaceutical company. William told me that Veezon took Hunter under his wing and spoiled the young man with his money. Hunter often took trips to Berlin to visit Veezon, and the man's bedroom.

David Marshall, age fifty-eight, ex-Marine. David had many secrets as a military man; Hunter Craig just happened to be one of them.

Timothy Pinion, age forty-seven, the owner of three restaurants in Rochester, all of which were successful. William explained to me that Hunter often took road trips to Rochester to visit the man, and his cock.

"You. You're the last one on the list, Caden. Number eight." William leaned back in his chair, crossed his arms in an astute manner, and said, "Now, Mr. Tuttle, tell me what you think."

I was speechless; any good man would have been, of course.

William explained, "A friend of mine compiled these facts about Hunter. It's true, my friend. You're just a random man on his list of other, older men who tend to take care of him."

"I don't take care of the young man," I retorted with slight frustration in my voice.

"Maybe you're his game. I think Hunter Craig enjoys you as an intriguing toy," William replied, which was a valid point, and could have easily been the truth.

"I don't know what I am to him. We all have our private lives. I have many friends he doesn't know about, and his list of so-called friends adequately proves that he also does." My tea was almost cold; no longer did I want it.

"I'm sure you do. But, how many boyfriends do you have?" He stared at me across the table with sincere eyes and a tight-lipped mouth, which followed his question.

"I don't have a boyfriend," I confessed. "Unless you count Hunter."

"I do count Hunter," William said. "He's the closest man to you right now. Unfortunately, he is also very close to seven other men. Did he ever tell you about his affairs with those other men?"

I shook my head. "Of course he didn't."

"As suspected, I assume."

"I should be careful with him," I stated.

My cohort picked up his tea, took a sip, placed his china cup back on the table, and affirmed in a direct tone, "You should, Caden. I would if I were in your shoes."

My mind drifted into a deep somewhere while seated across from William:

Scandalous, XXX e-mails from William started to arrive in my in-box. Seven- or eleven-minute pornographic films were attached to the e-mails. Titles to the brief films included: #31 Pinion Begging to Blow Hunter; #17 Sinclair Riding Hunter-Cock; #26 Style Eating Hunter-Ass; #10 Hunter Overtop Umberto; #19 Marshall Snacking on Hunter's Chow. Each homemade flick starred Hunter Craig. Each title described in full what the raunchy behavior of the movie entailed. Each e-mail stirred a boner inside my jeans or boxer-briefs. Each …

William warned, "You need to stay away from that young man, Caden. He's dangerous and ignorant. Hunter is only out for himself." Obviously, my sidekick was outraged, steering me away from my student's affection. William's pressing was rough and to the point. "I don't want to see you get hurt. You're my friend, Caden … and although Hunter is sexy as hell … he'll find a way to hurt you. Be smart and ditch him. Keep away from him."

Fury found the underside of my flesh. I was fuming and rattled off, "I really don't want to do that. He feeds me a fire I haven't felt in quite some time. I like his control. Part of me wants to be used by him, William. I adore it when he's around me. I like it when he seduces me because it makes me feel important. A young man like Hunter Craig is hard to come by when you're our age. I'm sure you know that. I'm quite sure you can relate to exactly what I'm talking about."

Silence. Stillness. I couldn't even hear my friend's breathing across the table. Was he ignoring me? Had I insulted him and not even realized it? Or, was he merely absorbing my rant and figuring out what to share with me next?

I wondered. Of course, I wondered.

What sane professor wouldn't?

Hunter was my drug, and I wouldn't throw him away like some piece of garbage. He was meth for me. Cocaine for me. Oxycodon. Some type of upper that filled my world with bliss. I was obsessed with him, just as he was obsessed with me. Part of me didn't care that he had a list of other men that he had wooed, seduced … whatever. When Hunter was with me, he was mine, not anyone else's. If he wanted to carry out a number of affairs with various men … I really didn't care. He enlightened me, played with me, and caused me to feel younger. His Alpha Boy behavior had worked on me. His game continued every single time our eyes met. Hunter would not be disposed of. I wouldn't hear of that. Although I didn't love him, I wouldn't accomplish such heartache and destruction in my life. I was smarter than that. Any man my age was.

# # # # #

For Christmas, I purchased a Fossil watch for Hunter and presented it to him early: a green aluminum face, compass included, a leather band, Chorono dialing system. The watch was fairly expensive, but I really didn't care. Money could not be applied to his cock, which supplied me with the greatest satisfaction. In fact, I told him once, "You can wrap your boner in a large red bow and let me eat it for the holiday. That can be your gift to me."

Hunter laughed, rolling his eyes. It was the first time I had seen him blush. His cheeks turned a blistering red, and a full smile took over his face.

"I'm serious," I said.

"I know. That's why I like you."

I wondered if he told all of his masculine and older encounters that. Honestly, I didn't put much thought into it, passed it off, and decided to kiss him, inserting my sliver of tongue into his handsome mouth.

William regularly called and hounded me about his discovered list of seven other men that Hunter was presumably fucking. I told him, "Go to Aspen and ski. Drop the topic of Hunter's sex-capades when he and I aren't together."

"Am I crossing a line?"

"Yes!" I barked at him, barely capable of listening to his call a second longer. "Go to Aspen, just as you have planned. Enjoy some skiing. Meet a great looking guy and get pounded. We'll talk when you get home around the middle of January."

"You make it sound so simple to ignore Hunter's sexual antics behind your back."

"Drop it," I said again and meant it.

William finally listened, and we shared hugs and kisses over the phone. He told me he would call from Aspen. It seemed rather blight how our conversation ended: so quickly, unemotionally, without any tenderness whatsoever.

In truth, I wouldn't speak to him for the next few weeks. Maybe our separation was meant to be. Distance did make the heart grow fonder, right?

PART 8 — HUNTER'S LESSONS

Lesson #1: Never underestimate the past.

I ran into one of Hunter's other lovers by accident. We just happened to bump into each other at Spindle Books on Rockland Street in downtown Merth. The bookstore was empty of customers except for the two of us. Our elbows happened to brush together while we reached for the same Peter Cameron novel, *The City of Your Final Destination*.

I thought nothing of it, of course. We were simply two men reaching for the same title in a queer book store. Much stranger events occurred on the planet: Princess Diana's death; crop circles; the birth of H1N1; Area 51; Stonehenge.

Truth was, I ignored the man at first. Why would I pay attention to him when he was just another fag in Merth? Instead, I took in the ceiling-high shelves of books, the walnut floors, and the lighted honeydew-scented candles. Spindle was small but very homey, a getaway place for relaxation and great books to scout. It was cozy for a man such as me, enlightening, and offered a rather Zen-like appeal.

"I know you," the man to my right said, holding a copy of *The Weekend* by Cameron and staring at me instead of the tomes on their upright shelves. "If you don't mind me being so bold, sir, what is your name?"

I studied him from head to toe: salt-and-pepper hair, six-two frame, 200 pounds, almost-gray-colored eyes, rigid jaw, and an asterisk-shaped scar on his right cheek. The stranger smelled like ash-scented soap and light perspiration. He was handsome, studious, and terribly astute. There was something about that scar on his cheek that I found rather odd but sexy. Perhaps I knew him as he claimed he had known me.

I held out my hand for him to shake and said, "Caden Tuttle."

His grip was strong and potent; it was refreshing to shake a man's firm palm. He beamed a bottled-white smile, seemed to glow, and replied, "We do know each other, Mr. Tuttle. You don't remember?"

# # # # #

Lesson #2: Always remember your lovers.

I didn't remember the man's name or who he was, even if he did seem familiar to me because of the miniscule scar on his right cheek. As I held the copy of Cameron's *The City of Your Final Destination* in my left palm, I continued to take in the gentleman and place him somewhere in the past events of my life. Failing to guess who he was, I inevitably shook my head, and defended myself with: "I'm sorry ... I really don't remember you."

"Us," he corrected me. "You should remember us. Let me caress your memory, if I can. Last summer. The professor's convention in Buffalo. I catered the food." The man leaned into me, discreetly looked behind us for any new eavesdroppers, and rattled off, "I fucked you in the bathroom, Caden. Tell me you remember that."

Timothy Pinion was at my service. The owner of three restaurants in the Rochester area did fuck me at the professor's annual conference inside one of the public restrooms. If memory served me right, his cock was almost eleven inches long, thick as a tire, and my ass hurt for days after his continuous banging.

He laughed at me now, and said, "You do remember me."

"I do now. How could I forget your dick when it practically ripped my insides apart?"

Pinion laughed at my comment and said, "You're seeing that student of yours, aren't you?"

How did he know that? Was Pinion aware of the other seven men that Hunter was sleeping with besides him? Did he, too, receive a call from someone like William Pike, a friend of a friend perhaps, and obtained a seven-person list of Hunter's sleepovers, men that he enticed with his body? Responding to the man's question, I said, "How can a man from Rochester know what transpires in Merth, particularly concerning my sexual affairs?"

The restaurateur/caterer/Caden-fucker heartily laughed, and said something crazy, "I'm here to visit my aunt for the day, not that that is any of your business. What is your business ... is Hunter Craig. The boy talks about you all the time when he visits me in Rochester. If I didn't know any better, I'd say he was in love with you."

# # # # #

Lesson #3: Know your Alpha Boy.

"He's not in love with me," I corrected Pinion. "The boy has other lovers, or men that he frequently fucks. I'm merely a toy for him ... Perhaps just like yourself."

Pinion dramatically shook his head and clarified, "Hunter is head over heels for you. And your mistaken about his other lovers or men that you think he randomly fucks. You're the only man he has bedded in the last sixteen months."

I was stunned, disbelieving what the gentleman had just shared with me. Quickly, I prattled, "You're mistaken, Timothy. I'm sure Hunter Craig is quite frisky with other, older men."

Pinion shook his head, determined to change my mind. "Know your Alpha Boy, Mr. Tuttle. Hunter only lusts for you.

When he visits me in Rochester, we only share dinners and conversation together. In fact, I have never kissed the man, although I have often wanted to since I find him terribly delicious. You're a lucky man, Caden. Eat that boy up and keep him. He's absolutely to die for in my opinion."

Pinion left my side, purchasing the hardback, first edition of *The Weekend*, which he held snugly in his right palm. Expectedly, he swished out of the bookstore and down Rockland Street. Perhaps I would see the man in the near future. Perhaps not. We were two men in a world of many who just happened to share the same planet, and the same passion for books, perhaps even men.

I did spend almost eight dollars on *The City of Your Final Destination*, which I wanted to give to Hunter as a gift. I had read the tome years before and adored it. Once Hunter read the novel, we would spend an evening watching the movie, which I also enjoyed, calling it one of my favorite films.

# # # # #

Lesson #4: Give those young men exactly what they want.

Over dinner at Humber's Pizza on Sash Street, I presented the tome to Hunter, who very much liked the gift. He thumbed through its pages, read a few passages under his breath, and said, "I think I'll enjoy reading it."

"I wrote something in the front for you."

He flipped to the first page in the book and read, "'For Hunter. May we travel to distant places together like the characters in this book, and enjoy each other's company for years to come. XXXOOO. Mr. Tuttle.'" He looked up from the tome and beamed with a smile. The young man then asked, "Where would we travel to together?"

"Buenos Aires," I replied.

"Moscow."

"Barcelona, Spain."

"Indonesia."

"Juno, Alaska."

"That's way too cold for me," he rattled off. "Let's go to Lima."

"Lima sounds very nice." I replied.

For the next hour, we talked of many places on the planet where we hadn't been but wanted to travel. Our feet mixed under the two-person table inside the pizza joint; perhaps the prelude to our naked bodies mixing together later that night.

After dinner, I watched him shower upstairs. He was heading out for an in-door soccer game with a few of his jockish buddies. There, hidden outside the bathroom door, beyond a screen of blue-white mist from the shower's potent spray, I admired the young man washing his solid pecs, thick thighs, sculpted stomach, and portions of his V-shaped back. Granted, his lathered body parts were mere shadows, since the mist was thick. Not that that deterred my voyeuristic nature, though. Instead, the mist only offered more of a turn-on for me, which occasionally exposed one of the young man's chiseled shoulders, his jaw, an inner thigh, and a sliver of his deflated cock between his powerful and soapy legs.

I gawked and studied his young beauty until he eventually turned off the shower's spray, stepped out of the shower, and fetched a towel. Quickly, I vanished from the bathroom's open door with a boner the size of a shovel in my jeans, which left me uncomfortable, overtly horny, and very much interested in mixing my skin with his yet again.

# # # # #

Lesson #5: Let him come home with you.

That evening, unseen by Hunter, I found my way into West End College's gymnasium, which was left open for students throughout the holiday break to exercise, do laps on the in-door track, or play soccer/football. There, I sat behind three hulking, young men who cheered the West End Chargers on in a game of soccer practice. Again, my stare consumed Hunter Craig, analyzing his work on the Astroturf: the shoulder feint, a jump cut, an inside hook, a Cruyff Turn, and an outside hook. Hunter was amazing on the field, a superstar soccer player with much zeal and skill. The young man seemed as if he loved playing the sport, but wasn't a show-off in front of his sexy-as-hell teammates.

He found me in the bleachers after his game. He was stoked and sweaty and …

"I'm coming home with you, and we can take a shower together," he whispered into my right ear, confirming with me that he was going to spend the night next to my skin, or overtop my skin, which would entail having rough sex together throughout half the morning hours.

"What do you want with an old man like me?" I asked, recalling my conversation with Timothy Pinion inside Spindle Books, still disbelieving the Rochester man and his knowledge that the soccer player next to me was possibly falling in love with me.

"I like you, old man," Hunter admitted.

"You're a fool," I chanted to him.

Discreetly, my student nuzzled up against my left ear, nibbled at its lobe, and whispered, "I'm not a fool, Mr. Tuttle. I'm a young man who just happens to like you. Why is that so bad?"

I kept quiet, stunned to hear his response.

Eventually, we made our way out of the gymnasium together, discovered my BMW, and I drove us back to my Tudor, where he promised to fuck me most of the night.

PART 9 — HUNTER, AWAY

December 15. William was in Aspen, and Hunter left for Berlin, Germany, to spend two weeks with Sinclair Veezon. How quickly the young prick escaped my world. How suddenly I was left alone. How depressed I became. Perhaps I was codependent for his youth, unintentionally hungry for the soccer player at all times. Maybe I was insane and lost a sliver of my mind, obeying my middle-aged thirst for his well-built skin. Shame on me for feeling as if I had lost my mind. My loneliness was unacceptable. I was a mature man with my own life. Before Hunter ... what did I have? Who was I? Had he changed a part of my interior that much, that I couldn't find myself while he was in Europe?

I could find another young man in my life if I wanted to. Was the desire there, though? Or, would I just hold out for Hunter's return and continue to enjoy his skin as I had carried out before he left for Germany?

Night after night I imagined he was in the Tudor watching me: standing over my bed while I slept; spying on me during my morning showers; gawking at me as I put provisions away; analyzing my naps in the middle of the wintry afternoons. Part of me truly believed he was at my side, next to me, an imaginary somebody who I felt was protecting me.

On December 20, five days before Christmas, I believed I saw Hunter in the front yard as he tromped through the thick snow, lifted his Timberland boots high, and dropped them into the fourteen inches of powder and ice. The figure was gone as soon as I noticed him near the snow-covered sidewalk. A blink of my eyes. A façade or mirage of sorts. Something or someone I couldn't explain. Details of a man that was so easily designed within the folds of my lonely imagination.

William's ski trip was cut short in Aspen. He argued with his temporary lover, was punched in his right eye and decided to take the first flight back to Merth. He claimed he was going to sue the shit out of the Aspen guy but never talked to a lawyer regarding the encounter.

In celebration of his unexpected return, I had a quaint dinner for William at my Tudor to exchange festive Christmas gifts with the man: braised Cornish hens stuffed with apricots, walnuts, and raisins; twice-baked potatoes; acorn squash lathered in butter and honey; and fig pudding for dessert. We drank a white, German wine, nibbled on expensive truffles throughout our evening, and unwrapped each other's gifts.

William gifted me a rare copy of *Of Mice and Men*, which I adored. He was delighted with the numbered and signed copy of a Steve Walker painting called *At Five in the Morning*. Both of us glowed with our presents like little boys, became slightly inebriated from the wine, and laughed most of the night away as friends in good company often do.

I told William that I was incapable of living without Hunter in my life. In response, my friend of many years simply called me a drama queen, which he insisted was normal behavior for me.

"I'm not thinking with my cock," I protested.

"I tend to disagree with that, Caden. What does the young man offer you besides his body?"

I was silent. Many things had entered my mind regarding the student: the way I felt with him when we woke up together, bubbly, younger, and with much spirit to live; how we enjoyed our candlelit meals together, which I found romantic and spine-numbing; the pleasure we found in making day trips with each other, prior to his jaunt to Germany; his beautiful smile and how it seemed to light up my world; the way his body collided so easily with my own, as if we were meant to be together. I felt

257

complete with Hunter Craig in my life, more alive, and most daring to take on new adventures, since the young man had entered my world and discovered a likeness for me. I was boundless, reborn in ways, and perhaps even more of a man who could envelop another man and discover peace together.

William laughed at me and insisted, "You're in love."

"I'm not. I know what love is and …"

He cut me off with: "Oh, Caden," and continued to heartily laugh. "You're being ridiculous. Love is in the air. This boy-thing has you exactly where he wants you. His Alpha Boy qualities have consumed you to the fullest. Face reality here … you're in love. I can't state it any clearer."

I was still silent, consuming his opinionated information. Love had never happened to me before. The previous boyfriends and masculine affairs in my life were only temporary flings. Never did I feel anything more. Some of those dick-hard boys and men did live with me for short periods of time, but never did I fall for them. Most were booted to the curb without any thought whatsoever. The truth was simple: if love stared at me, face to face, nose brushing against nose, I probably wouldn't have even noticed it.

"Think it over, pal," William suggested. "I'll be here to consume your results. Let it sink in."

My loneliness without the young man was devastating. Failure was discovered when I attempted to create new lectures for the following semester's courses because my mind was inhabited by a single student. I was weak and didn't feel like eating while Hunter visited Germany. I was helpless and unshaven, and my heart seemed to stop beating, which I found oddly uncomfortable.

Was William Pike right? Had I fallen in love with one of my students? Was I head over heels in romantic bliss for the Alpha Boy? What power did the soccer player have over me? How could he have possibly lured me into his web of lust, pivoting me into this current state of aloneness?

Hunter, away ... was my devastation.

Truth had unlimited powers and discovered me: I was in love with the young man, fully and without conditions.

Each day I received a different Facebook message from the young man in Berlin, Germany. Some were very short. Others were informative. Each were very different:

Visiting the Kaiser Wilhelm Gedächtniskirchen today, which is an inhuman reminder of World War II?

Missing your body next to mine. Cocks kissing.

Touring and eating at the Alexanderplatz. Staying near the Berliner Dom, a Protestant church, which was constructed in 1905.

Wish you were here. Beside me. Sightseeing my torso.

I've fallen in love with The Brandenburg Gate; could live next to it and stare at its beauty all day long.

Purchased a book of postcards from The East Side Gallery today; will send you one/two.

Thinking of you. Missing you. Want your dick.

Love you? I do.

William visited me at the Tudor and found me buried in a Greg Herron mystery. He helped himself to a whiskey, offered me one, which I kindly declined, and he snuggled inside my living room with his drink. The scholar wore a red-and-green striped sweater, chinos, and a snowman bowtie. One look at the man could surmise that he was queer.

"What brings you over here, chap?" I asked, placing the mystery to my right, on the Swedish sofa.

"I came to check on you. You're one step away from committing suicide without Hunter."

"You're overreacting," I chuckled. "I'm perfectly fine."

He looked around my abode, which wasn't at all tidy. Plus, I hadn't bathed in three days.

"You're quite ... depressed," William shared. "I don't want to be Dr. Phil here, Caden, but ... you need to pick yourself up and brush yourself off. Before you know it, Hunter will be back from Berlin, and the two of you can spend the rest of your lives together."

"I'm fine," I whispered, perhaps needing a whiskey like my friend to enlighten my mood.

Honestly, I wasn't fine at all. A breakdown of sorts had transpired since the soccer player's travels to Germany. My whole world had simply unwoven, and a tattered mess ensued. What was left could have easily been labeled depression. Maybe William was right: I did need to pick myself up and brush myself off.

William cleared his throat, consumed a sip of his whiskey, swallowed it down, and shared, "You smell, which tells me you need to bathe. For as long as I have known you, there hasn't been a day that you smelled. Perhaps this longing period you're going through over the soccer player is truly taking an effect on you."

"I'll bathe," I confessed, rolling my eyes. "And, I'll pull myself together."

"I suggest you also clean this pigsty."

"Done."

Again, he took a sip of his whiskey, which was almost gone. Once he swallowed the alcohol down, he said, "Tell me how much you love this guy."

I heavily sighed and replied, "I can't rid him from my system. I'm trying to get my thoughts and actions under control, but I'm not having much luck at it."

"Love will accomplish that, my friend."

"Love is strange."

"Indeed it is, Caden … Indeed it is."

# # # # #

I jacked off every day while Hunter was away: in my bed; on the living room floor; in the shower. Each time I imagined the student's palms on my shaft, working its excess skin up and down in manic waves. Repeatedly, I called out the young man's name in bliss. Speedy juts were always followed by heavy gasping. My hips jolted east and west into my imagined Hunter-palms and eruption after eruption was carried out. In doing so, Hunter's name was bellowed out again and again, sometimes even at the top of my voice. Then, each and every time I toyed with my dick, I fingered the man-goop up to my lips, opened my mouth, and licked the cream away. In doing so, I perceived it as my student's ooze, which was bittersweet, a sting to my system, and very much what I desired, since he wasn't at my side.

January 5. The New Year. I was awakened in the middle of the night by a car pulling in the driveway outside. A car door slammed. The front door of the Tudor opened, closed, and I heard commotion in the foyer: footsteps, a bang against one of the walls, and more footsteps. Within seconds, I bolted out of bed, flew into the hall, down the stairs, flipped on a light switch and …

Just as I suspected, the soccer player stood in the middle of the foyer with snow on his shoulders and the top of his head. Suitcases stood around his body. An excited smile was smeared across his face as he stated, "I made it home, Mr. Tuttle. You don't even know how much I missed you."

PART 10 — HUNTERSPELL

Both of us were extremely happy to see each other. We kissed as if we hadn't seen each other in years. Lust was present, which found a way of controlling us. My student actually had tears in the corners of his beautiful eyes upon his arrival.

Hungrily, he entrapped me in his arms and applied passionate kisses to my neck, cheeks, and lips. Hunter was chaotic with his movement, almost sloppy. He kept saying again and again, "I missed you ... I really missed you."

I helped him out of his winter jacket, boots, and collapsed against him. My palms pressed to his cheeks and I kissed him. No longer did it feel like nighttime, particularly three o'clock in the morning.

There, within the foyer's confines, we hurriedly stripped each other out of our clothes. In a matter of seconds we were naked and compressed our chests together. Arms entangled yet again. Nipples kissed. Bare cocks grew into firm erections. Hunter fell to his knees and plunged my firm cock into his mouth, clear down the back of his throat.

His to and fro motion on my nine inches was blissful and rough at the same time. My hips pressed diligently into his cavity, pulled free, and pressed inside again. His fingertips dug into my hips, keeping me upright. The man's lips were buried in my tangles of salt-and-pepper pubic triangle. Positioned above him, wavering east and west, I gasped for air, completely caught off guard by his famished desire for my naked body.

It was a rough beginning to sex without kissing and endearing pet names. Following a blowjob that almost caused me to burst my load, the young man lifted me and carried my naked body into the dark living room. There, among shadowy books, Prussian knickknacks, and Oriental rugs, antiques that I had collected throughout the years on my worldly travels, the soccer player consensually forced me over the Swedish sofa and spanked my bottom.

Three yelps escaped me within the night and echoed along the walls. My firm ass was struck again and again, somewhat heedlessly. I was sure welts were applied to my bottom, but I really didn't care, since I missed Hunter Craig. Truth was, whatever he wished to amply supply my body with ... I was game, full-heartedly.

Now fully positioned over the sofa, the place where I enjoyed winter tales on my Kindle, Hunter fell to his knees, pulled my rear open with his playful fingertips and palms, and politely shoved the tip of his warm tongue within my center.

Melodramatic groans of satisfaction escaped both of us. The connection at hand was nothing less than pleasurable for the two of us. Being apart for most of the month of December only prompted that sexual act of male-impaling-male companionship to be exactly what we desired to the fullest.

Tongue-dips drove me insane. My palms clamped on the sofa's expensive material. Feeling over-excited due to the soccer player's tongue-game with my bottom, sweat dripped from my forehead and decorated the sofa's imported cushions. Dip after dip ensued, which pivoted me into a state of moaning; a sound very similar to that of a post-Christmastime ghost's.

Following Hunter's deliberate and rump-numbing tongue-extravaganza, I was told by him: "My junk has been dying to be inside your ass."

"Do it!" I called out in the pitch-black room, semi-unconscious and horny as hell. "Pulverize my core."

And so it was done: Hunter found a condom and lube, which he used with appropriate skill. He then stood behind me, collapsed his left hand on my left hip, and directed his ten inches of rod into my opening.

Today, some years later, I barely remember the allure of his full ten inches being rammed into my epicenter. I do recall screaming into the night and digging my fingernails over the back of the sofa for fear of losing my life. Truth was I became woozy by my boyfriend's hearty size, which took the wind out of me and caused a rush of light-headedness to surface between my temples.

Frantically and robustly, in a meddlesome act, that young man pulverized my behind, just as I had instructed him. One thrust turned into dozens. Playful smacks to my ass were added like accessories to a formal tuxedo. Hunter became wicked behind me, heaving for breath, and in lust with our mutual act of naughty togetherness.

Yes, I was banged-a-plenty, prodded, slapped, and my shoulders were bitten when that young man leaned over me and used my skin like he was a bloodless vampire. Yes, my feet were kicked apart by his own feet, so he could have easy access to my backdoor compartment. Yes, he banged … banged … banged into me, out of breath, heedless with his unstoppable work, and so very greedy to get his rocks off with the use of my skin. And yes, he rode me like some farm animal, perhaps like a cowboy on a Stallion's back, enjoying his prairies, enchanting brooks, or Texas whatnots.

While those concurrent movements to my rump were so brutally, but enjoyably, carried out, Hunter decided to do a reach-around on my middle and grasped the cock between my legs with his right hand.

Jacks were processed to my inches. Rather, a man-milking process was enabled. The soccer player's right palm shifted north and south on the post between my legs. The jerky motion was hectic but enjoyed. While continuing to buck his weight into my rear, Hunter tugged wildly on my man-stick and called over my right shoulder, "I'm going to make you shoot, man."

Perhaps hypnotized by my student's Hunterspell, elation was discovered on my part. Not a dozen or more strokes later, euphoria waved throughout my system, spun in maddening circles, and caused an untimed orgasm to arise. Unbeknownst to the both of us, ooze flooded out of my tool and splashed against the back of the Swedish sofa.

"Shoot all of it out," the young man coached behind me, still banging my backside. "Don't hold it in, Mr. Tuttle."

I was drained in a matter of seconds. A rush of excitement emptied out of my body with Guinness record speed. Spurt was ejaculated with utter quickness, which caused me to grow spent and fall limp over the sofa, sweaty and in an untamable breathing spell.

# # # # #

What I thought of while being bottom-bolted:

Hunter is not in love with Marlin Dexter, Umberto Pasanna, Peter Style, Jack Springfield, Sinclair Veezon, David Marshall, and Timothy Pinion. The young soccer player is in love with me, and with me only. His short visits to those other men are nothing more than just that: visits. Those aged men are his friends, just as I have a handful of friends of my own. The Alpha Boy is harmless … needed … and causes me to feel much younger. The student (my student!) is a mystery to me and always will be. This is why I like him. And, William is right … I love him … I have always loved him, honestly.

Hunter exploded his load on my back. His sticky sap covered my spine, shoulders, and decorated the back of my head. In doing so, the man huffed and puffed behind me. Although I couldn't see him because the room was too dark, and because he was positioned at my rear, I only imagined the happy grin and beaded sweat covering his adorable face, his nimble hip-gyrations, and penis-tugging frenzy.

Once his cream-fest was finalized, the Alpha Boy pulled me up, spun me around, and connected our bodies together once again. A kiss was in motion for his return … two kisses … three kisses, and then a heart-tugging hug was carried out. Following our twosome connection, Hunter whispered into my ear, "We're filthy. We should really get a shower together."

I didn't object, following him upstairs, into the bathroom, and then into the shower.

Spent, side by side in the queen-size bed that we would share for the next few years together, until we decided to get married and purchase a bigger house, the soccer player danced his fingertips on his right hand between my firm pecs and asked about William. "How is he? What is he doing these days?"

I enjoyed the fact that Hunter inquired about my best friend. In response, I rattled off, "He's busy, as usual, and still on the search for Mr. Right." I then decided to share William's Aspen tale and his fight.

Following Hunter's laughter, he said, "We need to do dinner with him soon. I like that man."

"I'm glad you like him, Hunter. I think I can arrange that if you'd like."

"I would. Honestly."

He pulled me tight against his skin, applied a kiss to my forehead, pulled away, and stated quite clearly, "I likes you a lot, Mr. Tuttle. You're my favorite."

"I'm staying for as long as you decide to keep me," he said.

It was music to my ears. What forty-nine-year-old was liked by an Alpha Boy so contently? I was happy for the very first time in a long time. Professor Tuttle and his student had connected rather easily, falling for each other.

I confessed, "That sounds splendid, but ... I can't teach you this semester. The Dean will learn of our intimacy."

"We can keep it a secret from her. She doesn't need to know about it."

"Can we pull that off, Hunter?"

"We can try."

"It's sounds very risky. A lot is at stake, of course."

Hunter slid his right palm down and over my abs, into my triangular patch of pubic spirals, and discovered exactly what he was looking for. The soccer player rolled his palm around my limp beef and gave it a simple squeeze. In doing so, he said, "The Dean isn't going to jack or suck you off when you grow wood, Mr. Tuttle."

I laughed, crazy in love with the young man, completely caught up in his life and world, and just about everything that he was comprised of. "You're right, she would never do that."

"Case closed then. You can teach me this semester. I have three classes with you. I'll be your naughty student."

"The only way I want you to be."

"Under one circumstance, of course."

"Are you blackmailing me?" I inquired, holding him in my arms.

"Absolutely. I'll only be your naughty student if you let me move in and we can become a permanent couple."

"You're serious, right?"

"Perfectly."

"Are you teasing Mr. Tuttle again?" I didn't believe him and asked, enjoying his hand on my shaft as it carried out slow and smooth strokes.

"Not this time," he confessed, and brought my shaft into nine steeping inches again, having every intention of getting me off a second time, and many, many more times in the years that followed, spending them with me.

The Editor

Mickey Erlach is a full-time editor for STARbooks Press. He tries being Alpha, but his partner, Eric Summers, won't allow it.

ng any underwear. "Excuse me," I said, having a hard time looking

led by that bulge in his crotch, "but don't I know you?" "Maybe,"

of to   bout a m

Ray   God, you

ser?   in?" he as

"Lik   s stronges

body   e on Gree

he l   I ever sa

to t   any ideas'

king   he same

coul   ery long t

raci   ne swell.

with   e in store

go   behind s

see   in public

" he   vent to th

acy.   grabbed

d. I

raci   t, so firm

t, ha

h my   bing dick

ng, I   n cock, b

ound of unzipping filled the small space. I don't know who's hand

t before I knew it, I had his rod in my hand, and mine was in his. "

do?" he asked, his tone challenging. I knew exactly, and sank to